Karen McQuestion

A SCATTERED LIFE

PUBLISHED BY

amazon encore

Published by AmazonEncore
P.O. Box 400818
Las Vegas, NV 89140

ISBN-13: 9781935597063
ISBN-10: 193559706X

For Greg

ACKNOWLEDGMENTS

My deepest appreciation to my editor, Terry Goodman, for his enthusiasm, hard work, and attention to detail. Every author should be so lucky.

I am truly grateful to marketing whiz Sarah Tomashek for her guidance and expertise.

My thanks to the entire AmazonEncore team. I'm thrilled to be a partner in this innovative publishing endeavor and appreciate your efforts more than words can say.

Many wonderful people helped in the writing of this book. I'd especially like to acknowledge Vickie Coats, Kay Ehlers, Geri Erickson, Beth Knoelke, Felicity Librie, Cyndy Salamati, and the members of the Chapter One writing group.

My gratitude to the Ragdale Foundation in Lake Forest, Illinois, where portions of this novel were written.

And finally, I want to thank my husband, Greg, and our kids, Charlie, Maria, and Jack, for their unwavering love and support. You guys are the best!

CHAPTER ONE

Skyla's earliest memory of Thomas was linked with the smell of beer and the taste of blood. She was waitressing at a Mexican restaurant that semester, the one over on Brewer Street with the red tiled roof and the neon sombrero in the window. Enchiladas and fajitas were a novelty in small-town Wisconsin, where the traditional cuisine leaned toward grilled bratwurst, Friday fish fries, and coleslaw. The restaurant did a brisk trade, even if some of the locals did pronounce the J in fajita and said pollo as if it were a NASA mission. Skyla worked five shifts a week, five more than she wanted to.

Every day she intended to quit, but by closing time she'd change her mind. For weeks she carried a handwritten note in the pocket of her rust-colored, flouncy skirt. It said, "I, Skyla Medley, give Las Tejas restaurant two weeks' notice of my termination of employment." The note stayed the same except for the date, which she crossed off and changed from time to time.

It was the latest in a long series of jobs. Actually, a long series of everything—new schools, new jobs, new places to live. She was only twenty, but she'd always been on the move. Staying in one spot didn't have many advantages as far as she could tell, but the constant motion was wearing.

Getting a new job was never a problem. Neither was giving notice. Skyla wasn't quite sure what held her back this time. Somehow she'd misplaced her momentum. For the first time she wondered what it would be like to build a history in one place.

Still, the thought of quitting Las Tejas never left her mind. The boss, big Bruno, who wasn't even Mexican, barked orders constantly. She hated the yelling almost as much as she hated the hot plates and the sticky margarita glasses, which were top-heavy. She found it difficult to hoist the food trays very high and wound up resting them on her shoulders. The fajita meat was served on hot skillets that sizzled and spit next to her ear.

The wait staff sat at the tiled tables after hours, drinking sodas secretly spiked with rum and swapping stories of rude customers and messy children. They were mostly college students, half of them young men. The only thing that kept them coming back night after night was the tips—big wads of bills and handfuls of change.

Skyla was one of the younger ones, and she was so petite that most of her coworkers initially guessed she was in high school. And because she was quiet, they assumed she was shy. But neither was true. She was an observer of life and a college student majoring in art. The cooks and busboys joked with her, commenting on her reddish hair and pale skin ("Seen the sun lately, Skyla?") but couldn't get more than a smile out of her. She went about her business, clearing dishes and warning people about hot plates, and before long she figured out who was sleeping with whom and which bartenders were helping themselves to money in the till. People were pretty easy to get a handle on if you took the time to watch and listen.

The night Skyla met Thomas, she had just finished her shift. Business was slow that evening because the Green Bay Packers were playing on Monday Night Football. She'd lived in Wisconsin for almost a year and still didn't understand the natives' reverence for the Packers. Time card in hand, she headed toward the back room, but before she could punch out, big Bruno recruited her to wash glasses behind the bar. She didn't mind the washing too much, but the spongy floor mats were sticky and the air was thick with cigarette smoke.

She lowered each glass onto a sudsy revolving brush and dipped them into the rinsing sink before placing them to the side to dry. The process was so superficial it left her wondering if the glasses were really clean.

Because her back was to the rest of the bar, Skyla wasn't fully aware of what happened next. The sound of the football game muffled the noise of the commotion behind her. She remembered hearing a shout and turning to look. A flash of green flannel pushed against her with the force of a linebacker and threw her several feet. The back of her head hitting the edge of the bar broke her fall.

It was the talk of Las Tejas for weeks to come. The busboy with the bad skin liked to tell his version of the story. "I saw the whole thing," he said. "That guy in the plaid shirt was huge—had to be three hundred pounds and six foot five at least. He got mad when Bruno wouldn't give him another shot of tequila."

The busboy paused for dramatic effect. "That little Skyla was just minding her own business, just washing glasses, didn't have nothin' to do with it at all. Then that guy barged back behind the bar and crashed right into her." He slapped his fist into his palm. "*Bam!* Knocked her against the bar, and she hit the floor cold. One of her shoes even went flying. Blood everywhere. It took Bruno and two other guys to drag that drunk out of there. Then some guy sitting at the bar jumped over it like a damn pole-vaulter and went back by Skyla. I think he was a doctor or something."

Skyla remembered lying on the floor behind the bar and looking up at Thomas's concerned face. He appeared as if in a dream, kneeling above her saying, "Don't you worry about a thing; you're going to be fine." It was all so hazy and surreal she wondered if he were an angel, although she'd never heard of one with wire-rim glasses before.

She was vaguely aware of more yelling and the taste and feel of blood in her mouth, but it was background noise compared to Thomas's reassurances. "Who are you?" she tried to ask right before she lost consciousness, but her tongue was swollen where she'd bit it and the words didn't come out right.

CHAPTER TWO

"What's all that commotion?" Thomas called out from the other room.

"New people moving into the Jakubowskis' house," Skyla answered. From her spot on the screened porch it was hard to see much more than the moving truck. If she strained her neck she could see past Mrs. Williams's lilac bushes, but getting a better view would require actually getting up from the wicker table and leaving her coffee and newspaper. She wasn't that eager to find out about the new family. Four-year-old Nora was still sleeping, and there was a slight chance Skyla could finish the paper before she woke up. They'd find out about the new neighbors in good time.

"Do they have to play their music so loud? Don't they know it's Sunday morning?" Thomas shook his head and went back inside, letting the screen door creak shut.

Skyla took a sip of her coffee. It wasn't the music that upset Thomas; she knew her husband better than that. It was the old neighbors moving out and the new ones moving in. As far as Thomas was concerned, everything should always stay the same. He'd lived in Pellswick, Wisconsin, his whole life and didn't see any reason to live anywhere else. The same barber had cut Thomas's hair since he was a little boy. He had his car, chosen for durability, repaired by the mechanic who'd serviced the family cars for the last two decades. He taught at the same high school he had attended. Thomas was the most rooted person Skyla had ever met. Even the house he bought as an adult was a scant fifteen minutes away from his parents' home. He liked knowing when to expect the first frost, how often the rain gutters should be cleaned out, and what time to expect the mailman.

Thomas didn't like surprises. Even small changes caused him dismay. "Where did these come from?" he'd ask about something as mundane as new dishtowels.

"I bought them," Skyla would reply nonchalantly. She had learned it was better to be matter-of-fact about these things.

"What happened to the blue ones?" The pang of sorrow in his voice was unmistakable. Skyla wanted to feel sorry for him, but the whole thing was utterly ridiculous.

"The blue ones were threadbare. I put them in the rag box." She patted his arm. "Don't worry, you'll get used to these."

His penchant for routine took a while to get used to. She, who had grown up in a household that could change at any given moment, could never afford to get locked into how things should be, whereas Thomas derived great comfort from having things the same. He woke up at the same time every day of the week. Sleeping in went against his nature.

"I just can't do it," he said to Skyla one Saturday morning when she suggested they lie together awhile longer.

"There's nothing to it," she'd said. "You just don't get up."

It took about a year of marriage to get the basics down. Thomas had his own preferences in everything from food to bed making. Luckily, Skyla was adaptable.

✳ ✳ ✳

Skyla wanted to walk the long way home from church that day in order to pass the Jakubowskis' old house. "We might be able to meet the new people," she said. She glanced over at Thomas, who continued walking, still looking straight ahead. He wasn't the least bit interested in finding out about the new neighbors. Probably still inwardly grieving for the loss of the Jakubowskis—a loud, slovenly family whose teenage boys came and went at all hours of the night. Their departure didn't bother Skyla in the least.

What she was hoping for was a family with a little girl, a nice little girl. Preferably four years old like Nora so they could become the best of friends. It would make being an only child less lonely. This new girl and Nora would be inseparable, she was sure. The mothers would joke about the way those two always had to be together. Joined at the hip, they'd say. Of course, they'd have to caution the girls to use the sidewalk when they visited back and forth between the yards. Old Mrs. Williams, who lived in the house in between, was meticulous about her lawn.

Skyla had no illusions she and the mother of this fictitious child would become friends. Most of the women in the neighborhood were of the older, more sophisticated variety—professional working women or stay-at-home career moms. Nothing like Skyla.

When they left the house earlier that morning, Skyla spotted a few smaller bikes, a crib, and some other telltale kid signs coming off the moving truck. It was an odd Sunday. Nora had slept late, so late in fact that not only did Skyla get to finish the paper, she was able to fit a shower in. It was almost like the days before they had Nora.

Skyla rested her hand on Nora's caramel-colored hair. "If the new people are out, we can introduce ourselves. Maybe they'll even have a girl for you to play with."

"I hope she's the size of me," Nora said. She walked between her parents, holding on to the hem of her mother's skirt with pudgy fingers.

"They probably don't want to meet people before they've even moved in," Thomas said. "We shouldn't bother them." He jangled his keys in the pocket of his jacket.

"I don't mean we'll go up to the door," Skyla said impatiently. "Just if they're out, we can say hi."

"Still." Thomas frowned. "I'm sure they'll want to put things in order first."

"Let's just see."

"I think it would be best not to rush things."

"It won't be rushing—just welcoming."

They walked the next two blocks in silence. Nora seemed to sense her parents' disagreement and took a pause from her usual nonstop chatter. In the trees across the street a bird whistled in the way of a construction worker admiring a pretty girl. Skyla remembered being spooked by that kind of whistle the first time she'd heard it as a teenager, because she'd thought there was a man lurking nearby. The memory made her smile.

"A penny for your thoughts?" Thomas said.

"I was just thinking about whistling."

"Like this?" Nora puckered her little lips and blew out a slight squeak.

"Pretty good," Skyla said, squeezing Nora's hand as they turned the corner. From here they could see the new neighbor's house, just two doors down from their own. "My daddy was the world's best whistler. He could whistle while he was breathing in and out, so he never had to stop to catch his breath. He tried to teach me how to do it, but I never got the hang of it."

"Then he died."

"Yes, honey, then he died."

Half a block ahead, Skyla could see the moving truck still planted on the driveway at the Jakubowskis' old house. Country music blared from somewhere—Skyla couldn't pinpoint exactly where, maybe the garage. Circling the moving van, like covered wagons around a campfire, was what looked like every possession the new family owned. Bikes and dressers, toys and boxes, all of it stacked haphazardly around the van, some of it spilling onto the lawn.

"My God!" Thomas said. "They've been moving since eight o'clock this morning, and they haven't even gotten their things into the house yet?" Skyla knew he objected solely on principle. There was a right way and a wrong way to move. Clearly this new family hadn't figured that out yet.

They slowed as they approached the driveway. Behind one ring of furniture was another layer: bookcases and dressers and even more piles of boxes. Skyla couldn't imagine how many trips it would take to get these mounds of possessions into the house. The truck was a rental. Presumably there was no hired crew of strong, young men ready to converge on this pile.

"Hey, look," Nora cried out when they reached the end of the driveway. Her right arm let go of Skyla's hem and rose to point. "Mama, it's a boy. A little boy. Alls he gots on is his underwear."

Skyla didn't spot the little boy right away even though he was just a few feet in front of her. At first she saw only a pile of stuffed animals mixed with bedding. It wasn't until a few moments later that Skyla's eyes really focused and she saw the small boy in the heart of the pile. He was sucking his thumb and, despite the coolness of the day, wore only white briefs and a T-shirt. Because he wasn't in diapers, he had to be at least two or three, she thought. He had the chubby cheeks small children wear well. With the addition of white feathered wings, he could be a blond cherub on a greeting card.

Nora knelt down to talk to the boy, who regarded her with wide eyes. "Hi there. My name is Nora. What's your name?" The boy looked shyly at his feet, seeming to find new interest in his toes.

"I can't believe no one is with him," Thomas said. "He's so little he could run into the street and get hit by a car." His right hand in his pocket jangled his keys while he glowered at the house.

"Maybe his parents are close by," Skyla said, but she was doubtful. There didn't seem to be anyone around.

"I live in the house over there." Nora pointed. "Maybe you can come over sometime if your mama says it's okay." Even without a response she kept talking to the boy, who still hadn't taken his thumb out of his mouth. "Where's your mama and daddy?"

"It's odd no one is around. Maybe they don't know he's out here," Skyla said. She scanned the pile of furniture and possessions as if expecting to find an adult crouched nearby.

"Well, they should know. Good parents keep track of their kids. You never let Nora out of your sight."

"Actually, she never lets me out of *her* sight," Skyla admitted, although she was touched that Thomas put her in the good parent category. He wasn't big on compliments.

"If no one comes out in the next minute or two, one of us should go up to the house," Thomas said. "We can't just leave him here."

It was Skyla who walked up the flagstone walkway a few minutes later. As she stepped onto the covered front porch, she heard voices from inside the house. The wooden screen door rattled when she knocked. Probably jarred loose by the constant stream of the Jakubowski boys and their friends. So many times Skyla remembered seeing big gaggles of teenage boys sitting on the steps of this same porch, smoking and drinking when the parents weren't home. Their presence always bothered her—it didn't fit with the house. One of the oldest in the neighborhood, the house had leaded glass windows, a big bay window, and attic dormers. The wraparound porch was the kind of long, open porch Skyla would have liked for herself, although Thomas said their enclosed screened porch was far better. More privacy from people and protection from mosquitoes.

Skyla knocked again. Through the screen she saw an open staircase.

"Somebody get the door." A woman's voice called out from somewhere above. "Wyatt, you go down and answer it."

"Aw, Mom! We're in the middle of something. Get one of the little guys to do it."

"Why do you always have to argue with me? Go down right now!" The woman was agitated.

"But we just got started."

Skyla felt like she was eavesdropping. She ran her fingers over the dirty smudges on the wooden doorframe. Painting would be the first order of business if this were Thomas's house.

"Oh, for crying out loud!" A man's voice boomed out. "Do I have to do everything around here? I'll get the door."

Skyla heard the heavy steps on the stairs and had a view of a man descending—first his feet, then blue-jeaned legs, and finally his T-shirted upper body.

"Can I help you?" he asked. His booming voice fit his build.

"I live two doors down," Skyla said. "We were…"

"Hey, hey, hey," he interrupted. The screen door swung open, and he stepped out onto the porch. "It's great to meet you." He wiped his hand on his shirt before grabbing her hand and shaking it enthusiastically. He ran his other hand through a head of thick brown hair. The gesture revealed a damp stain under his left sleeve.

"We were just walking by," Skyla said, gesturing to the sidewalk.

He yelled through the doorway, "Roxanne! We've got neighbors." He turned back to Skyla. "She'll be so glad you stopped by." His voice dropped to a conspiratorial whisper. "The people we bought the house from seemed like complete jerks, if you know what I mean. No offense if you were friends with them or anything, but Roxy was a little worried about the people here. We've been in Wisconsin the last five years, so you'd think we'd fit in by now, but it's not so easy. Our last neighborhood the people were so uptight it was unbelievable."

"We noticed you were moving in…"

"I'm sorry, I never even got your name." He smacked his forehead with the palm of his hand. "Mine's Ted." He shook Skyla's hand again. "Ted Bear. But not Teddy Bear, if you don't mind. I've heard enough of that for one lifetime."

"I'm Skyla." Once her hand was released from his firm grasp, she pointed toward Nora and Thomas. "My husband and daughter and I were walking past your house, and we saw a little boy out front all by himself."

"A little boy?" Ted craned his neck to look past Skyla. From the end of the driveway, Thomas raised his hand in a halfhearted wave.

"Yes, a little guy with blond hair about two or three? He's sitting in a pile of toys down near the sidewalk. It's kind of cold for him to be outside in just his underwear…"

"Oh, for crying out loud!" He yanked the door open and bellowed in the direction of the stairs. "Roxanne! It's happened again. Dammit, can't you keep track of the kids?" He turned back to Skyla. "She keeps losing them, and yet she wants to have more. The woman is unbelievable."

"Ted, would you stop screaming? They're all up here with me." Roxanne's voice came down the stairs. "The twins are helping me put the beds together, and the little guys are unpacking boxes."

"Yeah, well do a head count. You're missing one." He turned back to Skyla and shook his head. "It's so crazy here."

"Moving is stressful." Skyla tried to commiserate, but secretly she felt no amount of stress could justify losing track of a child.

"I wish it were just from moving," Ted said. "Then the craziness would end. Oh well." He sighed. "Eventually they all grow up and move out, right?"

"So I've heard."

"Some days it seems like it won't happen soon enough."

※ ※ ※

From the moment the introductions were made, Skyla could tell Thomas wasn't impressed with their new neighbor.

"Hey, it's great to meet you," Ted said. Upon their approach, the little boy raised his arms and started whimpering. Ted hoisted the child over his left shoulder before shaking Thomas's hand. "Thanks for finding my kid. Most of the time it takes people a while to find out who the good neighbors are. Roxy and I figure that if we just scatter our kids around, the folks who bring them back are okay."

"We passed the test?" Skyla asked.

"Oh yeah. I'll let you know how you rate after I see what the other neighbors bring back."

"How many kids do you have?" Thomas asked.

"Five, including this one." He slapped the underweared bottom hanging over his shoulder. "This is a Gregory butt." The boy began to squirm and laugh. "Yep, five burly boys all like me."

"No girls?" Skyla tried to keep the disappointment from her voice.

"Nope, not a one. We only produce boys." Ted laughed, lowered Gregory so their faces were even, and gave him a loud, smacking kiss. "Obnoxious, dirty, noisy boys, just like their father."

"Sorry, honey, they only have boys," Skyla said to Nora. "My daughter was hoping for a friend," she explained.

"You can still hang by us," Ted said. "I've got one named Monty who's about your size." He held his right palm down next to Nora's head. "Almost exactly that tall." And then to Skyla he said, "Better watch your daughter, though. My wife wants a girl so bad, and yours is awful cute. She might try to steal her away."

Nora clung to her mother's skirt. There were times Skyla thought the child would climb back inside of her if she could.

"We better get home," Thomas said. "It looks like you still have some moving to do."

"Yeah," Ted said. He looked ruefully at the pile. "Roxanne's brothers came from Dayton to help us move. They were good about getting the truck packed up, but once it was unloaded, they left to get some beer and eats. I got a bad feeling they're not coming back. Roxanne says they're unreliable, but I call it like I see it—they're a bunch of drunks." He threw back his head and laughed, revealing a row of uneven white teeth.

Skyla saw Thomas stiffen. "How unfortunate for you," he said. Thomas cleared his throat. "We just wanted to make sure the little boy was safe. We'll be on our way now."

Ted thanked them again for finding Gregory before they headed home.

"It was great meeting you," Ted called after them. "Stop over later in the week and meet Roxy and the rest of the kids."

Skyla turned to smile and wave. "He seemed nice," she said.

"What a mess." Thomas shook his head. "I've seen their kind before. Believe me, it's best to steer clear of them."

"Their kind? That sounds harsh." Skyla twisted a lock of hair around one finger.

"As the man said, I just call it like I see it."

"Maybe they're just unorganized from the move," Skyla said. "You can't judge people in ten minutes."

"Sometimes you can." He was emphatic. "I know you always give everyone the benefit of the doubt, Skyla, but in this case I know what I'm talking about. I've seen their type. They go through life without a plan, and everything's willy-nilly. They can't even keep track of their kids, and their relatives are alcoholics. Who knows, maybe they are too."

"We don't know that." Even as she spoke, she knew Thomas had made up his mind.

Thomas picked up Nora and hoisted her onto his shoulders. The child interlaced her fingers to cover his forehead. "They're the type that'll pull you down if you let them. It starts out with small favors like picking up their mail when they go on vacation, and the next thing you know they'll be calling you from jail wanting you to post bail. No," he said, shaking his head, "nothing but trouble there. Good thing they don't have any girls—we don't have any reason to see them at all."

After supper that day, Skyla stood at the window in the cupola and watched the activity at the new people's house. Because of the way the street curved and the angle of the cupola, she had a good view of their driveway. A woman she guessed to be Roxanne was directing the rest of the family, pointing at bags and dresser drawers for the kids to carry in, all the while cradling a baby on one hip. Two older boys who looked to be at least nine or ten took turns helping Ted carry in larger pieces of furniture, while the child Skyla recognized as Gregory repeatedly carried the same lamp back and forth between the house and driveway. The scene reminded Skyla of the scurrying of ants on an anthill.

"Do you want me to get the binoculars?" Thomas's voice from the doorway made her jump.

"No, that's not necessary, smarty," Skyla said, although only a minute earlier she had wished for a closer view of their faces.

He stood next to her at the window. "They're making some headway, I'll give them that much. They better hurry, though, if they want to beat the rain."

"The news said we're not going to get it until late tonight."

"I don't know about that. The sky tells me it's coming any minute." Thomas put his arm around her waist. "I thought I'd take Nora for an ice cream cone. You want to come?"

"No, I think I'll just stay home and enjoy the solitude." Skyla kept her gaze on the window. "Go ahead without me."

She stood at the window and watched Thomas's car as it went down the street, and then she turned her attention to the new neighbors. Mesmerized, she didn't move for the longest time. As the sky darkened, the Bear family's pace increased until they were darting back and forth, throwing things into the garage. Once the rain started coming down, Roxanne shepherded the kids inside. Ted came out with plastic tarps. When Roxanne returned, the couple struggled against the wind to cover the remaining furniture. Skyla watched them until the rain against the window made it too difficult to see, and then she went downstairs and waited for Nora and Thomas to return.

CHAPTER THREE

Thomas's mother, Audrey, had always longed for a daughter. During each of her three pregnancies, she looked at little dresses and baby dolls and dreamed about braiding hair and setting up tea parties. She wrote different names on lined paper as if practicing her future daughter's signature: Natalie Marie, Francesca Rose, Carina Michelle. Walt chose their first two sons' names, and she accepted his choices without question. Thomas and Jeffrey were solid names, easy to spell and pronounce, and besides, she couldn't think of any other boys' names worth fighting for. But for a daughter—ah, there was a whole world of names out there for girls. If Walt had his way, a girl would get saddled with a standard name like Kristine Jane or Jennifer Ann. Audrey was not about to let that happen. Any girl child born to her would have a name befitting royalty.

As it turned out, all the hours spent contemplating names were wasted. She never had a girl. First there was Thomas, serious and quiet. He was a perfect firstborn, a son to make her husband happy and an easy baby. Audrey wasn't disappointed. She knew there would be other babies. Walt thought three was the perfect number, so there would be two more chances. Maybe the next one would be a girl, and Thomas could be the protective older brother.

Being a new mother was such a joy. Thomas was born in the springtime, and it was deliciously warm that year. She dressed him in cute sweater sets, laid him down in the stroller, and walked for blocks on the sidewalks in their neighborhood. Audrey enjoyed the feeling of warm air on her cheeks and the smell of lilacs. It felt so good to walk freely and have the baby on the outside of her body instead of under her rib cage, crowding out everything else.

Having her second, Jeffrey, was a different story. The first two boys were too close together, she knew that now, but things were different back then. That's just what people did. No one thought it was lunacy to have babies eighteen months apart—or at least no one said as much. There were a few people who clucked their tongues and said, "You're going to have your hands full." She agreed with them then but thought she was up to the task. She was young and healthy. How hard could it be?

Jeffrey's first year was a complete blur in her memory. Later she saw photos of herself at family gatherings she didn't remember and realized she had lived a year as if on autopilot. The sleep deprivation was the hardest part. Lack of sleep combined with being trapped in a wintertime house with a colicky baby and a jealous toddler was enough to push her into a deep depression. She resented Walt, who was able to go off to work. Even when he was home, Walt wasn't much help. When both babies were crying and she really needed him most, he found excuses to go out to the garage. Husbands were so useless.

After Jeffrey's first year things were better, but it took a long time before she felt like herself again. Having small children was such a worry. Danger was everywhere: the coffee cup too close to the edge of the counter, the vaporizer's cord trailing within reach of tiny hands. Walt didn't share her concerns, so she rarely left them alone with him. "You can't watch them every second," he'd say. Audrey knew different. You *had* to watch them every second. When each child learned to walk, she followed him around the house, ready to serve as a buffer between his head and the edge of the coffee table. She held her breath when they climbed too high on playground equipment and checked on them constantly, even when they were playing quietly in their rooms. It was exhausting, but a person couldn't be too careful.

Jeffrey grew from a fussy baby into an agreeable little boy. He was a contented child who adapted easily, unlike Thomas, who became upset if it rained on a planned zoo day or if the furniture was rearranged.

Oddly enough, she didn't get pregnant the third time until the summer before Jeffrey started kindergarten. She and Walt weren't doing anything to prevent it, and her fertility was never in question. Maybe sheer exhaustion was the best birth control.

Walt was quite clear there would be no more babies after this one. "No matter how much insurance I sell, we'll never get ahead if we have too many kids," he'd grumbled, and she agreed. Three seemed like plenty.

With that in mind, Audrey was sure the third one was going to be a girl. She'd paid her dues with the first two—they were good, healthy boys, and she was grateful for that, but certainly it was her turn to have a baby she could dress in pink. It almost made sense that the first two were so close together. Brothers that close in age would most likely be friends. A girl, though—oh, the possibilities made her heart sing! She bought a white linen baby dress trimmed with pink satin rosettes. Just the right size for the baby's first summer.

Audrey tried to explain her yearning to Walt. "Every woman needs a daughter," she said. "Do you think the boys are going to visit us when we're old and gray?"

"They damn well better, or I'll kick their butts," he said and turned back to his newspaper.

Audrey didn't have an answer for that one.

She had a mental image of her future daughter, a composite of all the features she admired in other people's daughters. Certainly she would have curly hair—not just waves, but actual curls. The color of the hair was important. She pictured her little girl as a blonde—not the bright blonde some people called towheads, more like the color of a jar of honey held up to the light. Green eyes would be nice. Blue and brown eyes were so common, she thought. Her daughter would be petite in size with delicate features. Audrey knew this physical combination was highly unlikely. Both Thomas and Jeffrey had straight brown hair and brown eyes and were of at least average height. Jeffrey, in fact, was almost as tall as his older brother.

Even with reality staring her in the face, she couldn't help wishing for her dream daughter. Lying in bed at night, she thought about a girl and rubbed her belly as if she could impress the desired characteristics upon the child inside.

It was a disappointment then when Dennis came out looking very much like the other two. She had not felt the intense joy most mothers experience when they find they've delivered a healthy child. She mourned the loss of that little girl for a long time. When no one was looking, she held the little white dress with the rosettes up to Dennis's body. He would have made a beautiful girl, she decided, even if he didn't have blond curls. She traced her fingers over the smooth satin of the rosettes and then folded the little dress and tucked it into the back of her sweater drawer. It occurred to her she could use it for a present, but the thought of seeing it on someone else's baby was too painful.

Despite the letdown, Dennis turned out to be a gift. The word that best described him, Audrey decided, was "charming." Even as a small child he knew just the right thing to say, reassuring other children when they cried and offering to help his grandparents with yard work.

"Goodness," a neighbor once exclaimed after Dennis complimented her new hairstyle, "my own husband didn't even notice." He was in grade school by then, and he was a favorite with his teachers, but not a stellar scholar. Thomas and Jeffrey were better students. They seemed to grasp new subject matter at a glance. Dennis was shortchanged of that talent, but he made up for it with attitude and perseverance.

What Audrey remembered best about Dennis's childhood was the exuberant way he came home after school, bursting through the door yelling, "Ma, I'm home." He always had something special to show her, a spelling test or art project he made. "Just for you, Ma. You can keep it!"

It amused her that he referred to her as Ma. The other two boys called her Mom, and as far as she knew, none of their friends called their mothers Ma. It was almost as if Dennis chose his own endearing nickname for her. While Thomas and Jeffrey diligently went upstairs each day to put their book bags in their room, Dennis tossed his down in the front hall and threw his arms around her waist. While the older boys would grab a quick snack and head outside to shoot hoops on the driveway, Dennis lingered at the table with his milk and chocolate chip cookies and told her about his day.

As a teenager he seemed to have a different girlfriend every semester and managed to stay friends with all of them, even after they broke up. The phone rang constantly during those years. Audrey and Walt rarely answered it when Dennis was home. It was seldom for them.

Dennis's popularity was a stark contrast with the quiet style of his brothers. Thomas and Jeffrey didn't have girlfriends during high school as far as she could tell. Thomas in particular was exceedingly shy and somewhat secretive. On the rare occasions when he was on the phone with a girl, he went into the study and closed the door for privacy. If Audrey asked who he was talking to, he'd mumble something like, "A girl from my Spanish class." Neither of the older boys went to dances and didn't seem to care. Dennis, on the other hand, never missed one. Anguishing over who to ask and what to wear was a routine with him.

She heard other mothers complain that their teenagers shared nothing with them. She should have been so lucky. At times Dennis told her more than she wanted to know.

"You be careful," she'd tell him after hearing about a narrowly missed car accident or a party that was busted by the police moments after he left.

"Oh, Ma," he'd say, laughing. "You don't need to worry about me. I can take care of myself."

If Audrey were asked to predict which of her three sons would live at home the longest, she would have said Dennis, and she would have been wrong. Thomas and Jeffrey went away to college, earned their degrees, and boomeranged back to inhabit their old bedrooms. Dennis went away to college too, but not to the University of Wisconsin like his brothers. He picked one clear across the country in San Diego. Within the first semester, he eschewed the dorm and found a pack of guys to rent an apartment with. When he called from the apartment, she could barely hear him for the loud music and voices of his roommates, the identities of which seemed to change from month to month.

When he graduated, Dennis stayed in California and worked at a job in sales making what he called big money. He still called her several times a week, and her heart leapt when she answered the phone and heard, "Hi, Ma." How could she not love someone who so clearly adored her?

Thomas and Jeffrey were good sons, but she was more than a little embarrassed when the years rolled on and they still lived at home. Walt didn't mind—if anything he relished having his grown sons home in the evenings, their bodies forming a triangle in the living room while they read the paper and debated world events. "See," he teased her, "and you were worried they wouldn't visit us in our old age. They don't have to visit—they're right here."

During Monday Night Football, Walt and the boys clustered in the den, the only room in the house that didn't belong to her. The walls were adorned with mounted fish and antlers and Little League trophies. A gun cabinet in the corner displayed rifles Walt insisted on keeping even though no one used them anymore. Audrey kept her distance, only stepping into the room to dust and gather up empty glasses.

Audrey thought it unnatural to be cooking and cleaning for two adult men long past the time they should be on their own. She sorted through piles of socks and found herself resentfully pulling them correct-side out. She printed their initials onto the labels of their white briefs with permanent marker so she could tell them apart. Her life had been molded around them when they were growing up. During their childhood, she only worked at Walt's insurance business during school hours so that she'd always be available. She'd tried to be the best mother possible.

Wasn't that enough? Now Audrey wondered if there was such a thing as being too good of a mother. No one told her this would go on and on.

By the time Thomas turned thirty, Audrey wearily resigned herself to the fact that her oldest boys were never going to move out. Their routines were as entrenched as the impressions their bodies left on their respective sofa cushions. Jeffrey rarely talked about his job as a computer programmer—or anything else, for that matter. Thomas, who taught high school mathematics, was less of a mystery. He graded papers in the evenings and on rare occasions had social invitations from coworkers, usually a wedding or party. He'd talk about it for days in advance, grumbling as if they had asked him to help move their sleeper sofa. "I guess if I don't go, it will hurt their feelings," he'd say.

Audrey knew something was up when Thomas started going out evenings without mentioning it at all. She'd look for him after dinner to tell him his favorite show was on or to hand him his mail (usually just catalogs or his *Scientific American* magazine), and he'd be gone, just gone. The first time it happened she walked through the house calling his name before she thought to look out on the driveway and saw his car was missing as well.

"Don't worry about him," Walt said. "He's a grown man." Which of course she knew as well as anyone. Audrey knew he could take care of himself. It was just so discourteous of him not to say where he was going.

Initially Thomas said he went to the library; later it was the hardware store. When she pointed out that he never came back with library books or tools, his story changed. Then he claimed he was going back to school to attend various extracurricular events. When pressed, he'd say he promised some of his students he'd come for the school play or a band concert.

After Thomas left one evening, Audrey commented that it was funny he had never felt compelled to attend these events before.

"Let it go, Aud," Walt said from behind his newspaper. "He's entitled to his own life."

"I know that," Audrey said, but still it gnawed at her. Why wouldn't he tell her where he was going? She tried so hard to be supportive and nonjudgmental. It was times like this she really missed Dennis.

Thomas traded in the plaid button-down shirts she'd bought for knit shirts of burgundy or navy. While sorting the laundry, Audrey noted that loose-fitting khaki pants replaced his usual cuffed navy blue dress pants. It didn't escape her that the smell of cigarette smoke emanated from his clothing after his evenings out.

Audrey noticed changes in his hairstyle and the cadence of his speech. He seemed happier in a way she couldn't explain. The hairstyle change was so obvious that even Walt and Jeffrey noticed.

"You almost look hip," Jeffrey commented between bites of a ham sandwich. Thomas had just returned to the house after a Saturday morning barber appointment and was sorting the mail on the kitchen table. "What happened to your Bob's Big Boy look?"

"Just time for a change," Thomas said, giving a thin-lipped smile.

"Why change now?" Jeffrey raised his iced tea to his lips and chewed on a piece of ice. "Something different in your life? Or maybe I should say *someone*?"

"Like I'd tell you." Thomas took a magazine and whapped Jeffrey over the head with a force that was more than playful.

"You can't fool me. I'm on to you," Jeffrey said, but Thomas was already heading up the stairs toward his room.

"If he's seeing someone, wouldn't he just say so?" Audrey asked after Jeffrey told her about the exchange.

"Not if she's a hooker," Jeffrey said. "Or one of his students."

"God forbid, the way you think." But it did make her wonder.

* * *

The idea to follow Thomas didn't occur to Audrey until his secret outings had gone on for several weeks. Even then she resisted the idea. Heavens, what kind of mother spied on her adult son? Probably the same kind of mother who was stuck washing his underwear when he was old enough to wear a size thirty-two brief, she decided.

Without knowing if she'd actually go through with it, she planned her course of action. She checked Thomas's car before and after his evening trips. The odometer was always seventeen to twenty-one miles higher than before he left. To get her bearings, she walked to the end of the driveway shortly after he left one evening (her excuse was checking the mailbox) and watched his taillights in the distance turn right onto the main road.

She'd use Walt's car. It was a dark blue, midsized sedan, less likely to be noticed than her white station wagon. Walt wouldn't think anything of it. Audrey often used his car when hers was low on gas or if she was going somewhere where parallel parking might be involved. Over the weekend she decided Monday Night Football would be the perfect time to slip out. With enough cold beers in the fridge and the chips and dip already set up, Jeffrey and Walt might not even notice she'd left.

Monday afternoon Audrey moved Walt's car onto the street so no one could park behind it, and she slipped her field binoculars under the front seat. It was unlikely Walt would move it before Thomas left. Since Walt retired, he was a creature of precise habit. If he hadn't left the house by noon, he was home for the day. With the Packers facing the Minnesota Vikings later that evening, it was doubtful he'd even leave his recliner.

After dinner Jeffrey and Walt settled down in front of the television set with cold bottles of beer and the orange and yellow plastic bowls used only for snacks during televised sports. Thomas moved quietly toward the coat closet, pulling out his corduroy jacket and noiselessly slipping it on.

"You're not staying for the game?" Jeffrey asked. He sat one seat cushion over from Walt. Both of them rested their right foot on top of their left knee. Until that moment, Audrey hadn't realized how much her middle son mirrored his father.

"No," Thomas said. "I promised a friend from work I'd watch it at his house. There's a group of us. Kind of a Packer party thing."

"Will she be there?" Jeffrey emptied a bag of chips into the orange bowl and smirked.

"Just give it up, will you?" Thomas's annoyance was punctuated by the jangling of his keys.

"There's nothing for me to give up," Jeffrey said. "I'm not the one sneaking around."

"It just kills you that I have a life, doesn't it? You sit in this house night after night. Nothing ever changes with you, and you think everyone else should live the same way. Well, I'm not going to be stuck sitting on that couch my whole life," Thomas said. He went out the front door and slammed it harder than necessary.

"Someone's a little touchy," Walt said. He reached over and plunged a chip into the dip, leaving a white splotch on the coffee table like a bird dropping.

"I guess he told me," Jeffrey said and laughed. He reached for the remote control and turned the volume up. "Mom, where's the other dip? The French onion one?"

"In the refrigerator," Audrey called from the kitchen, and then she pulled on her coat. She slipped out the back door and gently shut it behind her. The note she left on the kitchen table read, "Gone to the store—be back soon, Mom/Audrey."

She eased the car away from the curb, careful not to turn on the headlights until reaching the road. Her hand gripped the steering wheel as she peered over the dashboard, looking for Thomas's car. Darn it, why hadn't she made up an excuse to leave earlier and waited for him around the corner?

She turned right onto the main road. This spy business wasn't going to be as easy as she had thought. The streets were Packer-game empty, although if the truth were told, they wouldn't be much busier even if there weren't a game.

Good thing she was an observant driver. Walt said Audrey drove like a scatterbrain, and it was true she tended to sightsee while she drove. Walt, on the other hand, drove with an intensity that required absolute concentration on his part and silence on everyone else's. He drove with his entire body tensed and a tight grip on the steering wheel.

When the boys were young, Walt had driven the family car with one hand on the wheel, one on the stick shift, and a cigar clamped between his teeth. Even with the cigar Walt managed to cuss out the other drivers, who were usually going too fast or too slow.

Audrey and the boys would watch in fascination as the ash on the end of the cigar lengthened, seeming to defy the laws of gravity. "Your cigar, Walt, watch your cigar," she'd say.

"I know, I know," Walt always said, irritably flicking the end out the window.

"Next time, Ma," Dennis once suggested, "don't tell him and see what happens."

But she could never do that.

Audrey was miles from home when she lost sight of Thomas's car. She was ready to turn around when she spotted him under the bright lights of an overhang at a gas station. He held the nozzle to the side of his car and stared into space, a shock of brown hair hanging forward over the top of his wire-rim glasses. The mother in her wanted to pull in and tell him to zip up his jacket and put on his gloves, but she quelled that impulse and drove on, turning at the next corner and positioning her car to follow him.

A muddy pickup truck trailed Thomas's car out of the gas station, making it easy to follow without being detected. Audrey and the pickup truck drove behind Thomas for miles until he turned down a side road. The pickup truck kept going, but Audrey turned right along with Thomas down the side street and into the parking lot of a Mexican restaurant.

Alongside a neon sombrero in the window were multicolored tube letters that spelled out "Las Tejas." Audrey pulled over a safe distance from where Thomas parked. She watched him walk into the restaurant, hands in pockets. From where she sat, it looked like he was whistling. His slightly puckered lips blew out foggy breath in the cold night air.

This wasn't what she expected. A seamy hotel in the red-light district or a private apartment on the edge of town—those were the types of destinations that would have filled the gaps in her imagination. But this? Heavens, why would anyone lie about going to a Mexican restaurant? She realized ruefully she wouldn't even get a chance to use her binoculars.

A car behind her honked, and Audrey, startled, drove the car around back and pulled into a parking space. The rear of the building was poorly lit. A large green dumpster and loading dock made Audrey think the one doorway, situated at the top of a wrought iron stairwell, was the employee entrance.

Part of her believed the sensible thing would be to leave now and drive home. What if he saw her? What possible reason could she give him for being there? Thomas was testy as it was, and once he'd even accused her of being domineering. "I can't even breathe around you," he'd said, which made no sense at all. If anything, she'd always tried to give her boys space. The least they could do was find a place for her in their lives.

She stepped out of the car, locked the door behind her, and made her way across the lot.

"Lady." A young Latino came out of the back door, cigarette in hand. "You can come in this way if you want." He wore a grease-stained white apron over his T-shirt and blue jeans.

It was on the tip of her tongue to tell him he shouldn't be smoking (didn't anyone listen to the surgeon general?), but he was holding the door for her, so she ambled up the stairs, squeezed past him, and murmured thanks as she entered.

The air inside was thick with the cooking smells of spicy meats and onions. The bar area was open to the dining room, obscured only by a waist-high wall made of white stucco resembling whipped meringue. The sound of the Packer game was mixed with the sounds of piped-in mariachi music and the clanking of silverware.

Audrey's pulse quickened when she spotted Thomas sitting at the bar, alone. She would have known him even if she hadn't recognized his jacket. It was the way he sat, the curve of his shoulders, and the clean line of hair at the base of his neck.

The sudden presence of a hostess in a ruffled skirt and white peasant top forced a decision. "Just one this evening?"

Audrey nodded. No turning back now.

The hostess led her to a group of tables a half flight of stairs above the rest of the dining room. Like sitting at an indoor balcony, Audrey decided.

Two other tables were occupied, both by pairs of women who apparently didn't care about the game. "This is the only section that's open," the hostess said apologetically.

"It's fine." Audrey draped her coat over the back of the chair and picked up the glossy menu, a fine camouflage for a middle-aged woman spying on her adult son.

She kept the menu even after she ordered and the food arrived, ready to hoist it up if Thomas so much as glanced in her direction, which didn't seem likely since he hadn't moved since she came in. By the time she started her second strawberry margarita, Audrey relaxed and felt less like an interloper. She should go out like this more often, she decided, even if it meant going alone. Walt never wanted to eat anything more exotic than Italian. The only adventurous member of the family was Dennis. When he was in town, the two of them often drove two hours to the big city just so she could experience new things. Once they went to a new Thai restaurant; another time they ate at a wonderful place called the African Hut. Walt was never interested in joining them.

Audrey's gaze stayed on Thomas even as she dug into her taco salad and took slow sips from her margarita. From what she could see, he was drinking beer and eating from a plate of something covered with cheese and red sauce. She speculated that maybe he was meeting a group of friends from work, but he didn't seem to be with anyone.

Audrey turned the glass one fraction of a revolution with each sip, the better to taste the sugared rim along with the liquid. A roar from the bar crowd drew her attention to the TV hung in the upper left corner of the room. One of the teams made a touchdown, that much she figured, although the sport was alien to her. She had tried watching games with Walt and the boys on several occasions but could never quite figure out what the players were doing. They threw the ball, they all fell down, and then they all got up. None of it had any rhyme or reason as far as she could see.

Watching the fans was more interesting than the game. The crowd below Audrey cheered, raised their arms, and emitted sounds of disgust, all in unison. Almost as if they were all a separate part of a whole. The burly college student and his girlfriend wearing matching Green Bay Packer sweatshirts, the silver-haired man with the goatee, the two men who would have fit in at the production line at the brewery, the older lady resembling Mrs. Santa Claus—all of them watched this game as if they were marionettes grouped on one string. Their collective bodies leaned toward the TV as if they were being drawn into the action.

All but one, Audrey realized with a start.

Just one person at the bar had posture as straight as a librarian at a reference desk. Thomas.

His head wasn't turned toward the TV in the upper left-hand corner of the room, but in the direction of an employee washing glasses behind the bar. From where Audrey sat, she saw only the petite young woman's back and the rhythmical way she swayed from the waist, dipping glasses into twin sinks before setting them to the side. The young woman's auburn hair was pulled back into a ponytail, curly tendrils escaping on either side of her face. There was something oddly mesmerizing about the graceful way she moved. Thomas's head shifted a fraction of an inch with every movement. Audrey knew that if she could see his eyes, they would be following the ebb and flow of the girl's body.

Behind the bar a tall man with thinning black hair poured drinks. He leaned back to tell the young woman something, and she paused from her washing to turn and respond, giving Audrey a brief view of her face.

Audrey drew in a sharp breath of astonishment—she looked so young. She would have fit in with the girls who hung out at the custard stand after high school football games. From where Audrey sat, she looked seventeen, eighteen at most.

Jeffrey joked that Thomas was involved with one of his students, but Audrey hadn't given it much thought. She'd heard things like that happened all the time, but certainly not to her Thomas, who'd been sensible since the day he was born. Audrey preferred to think he wasn't associated with this girl at all, just distracted by her backside the way most men would be.

Audrey finished her taco salad, put her silverware lengthwise across the plate, and pushed it over to the other side of the small table. She picked up her margarita glass and finished off the last sweet sip. She couldn't see the point of staying any longer. Whatever secret Thomas had was going to remain his alone.

She pulled money out of her purse and looked around for her waiter. Her hands were sticky from her drink, and she wasn't sure where the ladies' room was located. How irritating that she'd forgotten to bring the wet wipes.

When her waiter did come, he bounded up the stairs, two at a time, as if he suddenly remembered the customers still lingering in the upper dining area. He held two beige checks fanned out like playing cards.

"One of these is mine?" Audrey asked.

"Yes." He held out her check and stared past her at the lower level. Audrey assumed he was watching the game until she heard an angry shout from below. A customer, a large man in a green flannel shirt, was gesturing and shouting angrily at the bartender. Drunk, Audrey thought. His shouting caused the other customers to look away from the game, their heads moving to the opposite side of the bar like spectators at a tennis game. The big man staggered to the far right side of the counter and moved bear-like behind the bar. Lunging toward the bartender, he slammed against the petite woman, who hit the side of the bar with a resounding whack. She slumped to the floor, disappearing from Audrey's sight.

"Oh my God," the waiter said and ran down the stairs with her check still in hand.

A group of men moved into the narrow opening on the left side of the bar to restrain the flannel-shirted man. The bartender and two other men dragged the drunk out into the dining room. His kicking and flailing knocked over an empty table and two cane-backed chairs. Silverware flew off the table and clattered onto the tile floor. Audrey stood up to get a better view.

"What happened?" A man in a white apron holding a metal-bristled brush rushed out from underneath the balcony. Kitchen help, Audrey surmised, as if she were watching a foreign film without subtitles.

"The drunk guy hit Skyla," the waiter said.

"Somebody call 911! Get the cops here." Now different voices hollered out at the same time, as if everyone thought of it at once.

Bar stools were abandoned and unfinished drinks deserted. People scurried around the dining room: the college girl handed tissues over the end of the bar, the two burly brewery workers dug cell phones out of their pockets, and a grandma-type lady righted chairs.

"Get an ambulance," someone yelled. This voice she knew. Thomas stood behind the bar holding a red-stained towel. "She's really bleeding. She needs to go to a hospital." His voice was loud and urgent, so different from the way he usually spoke. For an instant he glanced up to where Audrey stood, and she froze. Their eyes locked for a moment, and his face registered surprise; then he knelt down and she could only see the top of his head.

A group of people clustered around Thomas, but he didn't move. Audrey's gaze lingered on the swirl-shaped cowlick on the top of his head. He'd had it since he was a little boy. Funny, she'd almost forgotten about it until just now.

The hostess came into view and leaned over the top of the bar. "The ambulance is on its way. Five minutes they said."

Thomas glanced up and nodded, his eyes looking past her and at Audrey. This time his face was contorted in anger. She looked away, and he turned his attention back to the girl on the floor.

Audrey put her coat on and opened her purse. She pulled out a twenty and a five-dollar bill from her wallet and smoothed out the creases. She thought twenty-five was enough to cover the bill and a tip—probably way too much, in fact. It was hard to tell. The margaritas rattled her thinking, and she had the sick feeling she'd overstayed her welcome. Thomas's angry look left her feeling unsettled. All she had wanted was to be part of his life. Was that such a crime?

She walked down the stairs and through the crowd. A group of people clustered by the window, waiting for the ambulance.

A few others peered over the edge of the bar at the injured girl and Thomas. The people were a blur of green and gold—Packer colors.

Audrey exited out the back hallway, taking care to walk a straight line. It was important to pull it together and maintain control. It wouldn't do for people to think she was drunk.

CHAPTER FOUR

Spring in Wisconsin was like water in the desert, Skyla decided. The last week had been unseasonably warm—all the locals commented on it. A person couldn't check a book out of the library or fill a prescription at the pharmacy without someone ruminating on winter's demise. "Enjoy it while it lasts" became everyone's favorite parting words.

Winter had been long this year, interminably long. The cold soaked into her bones and stayed. After Thomas left for school in the mornings, she hiked the thermostat up to seventy-two degrees and still wasn't warm. The chill was always with her.

If it were up to Thomas, he'd keep it at sixty-six degrees round the clock. "You'd adjust if you'd just keep it cool all the time," he said. "Put a sweater on."

A sweater wasn't likely to do it, she told him. That still left her face and hands uncovered. Skyla hated being cold. Living in Wisconsin wasn't her idea, she reminded him.

Five years was the longest she'd lived under one roof, and it was in this house, the one Thomas bought right before they were married. He'd taken her to see the house right after the sellers had accepted his bid. On the drive to see it, Thomas turned onto Elm Street and watched her look at the neighborhood in awe. "I knew you'd love it," he said, parking the car so it aligned with the brick walkway leading up to the house.

The trees lining the street reached higher than the black curved streetlights. The homes themselves were stately. Some were Victorian charmers, while others were obviously additions from the twenties and forties—Tudors and bungalows mostly. Their house dated from the turn of the century and had a turret and leaded glass windows.

Skyla walked through the empty house, admiring the built-in china cabinet and bookcases and mentally furnishing the enclosed front porch with wicker furniture and ferns. To live in this house was beyond what she'd ever hoped for.

As a kid she had tried to imagine the lives of people living in middle-class suburban homes like this one. Places for people with money and no worries, her dad used to say. Growing up, she went to schools with kids who lived that kind of life. She listened to them talk and tried to imagine being part of their world. In the summer, they swam in backyard pools and rode their bikes around cul-de-sacs. Mid-afternoons their mother would bring out lemonade and frozen treats on a tray. When the father came home, he'd tousle the kids' hair and remind them to wash their hands before dinner. In the wintertime, the mother made sure scarves were properly wrapped and tied, jacket cuffs pulled over mittens. Each child was properly bundled before they were sent to the park, pulling their sleds behind them.

In Skyla's daydreams, she didn't bother thinking about the actual sledding. She'd experienced that, although the kids from her apartment complex used scraps of cardboard instead of sleds.

She skipped right over the sledding in her made-up scenario and thought instead about the tired kids trudging home afterwards, their boots crunching over white diamonds of snow. Her imagination focused on the mother who greeted them at the door, helping them take off their wet things, hanging damp mittens and hats by the radiator, warming their icy fingers between her own hands and asking if they wanted marshmallows in their hot chocolate. The mother part was the only thing she really envied, the only thing she wanted for herself.

❋ ❋ ❋

Skyla held the screen door open for Nora first and then pulled the door shut behind them. Out of habit, she braced herself for a gust of cold air that wasn't there. The spring breeze was warm and fragrant with the smell of lilacs and warm, damp soil. Old-timers in Wisconsin could always come up with some tale of springtime blizzards past, but looking at the purple and yellow crocuses blooming in her front yard, it was hard to believe it would ever snow again.

Skyla knelt down to button up Nora's red sweater. "Hold still a minute."

"Now can we go to the park?" Her daughter's voice was hopeful, excited.

Skyla worked each large button through holes the width of a quarter. "Yes, now we can go."

They heard the new neighbors before they saw them. Coming down the Jakubowskis' driveway was the blonde Skyla recognized as Roxanne Bear. Her new neighbor pushed a double stroller with a large canvas bag dangling off the back. A little boy walked alongside her dragging a stick. Trailing six feet behind him was the largest dog Skyla had ever seen.

"Hey," Roxanne called out as she reached the front of the Williamses' house next door. Skyla and Nora had just stepped off the paving stone walkway and onto the sidewalk. Roxanne clipped along so quickly that moving unobtrusively ahead of them was impossible.

"Hey back," Skyla said.

"Are you the one who found my Gregory on Sunday?"

"That was us." Skyla noticed Nora's face tensing at the sight of the big dog.

Roxanne stopped just short of hitting them. The front wheel of the stroller grazed the edge of Skyla's shoe. "I've been meaning to stop over or call and thank you, but I didn't know your last name, and it's been so hectic with moving and all." Behind her the dog rested his rear quarters on the pavement and leaned his boxy head to one side. A string of drool stretched from his mouth to his feet.

"No need for thanks," Skyla said. "We just wanted to make sure he was okay."

"Oh, yeah, they're always okay. I haven't lost one yet—at least not permanently." Her voice was tinged with pride.

"That's good." Skyla wondered about the standards of someone who boasted of not ever having lost a child permanently.

"The name's Roxanne," she said, thrusting out her hand. "Roxanne Bear."

"Skyla Plinka."

Roxanne gripped her hand firmly and smiled like they were old friends. "Skyla, huh? Cool name." She released Skyla's hand and rested her fingertips on the auburn head of the little boy standing next to her. "My two oldest boys are in school, but this is Monty, my middle child, and you know Gregory." She waved her hand at the toddler in the front of the stroller. "And snoozing back here is Ferd, the newest little Bear."

"This is my daughter Nora," Skyla said. "She's hiding behind me because she's not so sure about your dog." In truth, Nora was terrified of dogs.

"My dog?" Roxanne turned around. "Dammit, Buddy, I told you to stay in the yard!" She turned back to Skyla. "The damn dog listens about as well as the kids do." She grabbed his collar and tried to pull the dog to his feet. "Go home. I mean it, go back to the yard." She pointed toward her house. "Now, do it." Buddy whimpered and shook his head from side to side.

"He's saying no, Mama," Nora said. Her eyes were wide.

Roxanne looked at Skyla. "Would you mind watching my kids for a sec while I take him back to the house? I can tell he's not going to go back by himself." She clasped her hands together in mock pleading. "I'd really appreciate it. I'll be right back."

Skyla hesitated. "As long as it doesn't take too long. I promised my daughter we'd go to the park…"

"It won't be long. We were heading for the park ourselves. We'll walk with you, if that's okay." Roxanne grabbed the collar again. "Come on, boy, let's go home and get a treat. A treat, a treat, a treat!" Her voice took on a tone of false enthusiasm. The dog rose off its haunches and allowed her to lead him down the sidewalk. His sleek hindquarters swayed from side to side as he walked.

"What kind of dog is he?" Skyla called after her.

"A mastiff. It was Ted's idea to get him." Roxanne was shouting by this point. "He eats his weight in dog food and tracks dirt all through the house. Thank God mastiffs don't live that long."

✳ ✳ ✳

"So how long do they live?" Skyla asked when they arrived at the park. She and Roxanne sat at a picnic table while the three children played in the sandbox.

"Who?" Roxanne draped a receiving blanket over the top of the stroller where the baby slept. The striped blanket gave it the look of a traveling infant cabana.

"Mastiffs. You said they didn't live too long."

Roxanne sat down on the bench next to Skyla. "Oh that. Well, it all depends. Eight, nine years, something like that. With my luck, he'll beat the odds and set some kind of long life record." She made a face. "I know I'm terrible, but I really hate that dog. Ted and the kids love him, otherwise I'd be holding a dog raffle."

"Your dog, what's his name—Buddy? He's good with kids?"

"Depends on what you call good," Roxanne said and snorted. "He's pretty worthless as a guard dog, but on the other hand, he's not always jumping up on you and yip-yapping like some of those little dogs. You want something to drink?" Roxanne pulled a red, soft-sided cooler out of a canvas bag hanging from the back of the stroller. She unzipped it and peered inside. "I have juice boxes, Diet Coke, and a tropical wine cooler." She looked over at Skyla. "What's your pleasure?"

"I'll take the Coke."

"That leaves me with the wine cooler." Roxanne handed Skyla the red can and took out a slim bottle with a picture of a palm tree on the front. She wiped the sides of the bottle with her hand and unscrewed the cap.

"Your two older boys in school, how old are they?" Skyla asked. She pulled the tab back from the Coke and rested the can between her knees.

"They're twins. They'll be ten next month."

"Fraternal or identical?"

"Fraternal, but they look a lot alike. People get them mixed up all the time and say their names sound the same, which I don't get at all. They're Emmett and Wyatt—what's so hard about that?" She took a swig of the wine cooler. "I was reading a lot of westerns when I was pregnant with them, and I wanted to use the name Wyatt. Emmett seemed to go really good with it until months later when someone told me it was a clown name. Who knew? Anyway, the clown thing kind of fits. He's a way goofy kid." She smiled. "Ted said if they were triplets, we could have named them Emmett, Wyatt, and Dammit—and I think he was serious. Poor Dammit would have thought we were calling him all the time."

"Names are a tricky thing," Skyla said. "My problem is that with the last name Plinka, everything comes out sounding like that Muppet—you know the one, the Swedish chef?" She cocked her head to the side and spoke in a singsong voice. "My name is Skyla Plinka. My daughter's Nora Plinka."

"That's nothing. Try having the last name Bear. Any name you put in front of it ends up sounding like it's from a kid's fairy tale."

"Bear—that's a Native American name?"

"Nah, German. It was spelled different at one point, and somewhere along the line the *a* and *e* got switched around. One of those Ellis Island things, I think." Roxanne lifted the bottle and took a drink, her throat pulsing as she swallowed. She set the bottle on the table and stood up to yell in the direction of the sandbox. "Monty, you play nice, or we're going home! Don't you dare put sand in his pants." She shook her head and sat down. "That kid is going to keep driving me to drink. These boys are wearing me out. You don't know how lucky you are to have a sweet little girl. That's what I'm aiming for next time."

"You want another one?" Skyla tried to keep her voice neutral but was secretly aghast. "You must really love children."

"Children I can take or leave. It's babies that I'm nuts about. You don't have to give me that look—I know I'm crazy. Everyone tells me that. I just can't help it. Once my youngest gets past the baby stage, I want another one." She leaned in toward Skyla. "It's like a sickness with me. I can't help myself. I think it's hormonal or something. Every time I get pregnant, I tell myself that this is it, I'm done—no more. Then my youngest gets to be a certain age, and the urge comes back, and I think I'll die if I don't have another baby to hold in my arms."

"Babysitting for someone else wouldn't do it?"

"Not even close." Roxanne pushed the stroller back and forth to hush the baby, who had started to fuss.

Skyla shook her head. "I can't even imagine having five kids, much less six. I'm set with one."

"It's not as many as it sounds, really. At home I can manage. It's just when we have to go somewhere that it gets tricky." Roxanne finished the last of the wine cooler and threw the empty bottle into an anchored garbage can a few feet away. The bottle went in with a resounding clunk. She cupped her hands to form a megaphone. "Stop it, Monty. Don't you hurt your little brother. I mean it, you let go of his hair, now! Stop it!" She turned to Skyla. "Would you keep an eye on Ferd? I got to go break it up—he's gonna kill him out there."

Skyla leaned against the edge of the picnic table. The warm sun felt good on her face. Nora had left the sandbox during the brawl between Roxanne's boys and was sitting and rocking on a plastic horse mounted on a large spring. When she noticed her mother watching, she waved like a beauty queen from a parade float. Skyla smiled and waved back.

Roxanne crouched in the sandbox, holding Monty by his arms and speaking in a low voice. He said something Skyla couldn't hear and then nodded to his mother. Roxanne ruffled his hair, leaned over and picked up Gregory (whose face was red and blotchy from crying), and set him on his feet across from Monty. The older boy pulled Gregory up to his chest and kissed the top of his blond head. From where Skyla sat, Gregory didn't look like he was enjoying it. His face was scrunched and his arms were pinned to his side by his brother's embrace, but at least he wasn't crying anymore. Roxanne brushed the sand off of Gregory's back and then stood up and headed back to the picnic table.

"Well that's settled," Roxanne said as she sat down on the wooden seat. "I'm constantly telling them family is the most important thing there is, and that they should be good to each other. Just when I think they're getting it, they try to kill each other. But that's how it is with brothers and sisters, right?"

"I guess so," Skyla said. "I'm an only child, so I really wouldn't know."

"I'm so sorry," Roxanne said, her face softening. "So is that why you only want one? Because you grew up that way?"

"No," Skyla said, her face flushing. "It's just, I have this idea that if I have more than one, I'm just asking for heartbreak, you know what I mean?"

Roxanne looked puzzled. "Asking for heartbreak? How?"

Skyla rarely opened up to anyone, much less a stranger, but something about her new neighbor was comfortingly familiar. "When I was in kindergarten..." she began, and then the whole story poured out of her in one long rush.

That day, while she'd waited for her mother to pick her up after school, her father was home, numb from shock. He'd completely forgotten about her, and so she lingered, not knowing. Eventually her teacher, a kind young woman named Miss Sinclair, walked her home.

Although her memories of her mother from the same point in time were foggy, she clearly remembered the joy of having Miss Sinclair all to herself. She clutched her teacher's smooth, warm hand and looking up noticed a charm bracelet dancing on her wrist. The bracelet had a teaching theme—delicate silver charms shaped like pencils and books and an apple. Sometimes she liked to think the hand she remembered clasping had been her mother's, but no, she was fairly sure it was her teacher's—she remembered seeing Miss Sinclair's dark ponytail swing as they walked. They arrived at the apartment building to find a police car and ambulance in front and an officer blocking the front door. As they stood there, two men in dark uniforms carried out a covered stretcher. Miss Sinclair exchanged a few words with one of the officers as they came past. At his response, her face crumpled and her free hand covered her mouth. In the next moment, Skyla was lifted off the ground and had her head pressed against her teacher's shoulder.

Skyla's cheek rested against the raised pattern of Miss Sinclair's navy blue sweater, and her legs swayed back and forth as her teacher rocked her. She repeated something that sounded like, "Poor baby, poor baby. You poor sweet baby." The words came out like a cry, like Miss Sinclair was having trouble breathing. Skyla knew then her mother had left for good and nothing would ever be the same.

Just the night before, she had cried out in her sleep and her mother had come into her room to see what was wrong. "It was only a dream," her mother told her. "I'm not going anywhere." She remembered her mother sitting on the edge of the mattress to tuck her in and then stroking her hair, lulling her into a drowsy sense of false security.

After her mother's death, from a ruptured brain aneurysm, as it turned out, everything changed. Her father, who couldn't keep a job, was always convinced that a change of scenery would fix everything, so they moved over and over again. The hardest part of moving was keeping track of the simplest things: the name of her street, where they kept the cans of soup, the day of garbage pickup. Clues came to her in dream fragments in the phase of sleep just before waking up. It was then she dreamt of houses they'd yet to live in and people she'd yet to meet. When she was little, she never remembered much upon awakening except the images—the faces of people and pictures of houses like the fronts of movie sets. It was enough to make the new places and people seem familiar, like she was connecting with old friends instead of starting all over again. An affirmation she was in the right place. She used intuition to fill in the gaps left open by a lack of familiarity.

Growing up she had a best friend in every town along the way. When it was time to leave them she cried, but now she couldn't remember very many of their names. Life was so confusing. It was hard to keep track of things.

"My father died in a car accident when I was nineteen," she said, "and then I really was all alone in the world. Then I met Thomas, and now I have a home and a beautiful daughter. I'm the happiest I've ever been. Wanting more seems greedy. And you know, everyone I love dies." She wiped her eyes with her fingertips. "Not to be all melodramatic, but that's how it feels. Like I should just appreciate what I have. Having more than one child would just be tempting fate."

"Oh, you poor thing," Roxanne said, leaning over to give her a hug. "No wonder you feel that way. But I'm pretty sure that's not how it works. It seems to me you had your share of heartbreak already. You're due for only good things from now on."

✳ ✳ ✳

After Skyla finished the dinner dishes and helped Nora into her thermal-weave pajamas, Thomas gave them the litany of his day: The kid who always arrived late for his first-hour class was late again, unbelievable given all the warnings he'd had. A sophomore girl had transferred into one of his afternoon classes without any prior notification, just shown up with a note from the office. Additionally, Thomas grumbled, someone had taken the yogurt he'd left in the teacher's lounge refrigerator. All in all, it was not a good day.

"And what did you two do today?" he asked. Nora leaned against the foot of his recliner and paged through an alphabet book. Skyla sat across from them on the couch with her legs curled under her.

"We went to the park," Nora said without looking up from her book. "With our friends."

Thomas looked over his glasses at Skyla. "You have friends?" He sounded amused.

"We have new friends, Daddy," Nora said. "We had a picnic."

"Are these friends real people?"

Skyla laughed. "Yes, they're real. We went with the new neighbor and her kids, the one who moved into the Jakubowskis' house. You remember, we met her husband on Sunday."

He looked at her over his glasses. "Yes, I remember. The woman who doesn't keep track of her kids. The one I warned you about."

"Don't make that face at me. She's very nice, and Nora had fun playing with her boys. There aren't any other little kids in the neighborhood. Actually, it was nice to have another adult to talk to." Skyla ran her fingers through her hair, untangling the curls in the back. "And no one got lost, and I didn't have to bail anyone out of jail, despite your predictions."

"Not yet," Thomas said. "Mark my words—it's only a matter of time."

In truth, Skyla had marveled at Roxanne's mothering skills. Her canvas bag came equipped with provisions for every child-based contingency: Band-Aids, pacifiers, wet wipes, food. At the first mention of hunger, Roxanne pulled out sandwiches, napkins, cookies, and red grapes. Plenty for everyone.

Roxanne orchestrated the table arrangement for lunch. She helped little Gregory climb onto the picnic seat next to Skyla and directed Nora and Monty to sit on the opposite side. Roxanne doled out sandwich halves and clusters of grapes and deftly pierced the straws into the juice boxes' openings, handing one to each child before they even asked for a drink. All the while balancing a baby on one hip.

"I can't believe how organized you are," Skyla said. "I was overwhelmed with just one baby."

Roxanne shrugged. "Babies aren't hard. People just make it hard." She cooed to the baby perched on her side. "You're no trouble at all, are you?" She looked at Skyla and sighed. "It's when they get to be big kids that all the trouble starts. Then they start doing stuff like jumping off the garage roof and having farting contests."

"Farting contests?"

"Yeah, not too many people can do it on command." Roxanne said it with something like delight. "Farting and belching were the twins' main interests for about two years."

"I hope Nora never gets like that."

"She won't." Roxanne sounded positive. "Girls don't talk about gross body stuff—they just get all tattle-taley and whiny instead. Oh, I do want a daughter so bad. If I can't talk Ted into another one, I don't know what I'm going to do."

Skyla was overtaken suddenly by a surge of something like homesickness. Roxanne's no-holds-barred way of speaking was so reminiscent of the women she knew growing up: the lady friends her dad brought home, the women who lived on the other side of their apartment walls, the ones who gossiped while hanging wash in the neighborhood. She had a directness Skyla admired. Roxanne was every good-hearted neighbor Skyla had ever known, the kind who watched out for little motherless girls.

Thomas interrupted her thoughts. "I hope this isn't going to be a regular thing with this neighbor woman. It seems to me you could do a lot better." His forehead furrowed in concern.

"Actually, we're getting together tomorrow and taking the kids to McDonald's for lunch," Skyla said. "I really like her."

"Hmm," Thomas said, which was what he always said when words escaped him.

CHAPTER FIVE

Audrey never imagined that Thomas and Skyla would be married the summer following the incident at the Mexican restaurant. In fact, she hadn't imagined they'd get married at all. Skyla seem an unlikely match for Thomas, not his type at all, although she wasn't sure exactly what his type would be. For one thing, Skyla was so young, a full ten years younger than her son.

For another thing, they seemed to be complete opposites. She was an art student, an odd subject to be studying. Weren't artists a little flaky? And here Thomas was, a science teacher and as settled as the ground he walked on. What could they possibly have in common? The only theory Audrey had was that Thomas was fulfilling some kind of parental role for Skyla. The more she thought about it, the more she was sure it was true. Why, even how they met confirmed that. What could be more romantic than having a man come to your rescue and take care of you when you've been injured?

And there was the matter of finances. Over the last several years, Thomas had saved most of his salary by living at home.

Although Audrey wasn't sure of the specifics, it had to be a sizable amount. That must have had some appeal to Skyla, the impoverished student. He even bought a house while they were still engaged. And it was a beautiful old house too, right in the heart of the original section of town. Audrey was impressed, but Walt wasn't. "Old houses have old plumbing, old electrical, and everything else," he said. "Mark my words—it will be a money pit."

Skyla wasn't stupid. Her people had never even owned a house, for goodness' sake, traveling around like vagabonds. Certainly she must have recognized a sure thing in Thomas. And he wasn't savvy enough to see through her.

There was another thing that bothered Audrey. Skyla had these knowing eyes that made Audrey uneasy, like she knew all her secrets. Her future daughter-in-law was quiet, but not shy. She always seemed to be taking it all in. Conversations with Skyla were awkward. She talked about the movies, weather, and current events, but she never discussed her past. It was as if she was born the day she cracked her head on the bar and Thomas came to her rescue.

And what was the deal with her roommate? Audrey shook her head at the thought of him. Such a strange young man. Thomas had forewarned her, but still it was shocking to meet him at the wedding rehearsal on Friday night. He was a tall, thin man with skin the color of dark beer. His shaved head made his ears stand out.

"Who invited that guy?" Walt asked. He clearly meant it as an aside, but it was heard by everyone in the small chapel.

"Shhh," she said. "It's Skyla's roommate—her friend from art school."

"This is Oscar," Skyla said, introducing him to each person in turn. They made an odd couple. The top of her head only came up to his shoulders, and she was as fair as he was dark. "One of my closest friends. He's like a brother to me." When he shook Audrey's hand, his fingers totally engulfed hers. His grip was firm, and his skin was soft.

"I'm so pleased to meet you," Oscar said in a soft voice. Audrey was shocked to realize that he had a British accent. Did Skyla mention she was living with a foreigner? If she had, Audrey couldn't remember it. It seemed a pretty important thing to leave out.

"It's a pleasure to finally meet you," Audrey said, as if they had heard so much about him, when in fact, she only recalled Skyla mentioning him once.

The rehearsal and dinner afterward could have been a Plinka family gathering except for the presence of Oscar and Skyla. Apparently Skyla had no other friends or relatives, a fact that didn't surprise Audrey, but it puzzled Walt.

"Don't you have any relatives who will be coming to the wedding?" he asked Skyla. "Cousins, aunts, uncles, grandparents?"

"She knows what relatives are," Thomas snapped. "She just doesn't have any." He jangled the keys in the pocket of his khakis in what seemed to Audrey an angry gesture.

"Everyone has someone." Walt's voice matched Thomas's in irritation. "She had to come from somewhere."

"My parents and grandparents are deceased, and I'm an only child," Skyla explained almost apologetically. "I do have other relatives, but I don't know them very well, and they're all over the country. They tend to move a lot, and I don't know if I could find them even if I had to."

"Like gypsies," Walt said to Audrey that night when they were getting ready for bed. Audrey was pulling a sleeveless cotton nightgown over her head and had trouble hearing him.

"Like what?" she asked, coming through the head opening of the garment like swimming up for air.

"Gypsies," Walt said. "Skyla's family wandering around the country—seems highly suspicious. A likely story."

"You don't believe her?" Audrey nimbly fastened the last of the three buttons on the front of her nightgown.

"I'm not sure what to believe. She may be part of the witness protection program for all I know." He was sitting on the edge of the bed pulling off his socks and shoes.

"Oh, stop."

"No, I'm serious. That roommate of hers—didn't he look like he could be Secret Service or something in that dark suit? All he needed was some sunglasses and one of those ear phone things and he could be one of those guys guarding the president."

"I don't think so, Walt." Audrey was dubious. "He's not even American."

"That's another thing," Walt said. "That accent—did it sound real to you? It seemed to kind of come and go."

"I didn't notice that," Audrey said.

※ ※ ※

By the time they drove home from the wedding dinner the following night, Walt had a more positive attitude. "You know, I've never seen Thomas so happy. I don't think he stopped smiling once." His pudgy fingers gripped the steering wheel, and he leaned forward as if to see the road better. "Whatever he's got, I hope it sticks. It's a big improvement."

"He did seem happy," Audrey admitted begrudgingly. She twisted her anniversary band around so that the row of diamonds faced upwards.

Thomas had moved through the day as if being a bridegroom was his true calling. There was something odd about his appearance, something Audrey couldn't put her finger on until she realized that Thomas was uncharacteristically smiling with his teeth showing.

After the ceremony, Thomas enthusiastically shook Father Bob's hand and said, "Thank you for being part of the happiest day of my life." Several times he lifted Skyla up, her legs dangling like a doll's beneath the layers of petticoats. "She's all mine now," he said each time.

Later at the restaurant, before the food was served, the newlyweds walked from table to table—Thomas leading and Skyla hanging back a little—greeting each guest in turn. "Hey," Jeffrey whispered loudly from his place at the table, "check out Thomas working the room."

"He's supposed to do that," Walt's mother, Gram, said. "It's good manners." She was seated at the head table with the immediate family and Oscar. Her boyfriend Mike (odd to use the word "boyfriend" for an eighty-year-old man, Audrey thought) couldn't stay for the dinner. He begged off with another social obligation just before giving Skyla and Thomas a card they later discovered contained a check for three hundred dollars.

The tables with the other guests were positioned to fan around the head table where the family sat. "I declare, Skyla looks like one of those Irish Dresden statues," Gram said. Everyone at the table turned to watch the couple. She snapped her fingers. "You know what I mean. They stand about this high." She held her index finger four inches above the table.

"Those little figurines with the lacy porcelain gowns?" Oscar said to help her out. Until then he'd been as silent as moss.

Gram nodded. "That's it. She's so pretty, like a little bride doll." She turned to Jeffrey on her left. "You two boys are going to have a hard act to follow when you get married."

"I'm not getting married," Jeffrey scoffed. He rearranged the sugar bowl, creamer, and salt and pepper shakers so they lined up in an arc around his plate.

"Marriage is not for everyone." Oscar's voice, soft in volume, seemed even softer with the English accent. Audrey noticed that his hands fluttered when he talked, long, neat hands like the wings of a dark bird.

"You can say that again," Jeffrey said and stood up dramatically to lean across the table, shaking Oscar's hand and knocking over the pepper shaker.

"Marriage is not for everyone," Dennis repeated.

"You too, Dennis?" Gram asked, clutching her heart in fake horror. "I never would have guessed that there would be so many bachelors in this family. It's your fault, Audrey," she said, looking past Dennis to where Audrey and Walt sat together. "You've spoiled these boys."

"My fault nothing," Audrey said. "I'm through taking responsibility for anyone but myself. They're all grown up, and they can get married whenever they want as far as I'm concerned."

"When I said marriage isn't for everyone, I didn't mean to imply that I'd never get married," Dennis said. "I'll wait and see how it works out for Thomas. I'm biding my time, Gram."

"Well, don't bide forever," Gram said, unfolding her linen napkin onto her lap. "I'm getting older by the minute here, boys."

Aren't we all, Audrey thought.

CHAPTER SIX

Skyla had known all summer that Nora would be starting four-year-old kindergarten in September. They had shopped for a backpack (one so big that Skyla felt it violated some child labor law) and bought school supplies: crayons, scissors with rounded ends, a plastic ruler, and a box of facial tissue. Roxanne had the same routine for her third son, Monty, but she managed to find everything except the crayons right at home. She dragged down a half dozen plastic storage containers from up in the attic and rummaged in them until she found everything on the list. Even the Bugs Bunny backpack had belonged to one of Monty's older brothers at one time, evidenced by the fact that someone had given Bugs a handlebar moustache with a permanent marker.

It seemed to Skyla that Monty would resent hand-me-downs, but Roxanne said no. "When you come from a big family," she said, "you get used to it. I used to wait for my older sister to grow out of certain things so I could get them. One time I waited two years for this one sweater, and Jackie spilled grape juice on it before I could get it. On purpose I'm sure, so it would be ruined and I wouldn't get it. God, was I pissed."

The bus for afternoon kindergarten was scheduled to stop at the end of Roxanne's driveway. Skyla walked Nora down the porch steps after lunch and steered her in the direction of the Bears' house.

Roxanne and Monty were already waiting by the curb. Monty had on a Brewers baseball jersey and matching shorts. Roxanne looked incomplete with just one child at her side. The Bugs Bunny backpack was facedown in the gutter.

"Hey," Roxanne called out.

"Hey yourself," Skyla said. Nora was taking the lead now, pulling her arm and jumping over cracks in the sidewalk. "Did you lose a couple of kids?"

"Napping." Roxanne jerked her head toward the house. "Or at least they should be. I put them in their beds—hopefully Gregory hasn't crawled out yet."

Skyla nodded. She held her hand up visor-like to her forehead. It was hard to believe school was starting already. That was the trouble with Wisconsin. The warm months went by too quickly. And even when the temperature was good, there were too many mosquitoes.

"It goes so quickly," Skyla said, still thinking about the seasons.

"I know." Roxanne picked a thread off her tank top. "They grow up so fast. When they're babies, you think you'll never get a full night's sleep again, then you think they'll never get out of diapers, and the next thing you know they're off to school." She looked glum. "If only they could stay little forever." She reached over to tousle Monty's hair. "What will I do when they all grow up?"

"Get a job?" Skyla suggested.

"That's a good one," Roxanne said and harrumphed as if Skyla had suggested taking up sheep herding or brain surgery. "A job," she repeated and shook her head. "Not bloody likely."

Skyla knew Roxanne was talking about herself, but she still took the disparagement personally. She'd been toying with the idea of getting a job since Nora was a toddler, but Thomas hadn't been crazy about the idea. "What would you do?" he asked when she brought up the subject. She clearly remembered the way he'd looked at her over his glasses, a mixture of surprise and amusement on his face.

"There are lots of things I could do," she'd answered defensively, but when it came right down to it, she was stumped. Any job that involved nights and weekends would intrude on family time, and anything during the day would require a babysitter, which would eat up any money she'd make. Her mother-in-law, Audrey, had offered to watch Nora anytime she wanted, but this idea didn't appeal to Skyla at all. Audrey ("Call me Mom," she'd said, but that never came out easily) had a tendency to be controlling. There's no telling what she'd do given free reign with Nora. Probably dress her in fussy dresses circa 1965 and carry her around all day instead of encouraging her to be independent. No, that never would have worked.

Occasionally when summers rolled around she played with the idea of looking for seasonal employment. But Thomas had off then, and it seemed foolish to work when he was home and they could do things as a family.

Now that Nora was in school, Skyla decided that she was fresh out of excuses.

CHAPTER SEVEN

"You're kidding."

Skyla waited until dinnertime to tell Thomas about her new job. She'd cooked his favorite dinner and strategically waited until he'd speared the last bit of beef roast on his plate. It was Audrey's recipe—easy to do, just marinate in wine and cook slowly. It was delicious but wouldn't ever be found on a restaurant menu with a little heart next to it.

"No, I'm not kidding," Skyla answered, reaching to move Nora's milk glass away from the edge of the table. "We talked about this. Remember, extra money to put in Nora's college fund? Why are you acting so surprised?"

"We talked about you getting a part-time job," Thomas said, almost sputtering. "I pictured you at the library putting away books or selling Tupperware or something. Not working there."

Selling Tupperware? How could he even suggest such a thing? Didn't he know her at all? Skyla wrinkled her nose.

"You make it sound like it's a brothel or something," she said. "It's a bookstore. I'd have thought that'd be right up your alley."

"Barnes and Noble is a bookstore. Borders is a bookstore." Thomas pushed his glasses up the bridge of his nose. "Mystic Books is an opium den disguised as a bookstore." His voice was tinged with sarcasm. "That woman who runs it looks like a hobbit. She's let it get all run down. I don't even like walking past it anymore—it gives me the heebie-jeebies."

"It does have kind of a creepy ambience," Skyla admitted. Actually, the odd look of the place was what had drawn her into the store in the first place. She'd passed it several days in a row while taking her afternoon walk, a habit she'd started within days of Nora's kindergarten debut. Her walks were a secret indulgence. She'd avoided telling Roxanne about them for fear she'd invite herself along. As much as Skyla liked her neighbor and the boys, she didn't want her outings turned into extravaganzas—a stroller brigade complete with stops for snacks and searches for lost binkies.

Skyla walked the same route every day, a mile from home and all the way back again. The small downtown area was at the end of her route. The shops in Pellswick looked as if they'd been frozen in time fifty years before. The coffee shop sported vinyl-covered stools at the counter and a chalkboard listing the daily specials and the soup of the day. The barbershop had a revolving red and white striped pole just outside the front door. The photo studio displayed black and white images of babies and toddlers in a window fronted by a placard that advised calling for an appointment.

Further down the block she passed the bench outside the hardware store, which was usually occupied by two old men who were trading stories and smoking. Jawing, her dad used to call it. She'd walk by at a good clip, and they'd touch the brim of their baseball caps and call out, "Hey there," or "Afternoon." She'd nod and continue on. Nobody else ever seemed to be coming or going from the stores. It was amazing, really, that this small retail strip could stay in business when there was a mall, Wal-Mart, and fast-food restaurants just a few miles away.

At the end of her walking route was the bookstore. "Mystic Books—New and used books. Come inside, the adventure awaits," the sign said. Skyla resisted this invitation the first few days she passed by. Not an impulse buyer, she rarely entered a store unless she was looking for something specific.

After a few days she allowed herself to stop and look at the display window—a weird assortment of books, crystals, and what looked like a shrunken head. The backdrop was a draped gauzy material, the folds of which looked dusty, even from outside.

On a whim Skyla pushed open the screen door and entered. A bell attached to the door jangled, but from what she could see there was no one inside to hear it. Her first impression of the place—tall ceilings, dank smell, and dark paneling—reminded her of a cave. Even the hanging cylindrical light fixtures put her in mind of stalactites—or was it stalagmites? The store was narrow but deep, stretching back beyond Skyla's field of vision.

"Hello," Skyla called out. Her voice didn't echo as she half thought it would. She looked down at the floor and toed the old cracked linoleum. "Hello?" To her left a long mahogany counter held a cash register and piles of books. The rest of the store was a maze of bookcases of varying shapes and sizes situated at odd angles. Skyla thought it was a good thing Thomas wasn't with her. The store's layout would upset his sense of order.

A shuffling from behind one of the bookcases disrupted her thoughts. "Just a minute," a female voice warbled. Like a magic trick, a tiny woman popped out ten feet away from where Skyla stood.

The suddenness of the motion startled Skyla. The woman wiped her hands on the front of a white baker's apron, stepped forward, and then stopped and stared. Skyla suddenly knew what it must feel like to be tall. She, who had always been the short one, towered over this lady. From this angle she saw the top of her head, white hair laced with gray and pulled into a bun. The woman had pale skin and rosy cheeks, more from exertion than cosmetics, judging from the way she was breathing. "Oh, you're finally here," she said as if she'd been expecting Skyla. "I'm so glad you've come."

The woman's unrelenting gaze made Skyla suddenly conscious of the messy tendrils of hair escaping from her ponytail and the boldness of the bright floral sundress Thomas thought more appropriate for a cruise ship than a daytime stroll. "I think you must be mistaking me for someone else," Skyla said.

"No, I don't think so." The woman deftly untied her apron, lifted it over her head, and draped it over one arm. She walked forward and extended her hand. "I'm Risa Towers, the owner of Mystic Books. Used to be my husband and me ran it, but he passed on a few years ago, so it's just me now." She said all this in a rush and paused to catch her breath. "Everything's kind of a mess right now. I tried to rearrange the bookcases but couldn't move them too far. I have the worst time keeping order." She extended her stubby arm in a sweeping arc like a munchkin welcoming Dorothy to Oz. "Why don't you take a look-see, and then you can tell me what you think."

"Have we met?" Skyla was puzzled. Was this woman mentally ill or just confused?

"Not yet," Risa said. "You need to tell me your name."

"Skyla Plinka."

Risa beamed. "Lovely, perfect," she said, clasping her hands together in a way that Skyla found familiar. In fact, all of this—the odd little lady, the old building, and the dank smell—was starting to have that familiar feeling. She'd had this feeling often when she was a child, but as she'd entered adulthood, it had gone away without her even realizing it.

Now, at this moment, she felt it full force. "Déjà vu all over again" was the expression, but it was more than that. It was sensing that she was in the right place at the right time, that things were unfolding as they should. There was some comfort in that.

"I'll show you around if you like," Risa said. "Or if you'd rather go on your own…?" Her voice trailed off.

"I don't want to trouble you. I'll browse for a bit." Skyla looked at her watch. Nora wasn't due back from kindergarten for another two and a half hours. Normally she'd go home and do some laundry or cleaning, but there really was no hurry to get back. This day was taking an interesting twist.

As Skyla walked through the bookstore, the familiar all-knowing feeling spread through her like sips of hot chocolate on a cold day. The store's arrangement was hodge-podge—bookcases and an occasional chair strewn about like children's blocks. There was one central aisle though, and this was the course she took, pausing here and there for a closer inspection. Even without any seeming order she was able to anticipate what lay ahead and wasn't surprised to find out she was right. Some of the bookcases had small index cards taped to the side facing the aisle labeled with words like "Poetry," and "Health and Natural Medicine," and "Horticulture." She was aware that Risa Towers was watching her closely, but Skyla sensed more curiosity from the storeowner than suspicion.

Occasionally something on the shelves would catch Skyla's interest—a stone gargoyle the size of her fist next to a pile of gothic novels; an oversized book about the human body with transparency pages showing muscles, bones, and organs; an old-fashioned snow globe next to a section of children's picture books. Skyla picked up the globe. It was the size of a softball and heavy. Just picking it up made the snow inside it swirl around a miniature Swiss village.

"It's a music box, too." Risa's voice startled her. More than startled, really. Scared the crap out of her is how Thomas's brother Jeffrey would have put it. She hastily set the globe back on the shelf, relieved that her instinct had caused her to tighten her grip rather than release it.

"It's very old and valuable." Risa was at her elbow now.

Skyla nodded.

Risa continued, seemingly oblivious to the fact that Skyla had come close to smashing her antique snow globe. "My husband and I would travel all over the world and buy things for the store. It used to be Mystic Books and Gifts, but the gift part fell by the wayside after he passed on. I have enough trouble keeping up with the books now."

"Ahh." She filed this information away, but her mind was on the rest of the store, and she continued walking until she reached the back. "What is this?" Skyla peered behind a freestanding room divider hinged like bi-fold doors. Asian in appearance, its surface was black lacquer with gold lettering. Behind the screen was a round table, unexceptional except for the shimmery gold fabric that covered it.

"This is where we have our readings," Risa said. "I'm sure you've heard of them—everyone in town has."

Readings? Skyla's mind reeled. She couldn't imagine anyone bringing children here for story time unless their names were Morticia and Gomez. Could she be talking about a book club? She'd never heard of a book club in town. Pellswick was hardly a teeming metropolis, but there had to be some literary types around.

"Readings?" Skyla said. "I'm not sure I know what you mean."

"That's where Madame gives her readings," Risa explained. "She's so good—I'm surprised you haven't heard about her. Her psychic powers are amazing—amazing, amazing!" The little woman held up her arms like a gospel singer praising the Lord. "Everyone says so. She's been so helpful to me since my Bert crossed over. She's the one who told me you'd be coming in."

It took Skyla a moment to digest this information. "She knew I'd be coming in today?" Skyla was faintly aware of how ridiculous this conversation sounded. If Thomas had been there, it never would have gotten this far. He had a tendency to brush off eccentric people—well, any people really. She pictured him shutting down this conversation in the same way he firmly hung up on telemarketers mid-pitch.

In fact, he really wasn't open to possibilities at all, now that she thought about it. How very odd it was, she thought, to live your life so decisively, to be so sure of how everything should be, as if everything in life was black and white instead of various shades of gray.

"Well, she didn't say you'd come in today exactly," Risa said. "I'd just been praying for some help organizing this store. And Madame said that before the month was over help would come to me."

"Come to you?"

"Right through the front door, she said." Risa sounded jubilant. "And just as it was foretold, here you are."

"Here I am."

"You are good at getting things in order, aren't you? I can't pay much, but I'm sure we can work something out."

"Yes, actually, I'm very good at getting things in order."

"And you have an artistic eye. That's what Madame said—I'd get someone with an artistic eye. That's what I need to make everything appealing and draw people in, she said."

Skyla thought back to her art school training and the hundreds of boxes she'd packed for all of her childhood moves. Certainly, she was the right person for the job. Or could be, anyway. And she had thought about getting a job. Maybe it was meant to be.

Somehow it didn't sound quite so convincing as she was explaining this to Thomas later.

"But don't you see," she said at dinnertime. "It all works out so perfectly. She needs the help, I need a job..."

"Want a job," Thomas said. He was gathering up the dishes and carrying them to the counter even though Nora was still pushing her beef around her plate and had half a glass of milk. "You don't need a job. It's not as if we don't have enough money to live on."

"Well, of course not. I just meant that I have some time now with Nora in school, and we had talked about the whole college fund thing." Skyla felt like a teenager trying to talk her father into some oddball scheme, but of course she had no firsthand knowledge of this. Her father had never cared what she did. If anything, she'd been the sensible one, handling all the details of the household by the time she was nine or ten.

"Trust me, it will work out," she said finally, following him into the kitchen where he was putting the jug of milk into the fridge. He was opposed to keeping the milk on the table during mealtimes, preferring constant refrigeration. It wasn't until Skyla called Golden Guernsey's 800 number and got the statistics on milk spoilage that he reluctantly allowed her to leave the container out for short periods of time. But she still noticed him sniffing the open jug from time to time when he didn't know she was looking.

"I suppose it will be fine," Thomas said begrudgingly as he leaned over into the fridge. "If it starts to be a problem, you could always quit."

"I could always quit," Skyla agreed as she stood behind him caressing the downy hair on the back of his neck. But she couldn't imagine why it would be a problem.

CHAPTER EIGHT

"When I was a little girl," Roxanne said, "I dreamed of having a big, old house in the country with a bunch of animals and a dozen kids." She poured creamer into her coffee and stirred slowly. "And here I am, thirty-two years old with one stupid dog and seven kids short of my goal."

"A dozen kids?" Skyla was aghast. Already Roxanne's house pulsated with children. On a day like today, when the kids had off of school for an in-service day, it seemed like Roxanne had more than enough children. They were a blur of constant activity: feet pounding on the stairs (and there were two staircases—one in front and one off the kitchen), chasing, jumping, climbing. It made Skyla feel like she was in the middle of a dodgeball game. With five there was always someone chasing the dog or giving someone a wedgie or inflicting wrestling moves on their brother.

When Skyla was at Roxanne's house, she realized what people meant when they said they couldn't even hear themselves think. Sometimes she'd formulate a thought, and before it would reach her lips, the conversation would be interrupted by the news that Monty was bleeding or Wyatt had torn Emmett's shirt. She'd have to put her thoughts on hold for so long that she never would get the words out. It would nag at her later. *What was I going to say?* But it was no use. The thought was gone. It was impossible, somehow, to think that anyone could thrive on all that chaos, but somehow Roxanne did. "Knock it off, you guys," she'd say. "I mean it. I've just about had it." But her protestations made as much difference as a beetle on a soccer field. A dozen kids? Skyla couldn't even imagine it.

Roxanne pushed the cream pitcher across the table, but Skyla shook her head. She drank her coffee black. "Six boys and six girls," Roxanne said. "I read about a family like that in a book once when I was a kid."

"*Cheaper by the Dozen?*" Skyla asked.

"What?"

"The book—was it called *Cheaper by the Dozen?*"

"Yeah, maybe. Anyway, when I first starting going out with Ted, I told him my plans. I specifically said twelve children, and he said, *and I quote,*" she said as she leaned across the table for emphasis, "'Whatever you want, baby.' Those were his exact words. I thought it was all set."

From her spot at the table, Skyla could see Monty in the living room standing on a rocking chair and swaying, arms outstretched like he was riding a surfboard. On the floor next to him, Nora sat cross-legged looking through a book. "Do you want Monty standing on the rocker?"

"Yeah, it's okay." Roxanne sighed, swiping her hand through the air. "Now Ted says he never agreed to any such thing. That he never *dreamed* I actually meant twelve and that most people would think five is plenty. Like I care what other people think." From upstairs a stereo started up, the bass thumping so loudly that Skyla could sense the walls vibrating. "Damn it, they're going to wake the baby." Roxanne got up and lifted the coffeepot off its base. "Oh well, it's about time he'd be up anyway. You want more coffee?" Skyla nodded, and Roxanne brought the pot to the table. "Why in the hell would he think I'd say twelve children if I didn't mean it?"

"Maybe he thought you were kidding. Twelve is a lot of kids."

"So you think I'm insane?" Roxanne topped off her cup and Skyla's and then set the pot on a hot pad on the table.

"Certifiable."

Roxanne laughed. "I like you, Skyla Plinka. You say it like it is."

"Certifiable in a good way, I meant."

"Yeah, that's how I took it."

"Good." Skyla grinned.

"So here I sit, seven children short, and I don't know if I'll ever have a little girl. A big family is the only thing I ever wanted. I never had an answer when I was a kid and people asked what I wanted to be when I grew up. I'd say a teacher or nurse or something to make them happy, but all I really wanted was to be a mom." Roxanne pushed a stray lock of hair behind her ear. "You're so lucky to have Nora. I ache for a little girl. I saw this picture in a magazine once—they had all these cakes you could make for kids' birthdays, and I cut the whole thing out. I made a race car cake for Emmett and Wyatt and a teddy bear cake once for Monty, but the one I really want to do is the Barbie cake. Did you ever see it?"

Skyla shook her head.

"You bake the cake in a bowl and turn it upside down when it's done, and then you stick the doll in the middle of the cake so it looks like the doll's dress—like it's a ball gown or something. It's the cutest damn thing—they decorated it with frosting and these rosette things. When I find where I put the article, I'll show you sometime. Maybe you'll want to make one for Nora. It's so damn cute."

"My mother-in-law always makes Nora's birthday cakes," Skyla said. "I let her the first year to be nice, and now it's a tradition. I don't know how to get out of it."

"That's nice that she wants to."

"It's a compromise. If I didn't let her do the cake, I think she'd probably take over the whole day."

"At least you have as many kids as you want." Roxanne's voice was a grumble. "It's majorly unfair. I mean, Ted's getting what he wants out of life. He can go golfing and watch sports on TV until the cows come home, for all I care. It's not like it would make any difference. He comes and goes and does whatever. I'm the one who deals with the kids. Really, why would he even care?"

"Twelve kids sounds impossible to me. Why, imagine the laundry for fourteen people!" Skyla said, thinking about the pile of dirty clothes Roxanne already had in her basement laundry room. It was a mammoth mound of clothes, as big around as her dining room table and as high as Skyla's chin. After Roxanne showed her the pile, Skyla had gone home and re-created it for Thomas. "It's this big around." She paced in a circle to indicate the perimeter. "And this tall." She held her hand up in the air. "And she says no matter how hard she tries, it's always that size. She gets a few loads done and thinks she's getting caught up, and lo and behold, the pile's back up there again." Apparently Roxanne possessed the sorcerer's apprentice version of laundry.

Thomas just shook his head. "If she's having all these kids to get out of getting a job, she's doing it the hard way."

"I don't understand it at all," Skyla said, knowing she and Thomas were on the same wavelength as far as family size was concerned. They had both agreed on one child before she'd even gotten pregnant with Nora. "Who would want all that work? I never met anyone who loves babies and children like that." And it was true. Despite Roxanne's protests that she loved the babies best, Skyla could tell that the older children held her heart equally as well. She'd ruffle the older boys' hair as they walked past and search out Monty or Gregory for a kiss and hug for no reason at all. She hung their school artwork up and down the stairwell with pushpins, fussed over good grades on book reports and tests, and laughed at their knock-knock jokes.

"Sometimes," she told Skyla, "when they're at school, I feel like going and picking them up."

"Why?" Skyla asked.

"I don't know," Roxanne admitted. "Just for peace of mind, I guess. I like it better when they're here." At that moment Skyla saw Roxanne as someone who didn't need to venture out too far; she'd keep her world wrapped around her like a blanket if she could.

"I'm still seven children short," Roxanne repeated again over coffee. "But you know, Skyla, at this point I'd be willing to compromise and stop at ten or even eight." She paused and looked up at the doorway. Skyla turned around to see Wyatt coming down the back stairway holding the baby over his shoulder. The eleven-year-old carried him more comfortably than Thomas ever held Nora as a baby.

"He was crying, Mom," Wyatt said, handing him to his mother's outstretched arms. "Didn't you hear him?" His tone was accusing.

"No, but I'm glad you did," Roxanne said, taking the baby from his arms. Wyatt clunked back up the stairs while Roxanne settled the baby on her lap and reached for a napkin to wipe his nose. "Look at this face, Skyla. Even with his little snotty nose, isn't he the sweetest thing in the world?"

"He sure is cute," Skyla agreed. Ted and Roxanne did make adorable babies, she'd give them that much. Ferd was a smaller version of his brothers. He had the face of a round-eyed cherub and fuzzy blond hair. "So, did you tell Ted you'd be willing to compromise and have only eight or ten?"

"Yeah," Roxanne said glumly, "and he said he'd consider maybe one more if I could keep the house organized all the time. He says I should be able to keep up with what we have now. Tend the garden I already have instead of planting more flowers." She stuck her tongue out. "Ted's all like, 'Roxy, if you could keep up with the laundry and cook dinner most nights and have the house in order, then I'd say, sure—let's have another one.'" She smoothed the baby's hair. "Like that's going to happen. He just says that because he knows I'm not going to be able to do it."

"You couldn't sneak a baby past him?"

Roxanne whooped. "How do you think I got Gregory and Ferd? No, Ted's starting to be really careful. In fact, he's actually talking about getting a vasectomy. It would be pretty hard to get accidentally pregnant at this point. He's watching."

Skyla didn't ask for details. She'd heard enough.

CHAPTER NINE

The days were getting shorter and cooler now, the leaves changing from green to vibrant hues of orange, red, and yellow. Up and down the Plinkas' tree-lined street (Elm Street—although the trees were mostly maple, the original crop of trees having been killed by Dutch elm disease decades before), the change seemed to happen overnight. Skyla marveled at how quickly the leaves absorbed autumn's colors. Why, it seemed like only yesterday she was reveling in the green lushness of spring. She made a vow to pay more attention in the future.

Thomas thought this time of year was perfect—the lawn didn't need mowing or raking just yet, and the furnace and air conditioner could rest as far as he was concerned. Skyla, on the other hand, was chilly even while wearing the Packers sweatshirt she kept draped on a hook near the back door. Just hearing the whoosh of the furnace kicking in warmed her bones. Sometimes she stood over the radiator and held out her hands like a pioneer woman warming herself over a fire.

At the bookstore, it was different. There the physical work kept her preoccupied and warm. She'd settled into the job like it was her calling.

Within a few weeks, Skyla started thinking of it as her store. From the start, Risa, seemingly incapable of making decisions, gave her free reign. The first day when Skyla asked what needed to be done, the diminutive storeowner had thrown up her tiny, knotted hands. "Everything really," she'd said, shaking her head sadly. "It's all such a mess."

The word "mess" was an understatement. That became more apparent as Skyla went along: the bookshelves and light fixtures were dusty, the windows and walls were dirty, and books were arranged harum-scarum. Burned-out lightbulbs needed replacing. In the back of the store, sealed boxes were found to contain books and knickknacks from the store's gift shop era.

The cash register was a relic, a virtual antique of the type Skyla had seen in black and white movies. The buttons used to enter the dollar amount resembled the valves of a trumpet, and the numbers that popped up at the top reminded her of the cards judges held up at dance contests. The change drawer flew out with such force that anyone using it had to remember to stand at least a foot away. Risa stood on a stool to reach the buttons and then comically jumped off backwards right before the drawer opened. Skyla always had to stifle a laugh. Luckily, paying customers were rare.

Cleaning the store was such a pleasure, so different from the housekeeping she did at home where her efforts made no discernable difference. Skyla wore her oldest clothes and brought her own cleaning supplies. "Refresh my memory. What exactly is your job there, anyway?" Thomas asked, eyes narrowing as he helped her haul the vacuum cleaner and some rag-filled buckets out to the car one Saturday.

"Oh, a little of this, a little of that," she said brightly and wrestled the key into the trunk lid until it popped open.

"You look like the charwoman from the Carol Burnett show." His voice was a grumble. He lifted the Hoover and settled it on its side in the trunk, cushioning it with a blanket between the flares and jumper cables.

"You think?" Skyla said, but having never seen the show and having only a vague notion of what a charwoman was, she wasn't really offended.

It was hard to convey the feeling of satisfaction she got from this job. Oh, to see gleaming wood surfaces replace grime and dust! Skyla savored the smells of wood polish and soapy water as she worked methodically from the front of the store to the back. Clean, then organize, that was her strategy.

Along the way Skyla encountered what could only be called junk: mildewed books, broken knickknacks, board games, and puzzles with missing pieces. Risa vacillated when Skyla asked if they could be discarded. "Maybe it could be fixed," she'd say nervously, her forehead wrinkled in thought. Or she'd say, "Perhaps the pieces will turn up later." Worse yet was when Skyla's simple question ("Can I throw this out?") would ignite a long, wearisome story that would make her sorry she asked. "My Bert and I bought that in Honolulu in 1986!" Risa would say, her voice at the high pitch that meant she was excited. "Or maybe it was '87?" She'd look at Skyla questioningly. "No, it wasn't '87," Risa would continue, answering her own question, "because that was the year we went to Madrid. I specifically remember that because…" And she'd be off on a monologue that went on and on while Skyla stood waiting for permission to toss out a grass-skirted figurine missing a leg. Getting the conversation back seemed impossible—that line had been cast into very deep waters. Skyla learned to turn back to her cleaning while still making the appropriate noises. "Umm hmm" and "really" seemed to work in most cases.

She started making furtive trips to the dumpster in the alley when Risa was gone or otherwise occupied. Just disposing of the trash was a big improvement in the look and smell of the store. The dank mildew odor, which Risa had tried to cover by burning musk incense, was replaced by the fresh smells of soap and lemon polish.

Skyla saved the display window for last. She spent an afternoon emptying out the books and hanging crystals, pulling down the dusty gauze backdrop, which had been stapled in place, and using gloves to remove the shrunken head (a replica, it turned out). She was considering ripping up the backdrop to use as rags until Risa told her, proudly, that it was fine muslin "from England." With Risa standing behind her, Skyla felt compelled to fold the muslin and set it to one side. She would take it home with her—if it survived the washing machine, it might have some future use.

The back of the display window opened like cabinet doors. Once Skyla climbed inside to clean it, she was center stage, suddenly self-conscious in her ripped blue jeans and old denim shirt, red bandana wrapped around her head like the Aunt Jemima syrup bottle. Her presence in the window attracted attention from those outside. The two old guys, normally planted on the bench outside the hardware store, ventured down the block to watch her spray Windex on the glass, which she wiped in slow, exact swipes. One of them, cigarette clenched in his teeth, gave her the A-OK sign, thumb and forefinger together. "You're doing a great job!" he yelled a little too loudly, as if a wall divided them instead of glass. Skyla nodded and kept working.

The two old men stood there for a few minutes, thumbs hooked into belt loops, until they finally ambled back in the direction of the hardware store.

News of the goings-on at the bookstore traveled quickly. The afternoon she spent setting up the new display she felt like the main attraction in town. Young mothers pushing strollers, teenagers with backpacks, the retired men who normally hung out at the coffee shop yawing and doing crossword puzzles—they all took the time to visit, staring at her from the other side of the glass when she looked up from her work.

"Doesn't anyone around here work or go to school anymore?" Skyla asked Risa in irritation. She had taken a break to reload the stapler. "You could sell tickets out there."

Risa was standing behind the register, a habit she had even when there weren't any customers in the store. Skyla wasn't sure if this was wishful thinking or wanting to give the appearance of readiness in case someone walked in. "Madame said this would happen." Risa nodded knowingly. "You with your artistic eye— she said things would turn around for the business. People will come, she said."

"I think it's more that people are bored." Skyla snapped the stapler shut.

"Better they look at you than me," Risa said, resting her hands on the register. Standing on the stool she and Skyla were the same height. "They get a better view with you."

"Don't be too sure about that," Skyla said and returned to her work in the front of the store.

It wasn't that she minded the audience so much—she waved at babies and smiled at white-haired gentlemen who gave her the thumbs up. It was being observed without knowing it that made her uneasy. When she returned from her afternoon working in the window, Thomas gave her a play-by-play of what she'd done that afternoon. "How did you know all that?" she asked.

"My mother." He grinned. "Audrey Too-Much-Time-On-Her-Hands Plinka. She was *shopping* downtown and saw you working." Thomas put the word "shopping" in finger-gestured quotes. "She would have stopped in and said hello, but she didn't want to disturb you. She said to tell you to use newspaper instead of paper towels when you're washing windows. Actually, she had a lot of suggestions. I got an earful."

"I bet you did," Skyla said, remembering another conversation she'd had with her mother-in-law the month before. They'd been invited to Sunday dinner at her in-laws. Jeffrey was there as usual, as much a fixture of the house as the sunburst clock in the kitchen—now there was a guy who needed to get a life. The subject of Skyla's new job had come up after the plates were cleared and coffee was served.

"A job?" Audrey had said. "What put *this* idea into your head?" As if Skyla was prone to harebrained schemes and this was the latest.

"This isn't anything new. Thomas and I've discussed the possibility of my getting a job. I thought I'd put all my earnings into Nora's college fund." Skyla struggled to keep her voice even. "It just never seemed like the right time before. And now with Nora in school and the owner of the bookstore letting me set my own schedule, it all sort of fell into place." Walt and Jeffrey watched the two women in amusement, while Thomas meticulously laid his silverware across his plate.

"Hmm," Audrey said. Her lips were pursed in disapproval. "The owner of the bookstore—that Towers woman—she's a whole other subject. Don't get me started talking about her." She twirled her index finger alongside her head.

"She looks like a troll." This came from Walt, who rarely spoke up at family gatherings, preferring instead to migrate wordlessly from couch to table and back again. His main contributions to family discussions consisted of sports analogies and weather commentaries.

"I see her around town wearing winter boots all year round and talking to herself. I don't know why you'd want to be spending all your free time with her." Audrey stirred her coffee and tapped the spoon on the side of the mug as if making a point. Skyla imagined the taps as if someone was speaking out at a trial—*Objection, Your Honor!*

"Risa's treated me well," Skyla said after a pause. "She's very nice and doing the best she can since her husband died. It's not easy for her to run a business with her...disability."

"She's let that store go to wrack and ruin. But you know," Audrey said, reaching over and patting Skyla's arm, "it's not your responsibility to save the world. *Your* only responsibility is to Nora and Thomas and your home."

Jeffrey reached across the table for a cookie. "Oh, Mom, cut Skyla a break, would you? A job is a good thing. Everyone needs to do something out on their own." Skyla shot him a grateful glance. "Hey, Sky, what's the deal with that psychic who works there?" He broke the cookie in half before taking a bite. Jeffrey had a tendency to play with his food. "What's her name—Madame somebody?" He snapped his fingers. "Is she for real, or what?"

"Of course she's not for real!" Audrey sounded irritated. "Don't be ridiculous. No one can predict the future."

"I don't know about that," Jeffrey said and winked at Skyla. "There's a guy at work who swears she's the genuine article.

His wife was pregnant and that psychic predicted a bunch of things and was right on the money."

"Stuff and nonsense. It's all guesswork and putting ideas into people's heads that they themselves make come true." Audrey straightened her back. "Haven't you ever heard of a self-fulfilling prophecy?"

"If she really could do it, she wouldn't have to tell fortunes in the back of Mystic Books. She'd be making a killing betting on sports," Walt said.

"You check her out, Skyla," Jeffrey said. "Figure out what she's all about and give us the full report next time we get together."

"I can give you the full report right now," Audrey said. "It's no mystery. She's a fraud taking money away from pathetic fools." And before Skyla even had a chance to tell them she hadn't even *seen* Madame Picard yet, Audrey stood to gather up plates and silverware and abruptly left the room.

CHAPTER TEN

Even during the dream Skyla knew it wasn't real, or at least not the reality she experienced when awake. It had a blurred-edges feeling, with time passing in a slow, syrupy way. Unlike most dreams, she was present, meandering through the mist as if going for a walk. Her dream self was not surprised to encounter her brother-in-law Dennis walking toward her from the opposite direction. She knew it was him even though he was now Asian and slightly older. His face was rounder, and his hair was the glossy black she'd always envied on others. There was no discernable evidence it was him, but still she recognized him immediately. *How clever of Dennis to be wearing his Asian look today,* she thought, as if it was a wardrobe choice like a polo shirt or a linen suit. Dennis always was good at appearances.

"Skyla!" he'd called out upon spotting her, clearly excited, as if she was a dear friend instead of his older brother's wife. "How wonderful to see you!" Hearing his voice was like listening to music underwater.

She watched him for a moment, but he disappeared back into the fog before she could speak, leaving her with unanswered questions. "Wait," she cried out, but it was no use. He was gone, slipped back to wherever he'd come from.

She jerked awake to the sound of running water. The room was partially lit by the first rays of the morning sun, and she knew Thomas was showering in the bathroom right off their bedroom. It was only one of two modern updates the house had when they bought it: central air-conditioning and a full bath off the master bedroom. The previous owners had called it a master bedroom suite, but that was a stretch since the bathroom wasn't much larger than a closet and the bedroom wasn't all that spacious either. Still, there were plenty of nights Skyla was glad she didn't have to go down the hallway past Nora's bedroom to use the bathroom.

Thomas was humming in the shower. She listened for a few minutes and recognized his school's theme song. It was endearing the way he loved his job, the animated way he talked about students who got it, really got it when he covered a new concept, the dedication with which he fine-tuned lesson plans at the dining room table and wrote out recommendations for seniors who were applying for grants and scholarships.

She pulled his pillow toward her and clutched it to her front, taking in his scent, a mingling of Old Spice aftershave and woody soap. She swung her legs over to his still-warm side of the bed.

She was still lying angled on the bed when he came out of the bathroom, a blue-striped towel held to his front. His hair was wet and combed like a little boy just leaving the barbershop.

"Hey there," she called out softly, aware that her unused voice sounded creaky, sleepy. "Come back here." Skyla patted the space next to her, even though she knew it was pointless. Even though it was Saturday, he wouldn't come back to bed. Once he showered, he was up for the day.

"No, I think I'll get the paper and a cup of coffee." He covered her hand with his and pressed his warm fingers into her palm. "Want to join me?"

"No way," she said. "I'm not leaving this bed until you turn up the heat."

"Suit yourself." Thomas got up and opened a wide bureau drawer, getting out, she knew, a pair of boxer briefs and black socks.

Skyla burrowed under the comforter and settled in to watch him get dressed. Thomas pulled on his boxers and socks while standing, a feat that required balancing skills she didn't have. He was incredibly fit for someone who exercised only sporadically—running a few miles here and there only when he'd put on a few pounds.

Today he put on jeans and moccasins and was just pulling a turtleneck sweater over his head when the memory came back to her. Something about Thomas's head emerging from the sweater's opening reminded her of the dream.

"I had a dream," she said suddenly. "And your brother Dennis was in it."

"You're dreaming about my brother?" Thomas turned toward her. Even in the dim light Skyla could see the amused expression on his face. "I hate to be the one to break it to you, but he's gay."

"It wasn't *that* kind of dream," Skyla said. "And besides, I told you already, I don't think he is gay."

"So you said," Thomas replied. They'd had this discussion before and it had gone in circles, Thomas going on gut instinct and Skyla relying on the opinion of her former roommate, Oscar, who definitely *was* gay, and wouldn't he be able to tell? Thomas had said, "Who do you believe—Oscar, who met Dennis once at our wedding, or me, his own brother who's known him since birth?"

Thomas gave convincing arguments for his beliefs regarding his brother's sexuality: Dennis was neat, a stylish dresser, a great dancer, and a man who loved women but never made a commitment to any of them. If that wasn't enough, what about his lack of interest in team sports? What kind of man prefers playing racquetball to watching the NCAA championship? And the real kicker, the mother of all reasons, in Thomas's opinion, was that Dennis missed seeing the Packers win the Super Bowl because he'd gone skiing with friends. What was that all about?

Skyla agreed that Thomas made a good case, but she still wasn't wholly convinced. They argued back and forth until finally Thomas said it was a moot point. It really didn't make any difference. Dennis was Dennis regardless. And she'd agreed with that, but wouldn't it be nice to know for sure? Too bad asking would be considered bad form in Wisconsin. Thomas's take on it was that if he wanted them to know his sexual orientation, he'd tell them.

"It wasn't that kind of dream," Skyla repeated. "It was the kind of dream I used to have when I was growing up." She sat up in bed. "Remember me telling you how I always had those kind of freaky premonitions that came true?"

Thomas sat down on the edge of the bed. "When you were a kid?" He acted as if she'd never mentioned it before.

"Yes, I always had dreams and later on the things I saw in the dreams would come true. Small things, but they would be exactly the way I saw them. Like one time I knew that the house we would be moving to would have a patio with a big crack in it, and when we got there it was exactly the way I saw it." She clutched the satiny edge of the comforter. "And another time my dad said we were moving to North Dakota, but I saw cactuses—"

"Cacti."

"What?"

"The correct plural of cactus is cacti."

"Okay, whatever." Skyla was exasperated. "But the point is, I knew we were moving to the desert before my dad even did, before he even knew about the job in Arizona."

"But didn't you also say you weren't sure if you just remembered remembering—like once you knew it, it just seemed familiar? I wouldn't worry about it—a lot of people have that."

"What are you saying?"

"I'm saying I think what you're talking about is fairly common. People have random ideas or dreams, and later they only remember the ones that apply. Then it looks like they saw the future when in fact what they really did was rewrite the past."

Of course that's what he would think, Skyla thought. She thought of what her mother-in-law always said about her oldest son—*I never had to worry about Thomas. He's always been so sensible.* Sensible, reliable Thomas—funny how the same traits that were so appealing when she first met him could be so annoying now. "It's not like that at all," Skyla said. "It's just that I would forget the dream, and later seeing the thing from the dream would bring the memory back."

"You don't have to be so testy." Thomas lowered his voice, a contrast to her rising tone. "I was just trying to help you find a reasonable explanation."

"And by reasonable you mean…?" She didn't even attempt to temper her indignation.

He put his hand over hers. "Skyla, you're an intelligent person. Kids have vivid imaginations—you know that. You probably had dreams about snowstorms *and* palm trees *and* cacti." Here he put a bit too much emphasis on the word "cacti," Skyla thought.

"And later when you moved to Arizona, you just remembered the cacti one and thought, 'Aha, I'm psychic.' Everyone goes through stuff that like. When I was a kid, I used to lie on my bed and try to will myself to levitate. One time I closed my eyes and dozed off a little. When I woke up, it seemed like I dropped onto the bed. I could have sworn I actually hovered over the bed for a few seconds and then came down—it seemed that real to me."

"How do you know it wasn't?"

"Oh come on, Skyla." He gave her a condescending look. "I was like ten years old at the time. I still wanted to believe in Santa and those X-ray vision glasses you ordered out of the back of comic books."

"I just think," she said, "that it's good to be open minded."

"There's open minded, and then there's gullible."

"And I'm gullible? Is that what you're saying?" She heard her voice rising again and didn't care. "I'm just flaky Skyla with her crazy ideas and an art degree she doesn't even use."

"I never said you were flaky or gullible."

"You didn't have to say it. It came through loud and clear. You're always so quick to dismiss ideas that don't fit into your way of thinking."

The silence hung between them. Skyla knew Thomas was carefully formulating his thoughts before speaking aloud. He hated conflict. He rose slowly off the bed and took his glasses off the dresser and put them on before sitting back down on the bed.

"I didn't mean to sound dismissive," he finally said. "I thought I was being reassuring."

"You don't believe me." Her tone was flat.

He rubbed his temple and then rested his hands on his knees. "I'm not saying you're wrong." His eyes were cast down. "I know it seems real to you, but I think it's safe to say they weren't premonitions."

"Then what are they?"

"I don't know, Skyla. It's hard to say. Some people swear they've seen the Loch Ness Monster, or leprechauns, or fairies, or whatever. I'm not here to make judgments, but until I see proof, I don't buy any of it."

"There was a time," Skyla said, "when scientists believed the sun revolved around the earth." She gripped at the comforter like it was a lifeline. "And before that, most people believed the earth was flat. And they were positive they were right. Don't you think, then, that it pays to be open minded? The smartest people on the planet once believed things that were completely wrong. How do we know that there's not lots more out there we just don't know about yet?"

Thomas shrugged. "Time will tell, I guess. I'm not saying I can't be persuaded. I just haven't seen anything yet that I'd consider to be proof."

So that was it then. Skyla sighed. Another subject in their marriage to be filed under "agree to disagree."

From down the hall music from Nora's room could be heard—Disney songs. Thomas stood up. "Sounds like Nora's awake. I'll get her breakfast, okay?" He hesitated for a moment before walking to the open doorway.

"Hey," he said, turning before he reached the hall. "You never did tell me what Dennis was doing in your dream."

"Nothing much," she said, lying back down and pulling the comforter up to her chin. "He just looked like an Asian guy, and he was walking through fog." She could see that the whole thing sounded ridiculous now.

"Ah," Thomas said and nodded thoughtfully. "The fog part should be easy to corroborate. If you want, I can check online and see what the weather's been like in San Diego."

"Never mind."

"Okay," he said.

"Just don't forget to turn up the heat."

She listened as he padded down the hallway and stopped to talk to Nora. She heard Nora's childish squeal and "Daddy," and she knew from the sounds that followed that he had crouched down and scooped their daughter up into a hug.

CHAPTER ELEVEN

It seemed to Audrey that her family was falling apart. It was simpler when the boys were younger and living at home. Then it was easy to keep tabs on their coming and going. That was the only way a devoted mother could nip potential problems in the bud. She was needed then. And how. Why, without her around, heaven only knows what might have happened. Audrey took pride in making sure her boys were healthy—shots up to date, hearty meals, and plenty of nutritious snacks. The food police, Jeffrey had called her, mostly in jest, she thought. And yes, she would patrol. Someone had to, or they'd have been eating chips and cookies before mealtimes and taking food into the off-limits areas: the bedrooms and the living room. Sure they grumbled, but would they have wanted bugs where they slept? Yes, she was fastidious about crumbs, but at least they didn't live like pigs in a house with bugs and vermin. Audrey shook her head at the memory.

Back then she was so busy it made her head spin. She kept track of basketball practice, swim meets, and homework assignments. Audrey took pride in knowing when chapter tests and spelling bees were coming up. It was a chore to keep on top of things, but it was so necessary. She didn't understand mothers who didn't pay attention to these details—didn't they care? She heard other women comment that they forgot about the school's open house or neglected to send back the Scholastic book order on time. Incomprehensible. Drinking moms is how she thought of them. Whether or not they were was beside the point.

The boys didn't seem to appreciate her help, but that's how it was with children. Thomas in particular was prickly. He was an excellent student who preferred to study cloistered in his room. Dennis enjoyed having her quiz him on his Spanish vocabulary (*"Hola, Madre!"* he'd say), but he mostly studied with various girlfriends. Jeffrey—now that boy was a difficult one. A little lazy, in her opinion. When he graduated from high school, she had breathed a sigh of relief. She felt as if she'd carried him all the way through on her back.

"Just leave them alone," Walt would say in irritation when she was reminding the boys to start their social studies project or finish their book reports. "Let them sink or swim on their own."

Leave them alone? Mercy! Walt could be so dense at times. Leave them alone? Why? So they could fail? No, she was too good a mother to let her boys down.

Later when they all went on to college, got decent grades, and graduated, Walt couldn't resist getting a dig in. "See," he said at Dennis's college graduation ceremony, "you were so worried, and here all three got through. I told you they'd rise to the occasion if you'd let them." She'd been looking through the viewfinder of the camera watching Dennis bound up the stairs onto the stage as Walt spoke. What he was implying, she supposed, was that her efforts hadn't been needed, that she'd been nagging and overbearing for no reason at all. She turned to snap a reply in his direction and temporarily lost sight of Dennis. The interruption caused her to miss the perfect shot—the one of Dennis shaking hands with the dean and receiving his diploma. Trembling with anger, she settled for a shot of him crossing the stage and another descending the stairs. Her day would have been ruined if not for Dennis stopping on the way back to his seat, searching the audience for her, and then touching fingertips to lips and tossing a kiss her way. In his smile she read, *Thanks, Ma, I couldn't have done it without you.* At that moment she knew Walt was wrong. All her struggles setting things to rights had mattered. Single-handedly she had laid the groundwork for a lifetime of study habits and discipline for her boys. Any successes they achieved from this point forward could be traced right back to her. It was a proud realization.

But now her life was unraveling. Things seemed to be swirling around just out of her reach. Audrey was feeling at odds lately, pacing around the house, looking through closets and cabinets without knowing why. She'd taken to reorganizing drawers that really didn't need it and cleaning the oven when it was barely dirty.

Walt, on the other hand, was content coasting through his retirement days with nothing to show for his time. He had a routine of coffee and the morning paper, semi-regular trips to the hardware store, and evenings watching television. Heaven knows what he'd do without the history channel and ESPN. Sports in particular took up far more time than Audrey thought was healthy. Too much sitting, not enough moving.

"Do you want to go for a walk?" she'd asked Walt one evening after she'd cleared the dishes. He was already parked in his recliner, newspaper in hand. She noted the way his extra poundage had settled around his middle, making his tucked-in shirt bulge outward over his belt.

"A walk?" His tone was as incredulous as if she had suggested bungee jumping or rock climbing. "Why would we walk?" He looked at her over the tops of his bifocals in a way that she found infuriating.

"Just to get out. Get some fresh air."

He harrumphed. "Are you insane? It's dark, and your so-called fresh air is cold. It's an ass-blaster out there."

"It's not that cold. It's only the beginning of October."

"Too cold for me."

"Never mind." Audrey sighed. "I just thought it would do us some good to get a little exercise."

"You go ahead if you want," he said. "But I'm staying right here."

She hadn't walked that day or any time after that, although she often thought about it. Too bad the neighborhood was short of women her age. There really was no one she might connect with. Her one true friend over the years, Sheila Hansen, moved away years ago. She remembered how they'd chat for hours about their children and husbands. They took long walks around the neighborhood, often stopping at George Webb's to order hot chocolate and take in the smells of greasy burgers and hash browns. They talked endlessly about the things they'd do once the kids were grown. Sheila said she was going to take art classes and see the world if she could get Bob to go along with it. "He's a stick-in-the-mud," she'd say affectionately.

Audrey thought of her friend as a more vocal version of herself. Sheila would say things to Walt that even his own wife wouldn't. "Get your butt out of that chair, Walt," she'd chide. "There's a whole world out there. Really, I mean it." And she'd motion with upswept arms. "When we get back from our walk, I want to see you moving." Walt found her amusing, although he didn't change his ways. "Men," Sheila would say to Audrey when they were alone. "Selfish to the core. I've yet to meet one who wasn't." Such a kindred spirit, and then she had to go and move away. From Christmas cards Audrey received over the years, she learned that Sheila had divorced Bob, moved yet again, and married a guy with a long gray ponytail. In her last Christmas card photo, Sheila and her new husband, Dion, were standing in front of paintings at the art gallery they owned in Santa Fe. Walt thought the card was kind of show-offy, but Audrey looked at the card and couldn't quite shake the feeling that Sheila had somehow violated an unspoken pact and gone on ahead, leaving her behind.

The void in her life didn't show any signs of going away. Periodically she checked on it the way a child searches out the gap of a missing tooth with his tongue. Dennis was long gone—that was a source of sadness. He was so far away, and he almost never called anymore, only once or twice a week, if that. Jeffrey had long since gravitated to Walt's side. When those two were together, her presence was that of a fly circling the room—there but not really noticed.

And Thomas, well, he never really was hers, now that she thought about. Even as a boy his wide, unstaring eyes peered through his glasses toward her but not really at her. Always distracted, that was her oldest son. Half the time it didn't even seem like he was listening—not that he'd admit to it. And since he married Skyla, he was even less accessible.

Audrey liked Skyla well enough, but they never did hit it off. Her daughter-in-law didn't come to her for advice or ask for her recipes or do any of the things she'd hoped a motherless bride would do. And even though she'd told her several times, "Please call me Mom," Skyla persisted in calling her Audrey. Rude is what it was. Trust Thomas to marry someone self-reliant and distant.

When Nora was born, she'd hoped things would change. When Audrey first held the exquisite little bundle in her arms, she wished she never had to let her go. Nora was the tiniest baby, with a head the size of an orange and wrists as big around as Walt's thumb. They marveled at how perfect she was—the best characteristics from both sides, Audrey thought. As Nora grew, that was even more apparent. She'd inherited her mother's soft curls and petite build and Thomas's big brown eyes and firm chin. She also possessed both her parents' quiet ways.

Sometimes Audrey felt that Nora was just out of her grasp. She was a bashful child who clung to Skyla's side or played quietly with baby dolls during visits. When Audrey asked questions about toys or what she was playing, Nora politely answered in a barely audible voice. Audrey was certain she could break through Nora's shyness with a little more one-on-one time, but that never came to pass. She'd offered to babysit anytime, but Skyla and Thomas rarely took her up on it, saying they didn't want to impose.

"Impose?" she'd said. The thought was ludicrous. "Taking care of Nora would never be an imposition. I'm her grandma!" At that Skyla and Thomas had exchanged a glance that gave her the feeling there was more to it than that, but what it could be she really didn't know.

And now Skyla went and got herself a job. Audrey disapproved. She herself had never worked, unless you counted filing claims for Walt's insurance company and then only when the boys were in school. She always saw them off in the mornings, making sure they had their library books, lunch money, and anything else they'd need for the day. When they got off the bus, she was there to greet them at the door and ask about their day. She always offered snacks: freshly baked cookies, ants-on-a-log (celery with peanut butter and raisins), or trail mix, but it was never that processed, store-bought garbage that Nora favored. Fruit snacks! You could call it that, but in Audrey's opinion, they weren't any better than candy. Clearly Skyla had much to learn about parenting, but she didn't pick up on Audrey's suggestions, and Nora's childhood was already well under way. It would be a miracle if that little girl turned out all right.

Skyla's new job certainly wouldn't help matters. When Audrey voiced her concerns, Thomas seemed puzzled. "Skyla only goes to the bookstore during school hours or when I'm home," he said. "Her working doesn't interfere with Nora at all."

He clearly didn't get it. How could Skyla, who tended to be flaky anyway, justify leaving her family for hours at a time when her own house was run helter-skelter?

※ ※ ※

Audrey made it her business to check out Skyla's place of employment. It wasn't that she wasn't familiar with the place. Everyone in town knew about Mystic Books, the quirky store in the heart of downtown.

When Bert Towers was alive, it had been a fairly reputable little business. Big Bert was how he was known, and he was sorely missed when he was gone, even by Walt, of all people. Bert was a huge man with burly shoulders and a hearty laugh. Walt always said that if the storeowner had been a dog, he would have been a Saint Bernard. Whatever that meant.

Back then people flocked to the store to visit with Bert and invariably left with some book or knickknack the Towerses had brought back from Tahiti or Austria or some such place. Why, even Walt had once succumbed to Bert's salesmanship, buying a music box for her that played "Somewhere My Love," that theme song from the *Dr. Zhivago* movie. She still had it, too.

Mrs. Towers (Audrey never could remember her name) had been fairly normal back then, although she was lost in Big Bert's shadow and quiet as a mouse, which suited everyone fine. Since Bert died though, she'd turned weird and the store had gone to wrack and ruin. The sign hanging above the doorway badly needed a coat of paint, and the window display had been the same for three or four years now. Everyone in town commented on how the place had gone downhill. There was some talk of an out-of-town investor offering to buy the store—he wanted to open a sub sandwich shop. The story around town was that Bert's widow wouldn't sell. Which was too bad because the town really could have used a fast-food place.

Audrey drove by the store several times when she knew Skyla was working, but she didn't have the nerve to go inside. The fourth time she was rewarded by the sight of her daughter-in-law working in the display window. She drove past and turned around, finally parking across the street where she could observe Skyla without being seen.

Skyla was dressed shabbily: denim shirt, blue jeans, and a bandana around her head that made her look like those native women in *National Geographic*. Outside the window two old men, geriatrics in baseball caps, were ogling Skyla. One of them was yelling something through cupped hands. Skyla gave him a wave and a smile in response, but she continued spraying and wiping the glass. Periodically she'd pull another sheet of paper towel off a roll near her feet.

Watching Skyla clean in front of the two old men sickened Audrey. The whole thing was scandalous. This job would be fine for a college student or a senior citizen whose social security wasn't quite cutting it, but not for a Plinka. What would have provoked Skyla into accepting this sort of job? She knew Skyla came from modest means. Her people had been just plain common, if the truth was known, but still, why didn't Thomas put his foot down? She just couldn't understand it. Certainly Thomas and Skyla couldn't *need* the money. Given her son's talent for handling finances, that just didn't add up.

Audrey watched Skyla for twenty minutes or so, debated going inside, and then thought better of it. As she drove away, she wondered if Skyla had a gambling or drinking problem. It didn't seem likely, but she'd read that true addicts were masters at hiding their compulsions.

A week later, Audrey gathered up her courage and left the house with the intent of going inside Mystic Books. She deliberately went in the morning—she wanted to take a look-see when Skyla wouldn't be there. Audrey parked the car in a diagonal space just in front of the window. She stopped on the sidewalk to look over the display before she went inside. The glass sparkled, not a streak anywhere, she noted with satisfaction. Thomas must have told Skyla her newsprint tip. Inside the window, Skyla had arranged novelties from the store around books of the same bent. A stone gargoyle held a leather-bound book, *The Works of Edgar Allan Poe*, in its paws. Above the winged figure, taxidermied blackbirds were suspended on clear fishing line. The birds all had beady eyes, sharp beaks, and glossy wings. They swayed slightly as they hung, giving the impression of life. They looked more like garden-variety crows than ravens, but Audrey had to admit it was creepy.

To the right of the gargoyle sat a life-size skull candleholder. The red candle set into the top wasn't lit, but apparently it had been at one time because the wick was black and red dried wax oozed down the sides of the cranium. Books of ghost stories and haunted houses were propped up alongside the skull. Hanging above them were fabric ghosts the size of handkerchiefs. Audrey sniffed. She supposed the display was fine for now—after all, Halloween was coming up—but she hoped this wasn't the shape of things to come. Mercy, it was garish!

A brisk wind sent leaves skittering down the sidewalk past her feet. She regretted not wearing her winter jacket. It wasn't doing much good hanging in the front hall closet at home. Really, she should go inside now if she was going to. Before she could change her mind, Audrey took a deep breath and briskly entered the store. The door jangled shut behind her. To her surprise, there were other people in the shop. Some type of classical music played softly in the background. The little wizened woman who owned the place was behind the counter handing a bag to a man wearing a cowboy hat and a beat-up brown leather jacket. She nodded a greeting in Audrey's direction and then turned back to the customer in front of her. "The thing is," the man was saying, "not enough people have an open mind. There are some things in this world that just can't be explained..." As Audrey walked past, his voice receded behind her.

She hadn't been in the store for years and even then infrequently, but she could tell right away that the place was different. The closed-up musty smell that had been pervasive was gone, replaced by a fragrance like burning candles. Lavender or something floral like that. Audrey had heard that the place had gone from disheveled to filthy after Bert's death, but there was no sign of that now. The place gleamed; the wood surfaces reminded her of the old furniture polish commercial whose slogan promised it would make your table so shiny you could see yourself.

As Audrey walked down the center aisle, she noted how well labeled and organized the book selection was. Interspersed among the books and on shelves lining the walls were eye-catching mini-displays: a Victorian-style dollhouse completely furnished, South American pottery, a lamp with crystals hanging off the edges of the shade. As a bookstore it couldn't compete with the big chains as far as titles, but like shops in resort areas, it had a quaint look that encouraged browsing.

Audrey begrudgingly admitted Skyla had done a wonderful job. She proceeded down the aisle, stopping now and then to pick up books and inspect curiosities. Every price was clearly labeled, which was another change from the store's past. Big Bert encouraged customers to negotiate, a practice that always left Audrey uncomfortable. Why not just say how much you want for the thing? This was America after all, not some marketplace in Venezuela.

In the back of the store, Audrey's attention was drawn to the sounds of two women talking. No heads protruded over the tops of bookcases, and no bodies leaned in the aisles. The conversation sounded intriguing. The first voice, low and even, was answered by a second person who talked in exclamation points. This voice, the excitable one, was the one that caught her ear. She couldn't make out the words, but the voice was familiar. She was certain it was someone she knew. The conversation rose from behind a shiny black partition, some kind of Oriental thing from the looks of it, seeing as how it was covered with those gold symbols that passed for lettering in China and Japan. She strolled to the back of the store and eased in front of the last bookcase that was labeled, in Skyla's neat printing, "Horticulture." She plucked a book from the shelf, flipped it open in an attempt to look engrossed, and tilted her head to catch the words behind the screen. To the casual observer, she was an aging housewife in a beige cardigan sweater reading up on germination, but she felt more like Mata Hari than June Cleaver.

She strained to catch the words. "Really," the second woman was saying. "You don't say!" The other woman mumbled something unintelligible, and then there was a response: "You think it's a good idea then?" She heard more mumbles and a sound like cards being dealt.

The identity of the second woman came to Audrey like a snap of the fingers. Of course she knew the voice. How many times had she heard that same voice singsong, "Hello, Audrey!" stretching out the name to an ungodly length? That endlessly cheerful prattle would go on and on about what a beautiful day it was, stating every year that it was the best Christmas tree ever, like some idiot child who had yet to realize the downside of life. Audrey frowned. This was a voice that was always upbeat and spoke in clichés: making the best of a bad situation, counting your blessings, looking for silver linings, and on and on.

Whenever she started spouting these types of platitudes, Audrey found herself zoning out. Her mind wandered, and she made mental grocery lists or calculated how long it had been since she'd taken the comforters to the dry cleaners. She missed huge chunks of conversation that way, but nothing important, it seemed. Like one of those tedious soap operas whose storyline was easily picked up even after a lengthy absence, Audrey found she could resurface without having missed a thing.

How odd that she would be at the bookstore at the same time as Audrey. What were the chances of that happening? And from the sounds of it, she was with a friend, probably one of her casino buddies. Most likely someone she'd never bothered to mention to Audrey or Walt.

Audrey clapped the book shut and wedged it back into place. She adjusted her cardigan, pulling it firmly over her protruding midsection, and ran her fingers through the layers of her hair. She strode to the partition and poked her head around the edge.

"Gram?" she said expectantly. The sight of Walt's mother sitting there, purse clutched to her front, didn't surprise her. She would have bet the house that she was there. What she wasn't expecting was the outlandish appearance of her companion, a woman in her sixties with the teased hairstyle and excessive makeup of a Las Vegas showgirl circa 1965. Although, considering her wrinkled face and sagging jowls, she looked more like the showgirl's grandmother.

"Audrey!" Gram said and slapped the table with the palm of her hand. "What a wonderful surprise." She leaned across the gold lamé tablecloth. "Madame, this is my daughter-in-law, my older son's wife, the one I was telling you about."

"I knew that," the woman said, nodding her head so vigorously that her large hoop earrings swung back and forth. She extended her hand to Audrey. "How nice to meet you at last, Audrey." Audrey's ear caught a hint of an accent—Russian or Transylvanian or something. Shades of Count Dracula.

Gram looked from Audrey to the other woman, as pleased as if she'd met up with old friends on a cruise ship. "Imagine running into you here! What a nice surprise."

Audrey glanced down at the cards spread out on the table. Not regular playing cards. These had old-fashioned looking drawings of naked people and skeletons and a devil. She suddenly understood what this was all about, and her face reddened as she realized this was that awful psychic woman Jeffrey had talked about. Clearly Gram was here giving money to this charlatan and expecting to hear the future. Madame's hand was still out-stretched, every bony finger adorned with rings of silver and turquoise. Audrey wanted no part of this, but social courtesy required that she shake this woman's hand, even though it was a stretch to reach across the table. How typical of Gram to put her in such an awkward spot, all the while acting as if they were attending a tea party. "I can see that I'm interrupting," she finally said, glancing down again at the cards. "It looks like you're in the middle of something. I'll just get going." She buttoned her cardigan up as she spoke, a clear signal she was on her way out the door. "I'll see you later, Gram."

"Don't be silly," Gram said. She gestured to the chair next to her. "We're almost done. Have a seat."

"No thank you." Audrey pulled her purse to her side and lifted her head in what she hoped was a disapproving way. "I have to get going. I have some shopping to do."

As she turned to go, she heard Gram call after her. "Wait! Just give me five minutes and we can go out for lunch." Audrey grumbled an affirmative and headed up the aisle.

She was standing in the front of the store when her mother-in-law came breathlessly charging up to meet her. Audrey jingled her keys and tapped her foot. She made a point to look at her watch as Gram approached.

"How wonderful that you waited," Gram said. "This was so nice running into you. The two of us don't get a chance to get together very often." She pulled her scarf around her neck and knotted it as she spoke. "We can walk down to the coffee shop if you'd like. Lunch is on me."

Audrey nodded grimly and put her car keys in her purse. She followed behind as Gram pushed the door to leave, almost walking into her when her mother-in-law stopped to call out "Ta-ta!"

to the storeowner. A bit too cheerily, Audrey thought as she balanced on the balls of her feet.

"See you next week," the Towers woman called out from behind the cash register.

❋ ❋ ❋

Audrey gave Walt the lowdown when she came home that afternoon. He'd just settled down in the den with a beer in one hand and a bowl of Chex mix balanced precariously on his lap. The remote control was within easy reach on the end table next to him, but Audrey snatched it away before he had a chance to start clicking. "We need to talk, Walt," she said. "This is important." She blocked his view of the screen. Even off it seemed to have the power to draw his eyes away from her.

"I'm listening," Walt said. He flipped back the beer's metal tab and took a swig.

"It's your mother. You've got to talk to her." Audrey paced as she spoke. "She's out of her mind. You won't believe what she told me today."

"My mother? Where'd you run into her?"

"At the bookstore, Walt, the bookstore," she said impatiently. "Remember, I said I might stop by the bookstore after I picked up the dry cleaning?" She gestured with the remote. Walt gazed at it longingly. "I wanted to take a look at what Skyla's been doing all this time. I told you that right before I left this morning. Honestly, sometimes it seems like you don't even listen to me."

Walt held up his hand like he was stopping traffic. "Whoa, Nellie. Take a deep breath—slow it down." The Chex mix bowl tilted to one side, making a deposit on the ledge of his belly.

Audrey opened her mouth to object, but Walt pointed to Jeffrey's chair before she could get the words out. "You're getting ahead of yourself. Just sit down and tell it to me from the beginning."

She sat and waited while he scooped up the errant Chex mix and put it back in the bowl. He brushed the salt residue on his stomach off to one side, as if shaking it would make it disappear instead of transferring it into the chair's crevasse. "Are you ready?" she asked.

"I've been listening the whole time." Walt grinned. "Now what exactly has Mom gone and done this time?"

"She goes to see that psychic." Audrey set the remote down on the end table. "Every week she gives money to that woman at Mystic Books who says she sees the future. *Every week,*" she repeated when Walt didn't react. "Every single Wednesday she gets her hair done at the beauty salon and then goes to the bookstore and pays this fraud thirty-five dollars to give her advice about what she should be doing in her life. It's the most ludicrous thing I've ever heard. She's a regular customer, Walt, a regular. She's in this woman's appointment book every week at the same time. I tried to talk some sense into her, but it was like she didn't hear a word I was saying."

"Okay." Walt's tone was measured. "But on the bright side, she's not a heroin addict or an arsonist either."

"This is serious, Walt."

"I know, I know, Aud. I'm just trying to put it in perspective. Thirty-five bucks a week sounds like cheap fun to me." Walt shrugged. "It's not how I'd spend it, but it is her money."

"It's not the thirty-five dollars," she said. "That's the least of it. It's the fact that she gives that woman all kinds of personal information. She tells her about investments, where she keeps her valuables, when she's going to be out of town. For heaven's sake, for all we know that Madame Picard is some kind of con artist working with a gang of thieves to victimize old people. If you saw her, you'd be suspicious too." Audrey struggled with how to convey the oddness of the woman's appearance. "She's a real piece of work, loaded with jewelry and tons of makeup slathered on. And she has this suspicious-sounding accent, too. It doesn't sound real, if you ask me. I wouldn't trust her any farther than I could throw her."

"Does she have a turban?"

"What?" Audrey was confused.

"A turban—one of those head wrap things with the big jewel in the center and the feather sticking out of it?" Walt encircled the top of his head with his palm. "I kind of picture her like that."

"No, she doesn't have a turban." The look of amusement on Walt's face didn't escape her. Mercy, did everything have to be a big joke? Was she the only one with enough common sense to see when a situation was dangerous?

"Hmm, I thought every fortune teller had a turban." He took a swig of his beer. "Or maybe I'm thinking of a swami." He picked through the bowl of snacks and popped a few morsels into his mouth. "Now that I think about it, I'm pretty sure it is a swami. Aren't they the guys who charm snakes out of baskets?"

"She doesn't have a turban." Audrey spoke through gritted teeth.

"Okay, don't get so riled up."

"I think you're missing the point here, Walt. Your mother is putting herself at risk. The older she gets, the more I worry about her. First she starts going down to that casino and gambling—"

"Bingo once a week is hardly gambling," Walt interjected.

"—where she met that boyfriend, Mike, she's been seeing for five years who won't marry her."

"She's the one who doesn't want to get married."

"That's *her* story. That's what women always say when they can't get the men to commit."

"Whatever." Walt raised his hands in surrender. "I'm just going by what I heard."

"And now she's dabbling in the occult. What next?"

"I'd hardly call it the occult."

"You didn't see that psychic woman's cards, Walt. I did." Audrey's finger was pointed accusingly in his direction. "One of them had the devil on it and one had this hideous skeleton, and that's just what I noticed in the two seconds I was back there. Heaven knows what else there was." Audrey was agitated. Did something terrible have to happen before anyone would take her seriously? She picked up the remote control and wondered what Walt would do if she threw it across the room. "I don't appreciate your reaction. Here I'm worried that your mother is losing her mind, and you sit there grinning like an idiot."

"I can see you're upset," Walt said after a pause. "If it will make you feel any better, I'll have a talk with Mom."

"It would make me feel better."

"Okay then, it's settled. I'll call her." Walt set the snack bowl on the end table. "Can I have the remote back?"

"When? When will you call her?"

"Tomorrow." He held out his hand. "The remote please?"

"Do you promise?"

"I promise I'll try to get to it." He made his hand tremble in an exaggerated way. "Aud, show some mercy, would you? I'm going through TV withdrawal here."

Audrey sighed, handed him his clicker, and left the room to go into the kitchen. Clearly Walt thought the matter was settled. He was, she knew, hoping that she'd forget about the whole thing. "Just let it go, Audrey," seemed to be Walt's favorite expression lately. "Sometimes you're like a dog hanging on to a bone." Well, so what if she was? Someone had to keep this family on track, or heaven knows what would happen. She shook her head and opened the door to the freezer. Despite the waft of cold air, she stuck her hand into the stacked upper shelf and rifled through its contents until she found the pork roast for tomorrow's dinner. They probably wouldn't truly appreciate everything she did until she was dead and buried. Then they'd be sorry they didn't give her the credit she deserved, but of course, it would be too late by then. It occurred to her that she could follow Walt's advice and let everything unravel on its own. It might be interesting to see the bedlam that ensued. Left to their own devices, there was no telling what might happen.

CHAPTER TWELVE

It seemed to Skyla that people tossed around the word "friend" as casually as they'd fling a crumpled piece of paper into a wastebasket. Thomas talked about college friends or friends from work. Audrey mentioned running into friends at church or the store. These references always mystified her. If they truly were friends, where were they? Could they really be friends if they never called, wrote, or visited? She didn't think so.

Skyla preferred her father's definition. A friend, he said, was someone you could call in the middle of the night if you're stuck downtown and your car won't start. A true friend will come and get you without thinking twice about it.

For Skyla, Roxanne fit that definition. Skyla had never had a friend like Roxanne, unless you counted her college roommate, Oscar, who now lived out of state and rarely kept in touch except for the occasional e-mail.

In the space of just a few weeks, Skyla found herself leaning on her neighbor for the companionship she hadn't even known she was missing. She looked forward to their conversations. Roxanne had a million stories and a funny way of telling them. "I hope Ted gets home early tonight," she said one day when they were making sandwiches for the kids' lunches in the Bears' kitchen.

"How come?" Skyla stood at the counter and spread peanut butter as she spoke. She smoothed it in careful S-shaped strokes.

"I have to run to Target for diapers and stop at my aunt's to feed her cat." Roxanne was peeling an orange.

Skyla reached over and plucked a wedge of orange for herself. "Your aunt's on vacation?"

"Nah, she's in jail," Roxanne said and proceeded to tell the long, sad story of her aunt's addictions, one of which was a suave con artist named Wayne, the other any alcoholic beverage, especially beer. "So that's why," she said, "we all used to take turns watching out for her. My sister Jackie bailed her out of jail once. Another night we got a call that Wayne had abandoned her at some bar, without any money or anything, so Ted drove all the way to Sheboygan to help her out. Then there was the time my dad gave her six hundred dollars she supposedly needed for back taxes." Roxanne stopped and sighed dramatically. "This all happened like the same week, and none of us knew that the others had helped her. Finally we had a family meeting and decided enough already. She's on her own. So now all we'll do is cat duty if she's in jail or whatever. I don't mind the cat thing too much. I figure, why should the poor thing suffer just because its owner is an idiot?"

Skyla nodded as if this could be any family's story, even though she was sure that no one else in the neighborhood would be able to relate.

Thomas didn't appreciate Roxanne's stories. Skyla retold them for their entertainment value, but Thomas didn't take them that way. "It sounds like there's a certain white trash element there," he said, which was his roundabout way of putting Roxanne down while trying not to sound judgmental. Still, there it was—the term "white trash" in any sentence didn't come off very well.

It didn't help for Thomas to find a *National Enquirer* on the coffee table when he came home from school one afternoon. "What's this?" he asked as if he'd never seen a tabloid before.

"*Newsweek?*" Skyla joked. She regretted leaving the *National Enquirer* out where he could find it. If only she'd been thinking, she could have buried it in the newspapers in the recycling bin before he came home.

"You are so, so funny," Thomas said. He wrapped his arms around her and buried his face in her hair. His cheek was still cool from the outdoors, but his breath was warm against her ear. "I can see that the intellectual climate here is on a downward slide if we're buying trashy magazines."

"I didn't buy it. Roxanne gave it to me," Skyla said. Thomas pulled away from her and placed his hands on her shoulders. The look on his face made her regret having brought Roxanne's name into the conversation.

"Why doesn't that surprise me? I suppose she has a subscription."

"No, it's just an occasional fix. Junk food for the brain, Roxanne says. Just for fun." Skyla glanced down at the magazine. Minutes before it had seemed a harmless amusement—a story about a German shepherd that saved its owners from a house fire, a little celebrity gossip, some updated, though questionable, medical findings. Now, seeing it through Thomas's eyes, the newsprint pages and colorful headlines looked tawdry.

"I wonder if Oprah thinks it's good fun." Thomas let go of her arms and picked up the tabloid and read the cover. "Oprah balloons up to two hundred and fifty-six pounds. 'I'm out of control,' she tells friends." He tossed the paper back onto the coffee table. "Notice it's not two hundred and fifty pounds or two hundred and sixty pounds. It's precisely two hundred and fifty-six. That's how you know it's *real.*" His eyes widened in mock amazement. "I particularly like the choice of the word 'balloons.' Very dramatic. And of course they know exactly what Oprah tells her friends. I'm sure their unidentified sources are very reliable."

Skyla hated it when he got this way—prickly and self-righteous. "Okay, so it's probably not the gospel truth. You can't believe everything you read anyway."

"It's just not responsible journalism, Skyla." Thomas was speaking in his teacher mode now. "Someone gaining weight isn't even worthy of reporting. Not to mention that the photos look fake. This one on the cover doesn't even show her face. It could be anybody."

"Thomas, you're making much ado about nothing. If it offends you, I'll put it outside with the newspapers."

"It offends me."

"Okay then." Skyla couldn't help but wonder if he'd have been this sanctimonious if she'd gotten the magazine from someone else, maybe nice Mrs. Williams next door or even Gram, for that matter. Imagining Gram reading the *National Enquirer* wasn't too much of a stretch.

"You work in a bookstore, for God's sake. We live eight blocks from the library. We subscribe to *Time* and *Scientific American.* There's no shortage of reading material. You don't need to read garbage." He paused for a moment and looked at her face as if waiting for a reply. Then he spoke again. "I think you could do better for friends too."

"I said I'd put it outside!" The sharpness in Skyla's voice surprised even her. She snatched up the magazine and rolled it up so he couldn't see the cover.

Thomas looked startled at her outburst. "Good," he said. "Oprah and I thank you."

Then he walked out of the room, hands in pockets, whistling like he hadn't a care in the world. She recognized the tune, "What a Wonderful World," and knew he did it on purpose; it was his way of getting in the last word. How like him to try and make it look like she had overreacted when it really was him all along. And since when did he care about Oprah's feelings?

"You always said Oprah was a know-it-all," she cried out after him, waving the newspaper above her head. But all she got in reply was the sound of his footsteps plodding in even tempo up the front hall stairs.

CHAPTER THIRTEEN

Skyla had been working at the bookstore for more than two months when she finally met Madame Picard. By then the store was in good shape. She'd cleaned until it shone, painted walls, re-arranged fixtures into a semblance of order, and organized the merchandise. There were still boxes in the basement, but she was in no hurry to mess with them—whatever was in them was probably mildewed and decayed. All in good time, she'd thought, a phrase Thomas said Skyla used when she had no intention of getting to something, but in this case she knew she'd eventually tackle the store's lower level. If nothing else, the boxes could be discarded to free up some floor space.

She'd changed the window display twice since she was hired. Her first selection, a Gothic theme, coincided with Halloween and received many compliments from customers. The next time she decided to showcase the souvenirs from the Towerses' world travels and went with an international motif. A glossy world map served as a background. Overhead, shiny model planes were suspended by fishing line. She propped an atlas and travel guides in between the Peruvian pottery, the Swiss cowbell, and the various dolls in ethnic costumes. The November chill that had penetrated the glass persuaded her to work quickly. Skyla made a mental note to caulk around the glass once the weather got warmer.

She was proud of the way the window turned out. The front of the store was a beacon, she believed, calling customers and hopefully leading them through the front door, cash in hand. Risa said that sales had tripled in the past month, and she gave Skyla all the credit. When Thomas heard this, he said any increase was likely due to the approaching holiday season. That might have been true, but Skyla preferred to think her hard work had caused a turnaround.

She was alone in the store and had just put the finishing touches on the window when Madame walked in. Skyla heard the jangle of the bell, alerting her that someone had entered. Still on her hands and knees, she backed out of the window. She stood up and wiped her hands on her apron.

The older woman who stood there was unwinding a long crocheted scarf from around her neck and head. She was wearing what could only be called a cloak, a black covering halfway between a cape and coat. A few snowflakes littered her shoulders and the top of her bouffant hairstyle.

"Can I help you?" Skyla asked.

The woman smiled, perfect teeth contrasting with ruby lipstick. For a moment Skyla thought she was going to ask to use the bathroom.

"No, no, honey, I work here." The woman took off her cloak and draped it over her arm. She spoke with an accent Skyla couldn't quite place. "I'm Madame Picard, the intuitist." She held out her hand, and Skyla instinctively grasped it. Madame's skin was cool and papery. Her long, lacquered nails grazed Skyla's knuckles. "And you are Skyla."

* * *

When Skyla told Roxanne about it later, she found Madame hard
to describe. "She has this sort of presence, you know?" It was Saturday morning, and Skyla had been talking on the phone for the
last half an hour, freed up by the fact that Nora was watching a
new DVD and Thomas was next door feeding the cat for Mrs.
Williams, who was out of town. With the phone wedged between
her neck and shoulder, Skyla was able to talk and heat up chicken
noodle soup for lunch. "She sort of sweeps in like she's this movie
star from the fifties or something. And she has this very dramatic,
rich voice like she should be reciting Shakespeare. Maybe not,
though, because she has a little bit of an accent."

"What kind of an accent?" Roxanne asked. Skyla could hear
her as she went about her activities, changing the baby's diaper
one moment, pouring juice for Monty the next. The toilet flushed
at one point, but Skyla didn't question it. If Roxanne wasn't cleaning the bathroom, she didn't want to know about it.

"Kind of like the Count from *Sesame Street*," she said. "Or
maybe like she's from Romania or one of those Eastern European
countries."

"Okay." Skyla could picture the thoughtful look on Roxanne's her face. "So she looks like a movie star, and she talks like a
Muppet."

"Not like a real movie star—more like one who's not aging
well and wears lots of jewelry and makeup to compensate."

"Now she's sounding like a drag queen." In the background
Skyla could hear the sounds of the twins arguing. "Just a minute."
Roxanne covered the receiver. The sounds that came through
were muffled threats.

Skyla stirred the soup while waiting for her friend to return. She switched ears to stretch her aching neck.

Roxanne came back on the line. "So the big question is—is she the real thing or not? Cause if she is, I'm coming down there and getting a reading."

Skyla hesitated. "I don't honestly know. She doesn't usually work afternoons, so I haven't seen her much. All I know is that when her people walk in, they look all serious and concerned, and when they walk out, they're as happy as can be. That's got to be worth something."

"You got that right."

Despite the screaming and thumping in the background on her end, Roxanne continued the conversation, telling Skyla about a great aunt who used to read tea leaves at family gatherings. Skyla listened while pouring the steaming soup into bowls and tried to keep up her end, but she found talking above the noise level distracting. It occurred to her to tell Roxanne about the dreams she'd had as a child. Her friend certainly seemed open to the topic—no ridicule from Roxanne, that she knew for sure—but today, she sensed, wasn't the day they'd discuss it. Maybe they'd have uninterrupted time to talk when the Bear boys were grown and moved out of the house.

About the time Skyla was going to yell good-bye, Thomas popped his head around the doorframe of the kitchen. He was still wearing his jacket, and his knit cap (the one that reminded her of *Where's Waldo*) was dusted with snow. "You still talking to Roxanne?" he asked. His face had a frantic look she'd never seen before.

She nodded, alarmed. "Do you need to use the phone?"

"No, tell her that Gregory's on top of the van."

Skyla spoke loudly into the receiver. "Gregory's on top of the van." A clear picture came to her: three-year-old Gregory perched on top of the Bears' boxy full-sized van. Because the height of the vehicle made it impossible to store in the garage, it took up permanent residence in the driveway when Roxanne wasn't hauling her crew all over town. A metal ladder attached to the back curved up to the top for easy access to the luggage rack on the roof. Apparently, it also provided easy access for monkey preschoolers. Skyla looked over at Thomas. His eyebrows were furrowed in concern, his mouth a frown.

"What?" Roxanne asked. Behind her Skyla could hear the baby wailing and noises like a tub of wooden blocks being dumped down a stairwell.

"Gregory's on top of the van!" This time she screamed it.

"Oh my God!" The next thing Skyla heard was the sound of the receiver hitting the floor.

Skyla followed Thomas outside. "Should we go over there?" Thomas asked, pointing at the Bears' house. He jingled his car keys in his pocket.

"No, that might spook Gregory. Let them handle it." Skyla hugged herself against the cold. The turtleneck and sweater that had seemed so warm in the house weren't much of a barrier against the frigid air.

From where they stood, they had a clear view of Gregory standing on top of the van, his chin raised and arms outstretched. Roxanne had rushed out in her bathrobe and slippers, yelling for her husband. In response, Ted came running from the side of the house holding a snow shovel. Both of them called out to their son, who seemed oblivious to their presence. It was impossible to hear what they were saying, but the couple's pantomime reminded Skyla of police officers trying to talk a distraught person off the rail of a bridge. A gust of wind blew confetti snowflakes around the three.

Now the twins were outside as well, trailed by a crying Monty in stocking feet. Behind Monty came Buddy. The dog barked gruffly. His back haunches swayed back and forth in what looked like slow motion. Roxanne pointed toward the front door and shouted something that sounded like, "Get your ass in the house." Meanwhile, Gregory, arms still outstretched, started turning slowly in circles on top of the snow-dusted van.

"He's going to kill himself."

"That kid never listens," Skyla said, quoting Roxanne verbatim.

Thomas gave her an odd look. "It's the parents' job to make him listen. They need to get their act together."

As if Ted heard Thomas's words, he threw down the shovel and started climbing the ladder on the back of the van. Skyla watched and held her breath.

Hand over hand, Ted made his way to the top of the ladder until he was kneeling on the vehicle's back edge. A dark blue car like Walt's drove down the street and slowed in front of the Bears' house. Out of the corner of her eye, Skyla noticed it pause as it drove past. On top of the van, Ted inched forward on his knees and beckoned with curved fingers.

"Come to Papa," Thomas said softly, echoing Skyla's thoughts. She'd been leaning against him without realizing it, and now her tensed fist burrowed into the palm of his hand. The older Bear boys and Buddy now stood hushed. All the world was silent.

Gregory was still turning slowly around. His head was tipped back, and from where Skyla stood, it looked like he was catching snowflakes on his tongue. The snow falling on and around the fair-haired toddler gave him the look of an angel child.

Thomas tightened his grip on Skyla's hand at the same moment Ted lunged forward and grabbed Gregory around the waist. As if on cue, Monty began wailing while Wyatt and Emmett whooped and clapped. Still clutching Gregory, Ted eased backwards and down the ladder to where Roxanne stood, hands outstretched, ready to scoop her baby into her arms.

"Well," Skyla said, "thank God that's over." They'd been outside for only a few minutes and hadn't moved from their original spot, but somehow the whole thing left her exhausted. "All's well that ends well."

Thomas clucked his tongue disapprovingly. "All's well that ends well—this time." He gestured back to their house. "We better go in and see what Nora's been up to before we turn into negligent parents too."

CHAPTER FOURTEEN

In spite of everything Ted said, Roxanne knew there would be more babies in her future. There had to be. She carefully packed away Ferdy's outgrown sleepers and bibs, labeling each storage bin by size for future ease. She couldn't explain the immense joy that accompanied each new addition to the family. Finding out she was pregnant was a gift, better than winning the lottery. More like finding the golden ticket in her Willy Wonka chocolate bar. The actual state of being pregnant didn't do much for her, though she didn't mind it as much as some women, yibber-yabbering about their sore backs and varicose veins. Such big babies they were. What did they expect—they'd get the world's greatest gift for nothing? Clearly, some payment was expected. A little discomfort and a few stretch marks were the least of it, she thought.

Feeling the baby move was the highlight of the whole pregnancy experience. Two real people right inside of me, she remembered thinking when she first found out about the twins. She always imagined her babies in utero swimming, as if her body was the Club Med for the fetal set. A little floating, a little relaxing, and then a stop at the poolside bar for a renewing beverage.

She took her responsibilities as a pregnant woman seriously. She never drank alcohol or ate sweets. Her eating habits were exemplary. Oddly enough, the snack foods that normally called to her held no allure when she was expecting. She gave up the baked goods she loved, bypassing the Danish kringle and sugar-glazed crullers with nary a glance.

Her obstetrician, Dr. Davy, said she was the ideal patient. She gained the right amount of weight, took her horse pill vitamins daily, and wore her support stockings during the last month or so. He was so much better than the morose little weasel of a doctor who delivered the twins back in Dayton. Finding Dr. Davy had definitely been the high point of moving to Wisconsin five years ago. Sometimes she thought she loved Dr. Davy best of anyone in the world, Ted included. He was so kindly and concerned all the time. She associated him with her boys coming into this world. Dr. Davy had a voice like one of those guys on the audio books from the library. When he announced, "*It's a boy!*" a person would think it was the first time anyone had ever had such a thing. One time a student nurse actually clapped, that's how special he made it sound.

Going home was an event in and of itself—Ted coming with the kids, the whole tribe of them filling up the elevator and thundering down the hall to her room. There was always someone (usually a fresh-faced medical student or intern) who asked, "Are all these kids yours?" Their tone always indicated that someone really ought to slip this woman a brochure from Planned Parenthood. "All mine," she'd say happily to assure them it was by choice. Loading up to go home was a lengthy process. They always had to make a few trips to come back for plants and gifts and the freebies that the hospital gave out—the formula and samples of diapers and nursing pads. Usually Roxanne sat in the car with the babies while Ted took the twins back up the elevator to retrieve what was left behind.

The last time, when Ferd was born, was the only time she and Ted had an argument about names. Normally Ted would rubber-stamp whatever she chose, but this time he had an idea. ("God save us from men with ideas," she'd told Skyla later.) He wanted to name the baby Ferdinand if it was a boy. Ferdinand the Great was the king of Spain way back when, he explained, and since his grandfather on his mother's side was Spanish, he thought it would be appropriate. "A little family heritage, Roxy," he'd said, rubbing her shoulders and whispering in her ear in the way that drove her crazy.

Roxanne fought the urge to give in right away and countered by saying that Ferdinand was also the name of a bull in some kids' book, if she remembered correctly, and did he really want to saddle the poor kid with a name like that? They went back and forth like this for days, but in the end Ted won out. She really didn't have a better boy's name picked out, and besides, she was sure it would be a girl named Samantha. As it turned out, the baby came out looking like a Ferdinand, so that was okay. And Ted was right—they'd never have to worry about other kids in school having the same name.

Each time they came home with a new baby, Ted would tell her, "This is it, no more. Our work is done." She fought back an urge to tell him that the true work was just beginning—why scare him talking about everything that loomed ahead? Luckily, Ted came from a large family that loved babies. At his relatives' gatherings in Dayton, the arrival of an infant was heralded as if royalty had come to pay a visit. "Give me that baby," was what was most frequently heard, and not just from the women in the family either. Uncles, cousins, and brothers alike, all of them smooched the baby's cheeks and marveled over the perfect features and tiny hands. They fought over who would hold the baby and offered to change him or burp him, as the case may be. Unlike Roxanne's own family, the Bears were undaunted by a baby's cry. "Someone's hungry," they'd coo in baby talk before reluctantly handing the child over to its mother.

No one in his family commiserated with Ted. "I'm going to have to declare bankruptcy if Roxy doesn't stop having babies," he'd complain at family dinners. Roxanne would hold her breath, hoping no one would start quoting how much it cost to raise kids nowadays. One magazine article estimated it was over a hundred and fifty thousand dollars from cradle to high school graduation, but she knew that couldn't be right. Not unless the kid was wearing gold-plated shoes and eating prime rib for dinner. "I work night and day and still can't keep up with the bills," Ted would continue while eating the Jell-O and ham that were staples at these gatherings. "These kids just keep coming and coming. We just get one out of diapers, and another shows up."

"Don't you even say such things," his mother would respond, waving a finger in his face. "Babies are blessings. God wouldn't give them to you if you couldn't manage somehow." Roxanne couldn't help but feel a surge of love for her mother-in-law then, the little woman whose lumpy body and nondescript housedress covered a big heart.

Equally on her side was her sister-in-law Clara. Forty-two years old and single, Clara had just adopted a toddler from Guatemala—an adorable little girl with caramel-colored skin, shiny black eyes, and dark brown ringlets. Roxanne's boys were a blur of motion compared to tiny Analisa, an easygoing lap-sitter of a little girl who had the endearing habit of stroking her mother's cheek. "I'm so jealous of you having a daughter," Roxanne told Clara when mother and daughter first arrived home from South America. In true Bear fashion, a welcome-to-the-family party had been thrown at Ted's parents' house, and Clara had been showered with gifts, food, and offers to babysit.

"Ha!" Clara said. "Then we're even because I've been jealous of you and all your babies for years." Clara's whole face crinkled when she smiled. Like all the Bears, her face was more round than angular.

Clara would take Roxanne aside at family gatherings to tell her to ignore Ted. "He's been like this since he was a kid," she said. "He goes on and on about things as if he's all put out. The truth is he's crazy about those kids. I've never heard anyone brag about their wife and kids like Ted does."

"He brags about me?" Roxanne couldn't imagine what Ted would have said. She had a brief moment of panic wondering if he'd alluded to their sex life, but no, even Ted wouldn't go that far.

"All the time," Clara said. "You have so much patience. You're so good with the kids when they're sick and you have to stay up all night. He talks about all the art projects you do with them and how you help them with homework. He talks about how cute you look in the morning singing your wake-up song to the babies."

It was surprising to hear. Roxanne thought all he noticed were the unmade beds and the dishes in the sink.

"Have as many kids as you want," Clara advised. "Ted doesn't like change, but trust me, he'll adapt."

Roxanne was more than willing to take this advice, but it was getting to be increasingly more difficult to sneak babies past Ted. As a couple they were a fertile combination, and she'd always chosen birth control methods for their large margin of error. Her thinking was that if God wanted them to have another one, then she'd ease the way. Not that God needed any help, but she was sure he appreciated the thought.

Lately though, Ted was taking the bull by the horns, in a matter of speaking. He told Roxanne that she might as well throw out her diaphragm and sponges ("They don't seem to be working anyway," is how he put it) and came home with a box of condoms big enough to house a teapot.

"Two hundred count?" she wondered aloud as she read the box.

"Well, we don't want to run short," Ted said.

"Rubbers don't seem like much fun." In truth, rubbers seemed more like the wallet contents of horny teenage boys hoping for some backseat action. She didn't know any married couples who used them.

"These are *lubricated*." He took the box out of her hands and pointed to the word on the back. "And they have ridges. I think they'll be fun. Look, they're jewel-toned colors."

The look on her face must have been doubtful because he said, "We only have to use them at the end anyway. And it's just until I get a vasectomy." He used the V word casually, as if the surgery was already scheduled and it was no big deal. But Roxanne knew his fear of undergoing the knife was larger than his desire for sterility. In fact, he didn't like the word "sterile" at all, a truth that came out one night when the two of them were lying in bed in the dark.

"So what happens when they do a vasectomy?" she had asked. Roxanne lay on her side, her head resting on his shoulder. She made circular stroking motions on the bristly hairs of his chest.

"You don't have any more kids so you can get caught up financially, and you start to believe there really is a God."

"No, I mean what happens to the sperm? Where does it go? Or does your body not make sperm? How does that work?"

"I'd still make sperm—of course I would," he said, although he didn't sound certain. "I guess it just doesn't come out."

"So does it get all backed up, or what?" Roxanne pictured the clear plastic drain on the Liquid-Plumr commercial and imagined a tube in Ted's body clogged by some unidentifiable black grunge.

"I'm not exactly sure how it works." His yawning made her head and hand bump softly upwards. "I just know it does. Which is the important thing, by the way."

"Well, I guess we can ask the surgeon how that works," Roxanne said finally. "If it makes you sterile, the sperm has to go somewhere else besides out."

"Sterile's kind of a harsh way to put it." Roxanne felt his body tense, every muscle at attention.

"Well, what else would you call it?"

"I would no longer be fertile, but it really wouldn't make any difference since we have five boys already. I mean, it's not as if it's ever been a problem. If anything, just the opposite."

Roxanne sighed. "It's your surgery—call it what you want."

"I wouldn't call it surgery either. It's really more of a surgical procedure. Kind of a routine thing. Like having your tonsils taken out." He sounded as if he was trying to convince himself.

"Whatever."

That's how she left it. It was understood between them that since the vasectomy was Ted's idea, he would be the one to make the appointment. But she knew he never would. And that was just fine with her.

CHAPTER FIFTEEN

Once the Christmas season had officially begun, Skyla started working every afternoon. She created a display window with a politically correct holiday theme: books and objects representing Kwanzaa, Hanukkah, and Christmas. Risa had wondered at the necessity of including the first two. She'd never even heard of Kwanzaa, but Skyla was insistent that Mystic Books should include everyone. Her reasoning was so passionate that Risa threw up her arms and said, "All this talk is giving me a headache. Just do what you think best."

The bell that signaled the exit and entrance of customers at the store jangled constantly in the weeks before Christmas. Risa started ordering stock again and kept busy opening the UPS boxes as they arrived and putting new books on the shelves. She marveled at each shipment as if someone had sent her a present.

Skyla weeded through the contents of boxes in the basement in an attempt to find fresh merchandise. Occasionally she found a treasure—one carton contained a dozen miniature ceramic nativity scenes, and another was filled with cut-glass paperweights. But more often the boxes held musty, decayed baskets or used books that reeked of dampness. These finds required discreet trips to the dumpster in the alley.

In looking through her closet at home, Skyla rediscovered the clothes she'd worn during art school. Mystic Books seemed to be the perfect environment for the colorful tunics, funky jewelry, and hand-beaded vests she used to favor. She dusted off shoes she hadn't worn in ages and invested in stockings of various shades and patterns. Even after six years and Nora's birth, everything still fit. Wearing these clothes made her feel almost like a different person—she walked like a runway model and tossed her head on purpose to feel her dangly earrings caress the sides of her head. It was a shame that as a stay-at-home mom she'd fallen into the trap of pulling on jeans and sneakers every day. No wonder she'd always felt frumpy.

Even Thomas, not usually prone to giving compliments, was admiring. "You look really glamorous," he said one day while Skyla was getting ready for work. He leaned against the door-frame of the bathroom and gave her an appraising look. She'd just pulled on an outfit she hadn't worn in years: a white top under a plum-colored Asian-style jacket with matching gathered pants. She piled her hair on top of her head and inserted what looked like chopsticks through the loose cluster of curls to hold them in place.

"Thank you very much, sir," she said, not looking away from the mirror. She leaned forward and applied rose-colored lipstick while he looked on.

"I remember that outfit." He said it shyly, like they were acquaintances rather than husband and wife. "You wore it the Christmas you met my folks. My mom said you looked like a red-haired Chinese harem girl."

Skyla laughed. "Good old Audrey. Always an opinion." She slid the cylindrical cover back over the lipstick tube until it clicked shut. "Sometimes," she said, "I get the feeling that your mother doesn't like me very much."

"Don't take it personally. She doesn't like much of anyone." Thomas paused. "But really, you look great. I think this job is a good thing. It's brought out the best in you." He said it as if he hadn't been sure until just that second.

It did bring out good things in Skyla—she'd stepped outside herself and discovered a new passion for life. Her enthusiasm carried over at home. The house didn't feel so confining anymore. Instead, it was a haven from the outside world. Spending time with Thomas and Nora felt more like a reunion or some sort of rediscovery than part of her everyday routine.

At work she thrived on the hours she spent interacting with customers, straightening the shelves, and brainstorming ways to improve the business. Because of Skyla, Risa now offered gift wrapping and accepted credit cards. She hadn't taken Master-Card or Visa until that point because, as she put it, "I don't really know how that works." Skyla didn't either, but she figured it couldn't be that hard—practically everyone accepted them except Girl Scouts selling cookies, and that was only a matter of time. She asked around—it was amazing what people would tell you. The owner of the diner down the block gave her advice on setting up the store for charge cards. The florist suggested that Risa have a coupon included in the direct mail packet that was sent to every homeowner in Pellswick, and the two old guys from the hardware store came and painted the Mystic Books sign that hung over the entryway and only billed them for supplies. Yes, it was amazing what she could accomplish once she set her mind to it.

The only area of the store Skyla never touched was Madame Picard's eight-by-eight-foot corner in the back. There seemed to be an unspoken rule that it was off limits, which was fine with her—one less thing to worry about. As it was, the spot didn't need any sprucing up. The shiny black partition that shielded Madame's table from the rest of store was so attractive that more than one customer unwittingly asked if it was for sale.

With the store's increased traffic, Madame's appointments picked up to the point they spilled into the afternoon. Skyla passed the psychic's nook when she hung up her coat and later when she made trips to and from the stockroom. She found herself occasionally pausing to eavesdrop on conversations behind the screen. She began to associate Madame with the cackle of laughter, the shuffling of cards, and the smell of musk incense. Whatever wisdom was being served in Madame's small corner of the world, the customers ate it up. Women with long faces, teenage girls with sullen looks, and men looking bored or anxious all shuffled in like they'd misplaced hope, and they came out from behind the partition with a look of contentment and a smile. "What she sells back there is peace of mind," Risa confided in Skyla. "You get a lot of peace for thirty-five dollars—believe me, I know." She nodded, and her head reminded Skyla of one of those head-bobbing birds she still saw occasionally on the dashboard of an old car. "A lot of peace," she repeated.

Skyla was carrying a bag of trash out to the dumpster one day when she almost collided with Madame Picard, smoking by the back door.

"It's okay, honey," Madame said after Skyla gave a flustered apology. She dropped the glowing cigarette and ground it out with a twist of her toe. "I shouldn't be doing this anyway. It's a very bad habit." She pulled her fuchsia shawl tightly around her shoulders.

"I get to where I want it so bad I'm huddled in doorways of back alleys like a homeless person or a criminal." She pronounced the last word "creeminal."

"Where exactly are you from, anyway?" Skyla asked. She had dashed out without her coat. The wind whipped through her thin skirt, but curiosity made her linger.

"Manitowoc."

"Manitowoc, *Wisconsin*?"

"Is there any other?" Madame laughed. "Grew up on a dairy farm, no less. Can you picture me milking cows?" Her Eastern European accent had melted away and was replaced by a decided Midwestern twang.

Skyla stared at Madame's bouffant hair, hoop earrings, and bright clothing. Finally after a moment she said, "No, I can't." The weight of the garbage bag pulled at her hand. She set it down on the snow-covered asphalt.

"Used to do it every damn day," Madame said. "Five thirty in the morning, rain or shine. That farming life is tough. Hard to go on vacations. Even when I got married, my folks had to find someone to cover for them that weekend." She shook her head disapprovingly. "When my daughters were growing up, I always told them never to marry a farmer. It's a hard life."

"But your accent," Skyla said. "I thought you were from another country or something."

"Oh, no, no, sweetie." Madame placed a firm hand on Skyla's arm. Skyla glanced down and noticed that today her long, manicured nails were encrusted with rhinestones. "That's just part of the job, part of what I do. People like it. They want a little drama in their lives. And I give it to them." She chuckled. "I give them a damn good show, if I do say so myself."

Skyla looked at her questioningly. "So you don't see the future?"

"No one really knows the future." Madame gave Skyla's arm a little squeeze. "Life is uncertain. Who knows what tomorrow will bring?"

Skyla pulled loose from her grasp. "But people think you know. That's why they come to you."

"They come to me unhappy in their marriage or worried about bills. I tell them things will get better. There's no harm in that. And you know what? Most of the time it does get better. Life is funny that way—it goes in cycles."

Skyla stared at Madame and struggled with how to make sense of this. "But those people trust you. They pay you. They listen to your advice."

"Oh, honey." Madame sounded like a mother about to tell a child the family pet died. "You seem like a smart girl. You must know that only a fool mistakes longing for reality. No one really believes if they don't want to." She shrugged.

Skyla had trouble believing what she heard. "But it's just not right. You're deceiving people." So it was all a fraud? She thought of all the people who earnestly laid down cash expecting answers in their lives. Skyla had heard their voices from the other side of the screen, asking questions like "Should I break up with my boyfriend?" and "Is now a good time to move?" or "Is my husband cheating on me?" What kind of person would lie to such trusting souls?

Madame lifted her palms skyward. "They should have faith in themselves. Most people know what they should do. They just want confirmation. I never lie to them. I always say I'm an intuitist—I use my intuition. Sure, I get little flashes now and then, but you can't count on that." She shrugged. "I give advice freely, and they're just as free not to take it. No one's holding a gun to their head." She smiled. "Most people have everything they need to be

happy. They don't need me. But if it makes them feel better..."
Madame looked at her watch and headed back into the store,
leaving Skyla standing next to a snow-dusted Hefty bag.

※ ※ ※

Most people have everything they need to be happy. The words
latched onto some part of Skyla's brain. She repeated the phrase
to herself while she rang up books and stocked shelves. It had a
certain resonance to it, but she doubted it was true.

That night after Nora was tucked into bed and the dinner
dishes were done, Skyla approached Thomas, who was sitting in
his recliner engrossed in the latest John Grisham novel. She stood
over him and watched his eyes flick back and forth across the
page. He seemed unaware of her presence. Gently she lifted the
book out of his hands, set his bookmark firmly in place, and put
the closed book on the end table to his side. He looked up expectantly. She said, "I need your opinion about something. What
do you think of someone who makes money off of telling people
lies?"

"We're talking politicians, I take it?"

"No, smarty." She sat on the couch across from him. "Psy-
chics."

"That woman at the bookstore?"

She nodded.

Thomas gasped dramatically. "What—she's not for real?"

Skyla leaned toward him, rested her hands on her knees, and
told him about the conversation in the alley. "And then she says,"
Skyla concluded, "that no one really believes what she says unless
they want to and that they should trust their own instincts. As if
that makes it okay."

"She's got a point," Thomas said. "Look, Skyla, I know you tend to be more open minded than I am." He paused and looked upward as if the right words might be printed on the ceiling. "But—"

"You mean I'm gullible."

"More open minded," he repeated. "But I'm still not sure why you're so upset. I can't imagine that anyone believes it. The whole thing sounded fishy from the get-go. I mean, come on, the woman has a crystal ball, for God's sake."

"I knew the crystal ball wasn't for real. I thought it was for ambiance!" Skyla felt like crying. "I'm not that stupid. I just thought she had some insights."

Thomas's hand crept over to the cover of the John Grisham novel. "So what do you want to do? Report her?" Skyla knew the subject was just about closed. "If you want, I can ask around and find out if she's breaking some kind of law."

"No, forget about it." She swallowed her disappointment. "I guess it's not important."

CHAPTER SIXTEEN

Audrey started driving by Skyla and Thomas's house nearly every day. Sometimes she stopped over on the pretense of dropping off muffins or raspberry kringle, but more often than not she just drove past. She looked longingly at the house and made note of the fact that their front drapes were always closed when they could be taking advantage of the morning sun's natural heat.

Sometimes after leaving Thomas's neighborhood, the car went, almost as if on autopilot, in the direction of Gram's place. Audrey never stopped at the house, only slowed. She took note of the thick layer of snow on Mike's parked car, which could only mean he'd been there all night. It seemed indecent that Gram let him stay over like that. All the neighbors must know what was going on in there. How much trouble would it be to put his car in the garage?

Her furtive outings made her feel more in touch with her family. She came home knowing that Thomas and Nora had built a snowman in the front yard or that Gram had indeed hung the Christmas wreath Walt and Audrey gave her on her front door.

There was some satisfaction in knowing these tidbits. If only they would include her, she wouldn't have to resort to all this undercover activity. Maybe someday they would trust her enough to include her in their lives. It was odd that both Skyla and Gram used such poor judgment in choosing those closest to them. Audrey pictured how distraught Gram would be once she realized her five-year relationship with Mike was a sham. Audrey had him pegged as a con artist right out of the gate. She couldn't imagine there was an actual romance between them. And if there was, why didn't they get married? (Of course, Gram said she was the one who didn't want to get married. Hah!)

Mercy, the more she thought about it, the more she was certain that Gram's money had to be the main attraction. When Gram did wake up to Mike's conniving ways, Audrey would listen sympathetically to the phone call that would follow. She wouldn't say I told you so, even though it would be tempting.

Skyla was another one. With no mother to guide her, it was a miracle she'd done as well in life as she had. Marrying Thomas had been her saving grace, Audrey decided. And though Skyla wasn't half bad as a mother, she did have a tendency to baby Nora. Heavens, the child couldn't walk past without her mother reaching out to stroke her cheek or pull her close for a kiss. Audrey mentioned this oddity once to Thomas, and he brushed it off as being Skyla's way. "Women raised without mothers are often overprotective mothers themselves," he'd said. That motherless thing was the same excuse he gave for their decision to have an only child. "Skyla wants to do it right," Thomas had said, adding that it was a mutual decision.

As far as Audrey was concerned, Skyla had been doing just fine until she hooked up with that neighbor Roxanne. The family with all the teenage boys who lived there before was bad enough—who could have thought anyone could have topped them? Just driving past the house a person could see that this Bear family was low class. The garbage cans, rolling sideways in the road, metal lids haphazardly lying on the sidewalk, were still there at the end of the week when pickup had been Monday.

The Bears' snowman had maternity underpants draped over its head, and the front walk looked like it had never been shoveled. And heaven only knew how a scattering of toys got on top of the two-story roof. And this was the woman Thomas said was Skyla's best friend? Audrey sensed he didn't approve of Roxanne either, though it was typical of Thomas not to come right out and say it, even when she provided him with plenty of openings.

One afternoon Audrey turned the corner onto Elm Street just in time to see Nora's bus pull up in front of the house. Panic-stricken at the thought of being spotted, she decided to stop and visit. Maybe she'd say she was in the neighborhood and wanted to see their Christmas tree. It was a plausible excuse. Most daughters-in-law would have invited their husband's folks for dinner and tree viewing by now, but since no invitation had been extended, she would take the matter into her own hands.

She pulled up behind the bus, mindful to keep back a few car lengths. The bus was a presence on this quiet winter day. Exhaust fumes darkened the air in front of the car, and the engine noise had an industrial sound to it. Inside the smeared back window, Audrey could see the outlines of children moving like Mexican jumping beans. How safe could that be? She remembered reading, years ago, reasons why seat belts couldn't be used on school buses, but now, for the life of her, she couldn't remember what they were.

The door of the bus opened with a squeal, and like cereal out of a box, children poured out. Nora was last, and Audrey looked to the house expecting to see Skyla in the doorway, but she wasn't there. The other kids, mostly bigger boys, were now heading down the sidewalk in the direction of Audrey's car. One of them kicked at a garbage can lid as he passed. Nora stood hesitantly on the walkway, looking first at the house and then at the empty driveway where her mother's car was usually parked.

Audrey was fumbling with the electric door locks, ready to step out of her car and call her granddaughter over, when she heard shouting.

"*Nora!*" a woman's voice yelled. "Over here!"

Audrey saw a blonde woman in a T-shirt and jeans standing on the porch of the Bear house, motioning the little girl in her direction. Shifting back in her seat, she turned in time to see Nora's face light up. The little girl moved quickly down the sidewalk, stepping over a garbage can lid with a skipping step and turning up the Bears' front walk. Audrey noticed that the drifts her granddaughter slogged through were knee high.

Audrey stepped out of the car. "Excuse me," she called to the woman she assumed was Roxanne Bear. Even from this distance Audrey recognized the frowsy look of a woman with poor housekeeping skills. "Excuse me," she called again, this time with sharp authority.

Nora stood next to the woman on the porch. Roxanne's hand rested on her shoulder. "Yes?"

"Nora is my granddaughter. Is there something wrong at the house?" Audrey walked around the back end of the car and made her way up the walkway.

"Hi, Grandma." Nora's voice was kitten soft. She waved a mittened hand.

"Is Skyla ill?"

Roxanne hesitated and then spoke slowly. "No one's ill. Everyone's fine. Nora just comes over to play with my boys."

"Skyla's not home?" Audrey was close now, just two steps down from where Roxanne and Nora stood on the porch. She could see her granddaughter's breath and the goose bumps on Roxanne's arm.

"Roxanne's babysitting me," Nora said. "Sometimes I forget which days, though." Her face was so precious, like a little Shirley Temple.

"Skyla's not home?" Audrey said again to Roxanne. The cold penetrated right through her gloves.

"No, she's at the bookstore." Roxanne opened the door and spoke to Nora. "Go on in, honey, and get your wet things off. I'll just be one minute."

It seemed to Audrey that Roxanne hustled Nora inside the way a person would scoot a child away from the entrance of a pool hall or an adult bookstore.

"Bye, Grandma," Nora said, and she obediently went inside, letting her backpack slide off her arms as soon as she was through the doorway. Inside a dog barked, a baby wailed, and a stereo pounded.

"You don't need to watch Nora," Audrey said. "It looks like you have enough going on already, for heaven's sake. I'll take her home with me now." Having an unreliable neighbor babysit for Nora was ridiculous when she and Walt lived only fifteen minutes away and were always available. How many times had she made the offer to Thomas and Skyla? What a slap in the face this was to have her only granddaughter languishing at the neighbor's house when she could be spending quality time with her grandparents.

Roxanne folded her arms across her chest. From her vantage point on the porch, she towered above Audrey. It was hard to tell if the look on her face showed disdain or pity. "That's real nice of you to offer." She spoke like she was choosing her words carefully. "But I really couldn't do that without Skyla's permission. We have this arrangement for me to watch Nora, and I can't just up and change it without checking with her first."

Nice of her to offer? She was Nora's grandmother! "Let's call Skyla then," Audrey suggested.

"Oh no, I wouldn't do that." Roxanne responded as if a simple phone call was a *very bad idea.* "It gets so busy at the store, and I wouldn't want to bother her. I think we should just let it go for today. Nora's really no trouble. I don't mind watching her." And as if the matter was settled, she opened the screen door and eased her way into the house. "It was nice meeting you, Mrs. Plinka," she called, almost an afterthought, and pulled the door shut.

It occurred to Audrey, as she stood there in the snow, the door shut in her face, that she'd never been treated with such disrespect. That woman had stood there and taken her granddaughter into what had to be a filthy house and shooed Audrey away like a pesky cat. It showed a complete lack of respect for her stature as a grandparent. What an awful way to be treated, especially by someone to whom she'd never been properly introduced.

She walked back to her car, careful to avoid the deepest deposits of snow. A crust of ice beneath the drifts made walking treacherous.

Did Thomas know where his daughter was spending precious hours during her most formative years? Probably not, she decided. Skyla managed everything in that house, including Thomas.

Audrey could mention it to him, but she doubted he'd do anything about it. His first loyalties were always to Skyla.

Walt wouldn't be any help either, that she knew. Unless his recliner caught on fire, he wasn't moving. If anyone were to safeguard Nora, it would have to be Audrey herself. She was the only one with the life experience to see what would be best. This time she was on her own.

CHAPTER SEVENTEEN

When Christmas was only a week away, Skyla and Thomas spent a Sunday decorating the house. After church Thomas wrestled a spruce into the tree stand, and Skyla wrapped boughs of green around the spindles of the open staircase. Decorating the tree came next. Nora trailed after each of them in turn, happily holding the end of garland like the leash of a beloved pet and offering opinions about ornaments and lights.

By afternoon the house had been transformed. "I don't think we've ever waited this long to decorate," Thomas said after he'd returned from putting the empty storage boxes in the basement.

"We haven't," Skyla said. "I'm behind in everything because of the bookstore. It's cutting into my Martha Stewart time. I haven't baked any cookies or sent cards out either, and I don't think I'll get to it."

"Better no cards than one like the Bears sent. That was a fiasco."

She laughed. "I told you that was a mistake. They never would have sent it out if they'd noticed." Skyla had heard all about what

Roxanne called "the annual Christmas photo ordeal" long before they got the holiday card in the mail. Roxanne gave her the lowdown during one of their usual morning coffee klatches.

"Do you know how hard it is to get five boys in the same room, much less sitting together and smiling for the camera?" Roxanne had said. "I've given up on taking them to a portrait studio. We've done that before, and it's always a freaking nightmare. I don't even dress them up anymore. If they're all wearing clothes and they're fairly clean, I put them in front of the tree and click as fast as I can, praying to God I get at least one shot where everyone's looking at the camera and no one's crying."

"Sounds reasonable." Skyla was always amused by Roxanne's stories.

"Yeah, you'd think so, wouldn't you?" she said and bounced the baby on her lap. A thread of saliva stretched from his toothy grin to the front of his shirt.

"This year I wanted to do it nice and early—get it over with. We didn't have the tree up yet, so Ted says, 'Why don't we put them in front of the fireplace and hang the stockings on the mantel?' I'm like, that's brilliant! So, we get all the boys lined up, and they're wiggling around and poking each other, and the baby is crying. I'm about to give up, and then Ted says, 'Hey, why don't we put Buddy in the shot?'" Roxanne rolled her eyes. "He thinks it will look cute. You know how I hate that dog. I'm thinking it will be a pain—now we'll have to worry about the dog *and* the kids looking at the camera—but Ted says it will help settle the kids down."

Skyla nodded thoughtfully. Her main experience with Buddy was the persistent way he backed his rear up to her legs and then sat on her feet. Roxanne assured her it was just something he did.

He wasn't targeting Skyla in particular or anything, but knowing this didn't make it any more pleasant. "So I drag the stupid dog over to where the kids are, and we get him to lay down in front of the boys." Roxanne motioned toward the floor. "And I guess Ted was right, it did settle the kids down a little bit, because after that the baby stopped crying and we only had to stop twice, once because Monty stepped on Gregory's foot and another time when I had to light a candle because one of the big boys farted and they were all laughing and holding their noses. You know how that is."

Skyla nodded even though she didn't quite know how that was. Nothing comparable went on in the Plinka household. Thomas was such a gentleman he even ran the water when he was using the toilet and someone was in the next room. When Nora burped, she daintily covered her mouth with her hand and said, "Excuse me" right away. Roxanne's household, on the other hand, seemed to generate an exceedingly large amount of flatulence, which led to an even greater amount of commentary about the strength of the smell along with speculation about the identity of the guilty party.

"So out of thirty-six shots there are only two where they all look halfway decent, and of course the damn dog is in both of them. Ted prints the cards to say, 'Merry Christmas from the Bear family.' So now we have sixty Christmas cards that make it look like the dog is more part of the family than Ted and I are."

"I'm sure people will know the word 'family' includes you and Ted," Skyla said to reassure her. "Most of the Christmas photos I get just have the kids on them. Parents usually don't want to be in the picture."

Thomas was opening the mail in the kitchen the day the Bears' card arrived. He sorted the stack by size and then type (bills, personal correspondence, ads) and opened them using a silver letter opener from a desk set his parent's gave him for high school graduation.

"Well, this is interesting," he called out to Skyla, who was emptying the dishwasher.

"What?"

"The Bears' Christmas card. Unbelievable." He sounded disapproving.

"Yeah, Roxanne said it was a huge ordeal." She lifted coffee mugs out of the top rack and set them upside down inside the cabinet. "If they look funny, it's because it was a nightmare getting all of them to settle down and behave long enough to take the picture. You know how those boys are."

"The boys are fine," Thomas said. "But the dog is disgusting. My God."

Skyla racked her brain, wondering how Buddy could be disgusting in a still shot. Drooling, maybe? Or did the flash give him red eye, making him looked deranged? "What's disgusting?"

"You've got to see this."

She wiped her hands on a dishtowel before walking to the table and looking over Thomas's shoulder. He held the photo up, thumb and finger pinching the edge.

Skyla first looked at the dog's head—it was tilted to the side with his mouth slightly open, Gregory's hand resting on Buddy's ear. "What? His tongue hanging out?"

"You're looking at the wrong end," Thomas said and pointed to the dog's underbelly.

"Oh my God." Unbelieving, Skyla took the picture out of his hands and held it closer to her face. She pulled out a chair with her free hand and sat down next to Thomas. "Oh my God." No other words came to her. She covered her mouth with her hand and looked over at Thomas, who was grinning. "I really don't think this is all that funny," Skyla said, trying to sound stern. "Roxanne's going to die when she finds out."

"I'm sure she already knows. It's probably her idea of a joke."

"I'm sure she *doesn't* know." A sudden thought came to Skyla. "Oh God, and they had sixty of these printed up. I wonder if they mailed them all at once."

"She has to know," Thomas said. "No one can mail out sixty Christmas card pictures of their dog with a hard-on and not notice. They're not the classiest people, but they're not completely brain dead. At least I don't think they are."

Skyla looked at the photo again. The three oldest boys sat on the ledge of the fireplace. Emmett held baby Ferd while Gregory stood in front of Wyatt and waved at the camera with one hand while petting the dog's head with the other. Buddy lay on his side, top rear leg slightly raised. It was hard to imagine someone could look at this photo and not notice the rod projecting outward from the underside of the dog. "Wiener" was what Roxanne's boys called it, but the word "bratwurst" would be a more appropriate description in this case. He was a big dog, and the thing was proportionate. Still, Skyla was sure Roxanne didn't know. She couldn't imagine Roxanne would have left *that* detail out of the story.

"I have to tell her," Skyla said. "She's going to die."

"This might be the start of a family tradition." Thomas smirked. "Hereafter in Bear folklore this will be known as the year of the Christmas hard-on," Thomas continued. "In time they'll start to incorporate genitalia into all their holiday traditions. Other families have gingerbread houses or go caroling, but not the Bears..."

"I'm going over there," Skyla said. "I'd call, but I want to see her face when I tell her." She took her jacket off the peg by the back door and slipped her arms through the sleeves.

"They'll be putting up their phallic symbol wreath every December," Thomas continued, as if he didn't hear her. "Their Advent calendar will be more like *Playboy* calendars. The boys will lift up the little flaps," he said, gesturing with a pulling motion, "and instead of holiday pictures, there'll be—"

"I get it already." Skyla covered his mouth with her hand and kissed the top of his head. "Could you hold down the fort for a bit? I won't be gone long."

"Do what you have to." He sounded amused. "I'm just going through the mail."

CHAPTER EIGHTEEN

Audrey wondered if she were in the throes of a midlife crisis. Of course she was stretching the term "middle-aged" a little since people rarely lived a hundred and twenty years, but what else could explain her feeling of emptiness and yearning for change?

Christmas had always been her favorite holiday, but this year she couldn't muster any enthusiasm for the usual baking and decorating. Maybe her depression was due to the overcast days or the bitter winds that assaulted a body as soon as they set foot outside the door. Mercy, winter got longer every year.

Gram would be gone on December 25 (off on a Panama Canal cruise with boyfriend Mike), so Audrey had everyone over for Sunday dinner a week before Christmas. Jeffrey was home already, of course, and Thomas, Skyla, and Nora said they would come after they finished putting up their Christmas decorations. "You're just putting up the tree today?" Audrey asked during their phone conversation and listened politely while Thomas explained about how hectic everything had become with Skyla's new job. The same job they'd sworn wouldn't make any difference to their family life. So this is what it got them. Audrey offered to come and pick up Nora early so she'd be out of their hair when they were working, but Thomas declined, saying that Nora would be upset if she weren't there to help. As if a kindergartner's efforts could make a difference.

How they babied that little girl! In a way, Audrey couldn't blame them—the child looked like a princess from a fairy tale. When they walked in the door late that afternoon, Audrey again marveled at her beautiful granddaughter, all rosy cheeks, curly hair, and big eyes. The effect was somewhat spoiled by the fact that Skyla had dressed her in play clothes. No accounting for some tastes.

Walt's mother arrived a little later, trudging into the front entryway with her big purse slung over her right shoulder and singing Christmas carols in a way that made her sound a little loopy. "Jingle bells, jingle bells, jingle all the way," she belted out in an alto voice that wasn't beautiful in her younger years and was now cracked like aged china.

Gram hung her coat in the front hall closet and then pulled brochures out of her purse and fanned them out on the coffee table. "This," she said, pointing to an enormous boat, "is where I will be on Christmas Day." The younger people crowded around to take a look, and from there it went on a sliding slope as far as Audrey was concerned. Gram told them far more than they needed to know about her cruise: the ports of call, food, and activities. It went on and on. Apparently not everyone found it as tiresome as Audrey did: Jeffrey seemed intrigued by the trip, and even quiet Skyla started talking about traveling and all the different places she'd lived as a child. The palm trees in the brochures reminded Skyla of San Diego, one of the ports of call resembled the forests of Idaho, and the description of the equator's sun was similar to what she remembered of southern Texas.

"What a scattered life," Audrey finally said in her *enough already* voice. "You certainly moved around a lot." Skyla grew silent, probably reflecting on her good fortune at having escaped *that* kind of background. She was lucky to land a catch like Thomas and become one of the Plinkas—a family of tradition with anchors to the community.

To shift the conversation in a different direction, Audrey brought out Dennis's Christmas card and holiday letter. He'd done a beautiful job detailing all his news: projects at work, trips he'd made, and a comical story about an attempt to make wine from the grapes that grew behind his apartment building. Enclosed was a photo of Dennis with an Asian friend (Austin, it said on the back) taken on one of his weekend trips. The two were dressed in ski gear and stood at the bottom of a hill surrounded by a weird fog. Their skis were angled and poles held upright. Both Dennis and his friend grinned. It was an odd photo to pick, Audrey thought.

The rest of the family—except for Walt since he'd already seen it—turned away from Gram's brochures to look at Dennis's card and letter. Thomas studied the photo for a minute or so and then nudged Skyla. "This is interesting. From now on I'll be more open minded when you tell me about your premonitions." He raised his eyebrows and handed her the picture.

Skyla looked at the photo and remembered her dream: Dennis in his Asian look approaching her in the fog. And here he was, with his Asian friend, both of them surrounded by fog. It was like she'd envisioned this picture but got the details mixed up. She grinned at Thomas. "I love it when I'm right."

"If you ask me, we're both right," Thomas said, pointing to the two men's matching patterned ski hats.

"What?" Audrey asked. She glanced over just in time to see a knowing look pass between Thomas and Skyla.

"Private joke," Thomas said.

"Nothing really." Skyla handed the photo to Gram. "Just some stupidity."

Audrey knew enough not to pursue it, but still it rankled. What was the big idea? Why the secrets? If it really was nothing important, why couldn't they tell her? Heavens, it was a sad thing to feel like an outsider in her own home.

CHAPTER NINETEEN

As soon as the kids were asleep, Roxanne wordlessly led Ted into the bedroom and locked the door behind them.

"I'm going to get it, aren't I?" he whispered, lips brushing against her ear.

She wrapped her arms around his neck and pushed up against him. "You got that right." Roxanne had wanted him all day. She'd called him on his cell phone that afternoon asking, "What are you doing *later*?" His response, "You tell me," let her know he understood.

She noticed he came home earlier than usual that night and was an unusually diligent father: helping with homework, doing baths and getting the little ones in their pajamas, reading bedtime stories. As they passed each other in the hallway, she felt his hand graze her bottom and noticed him looking at her with longing. "Later," he mouthed to her while carrying a towel-wrapped Gregory out of the bathroom. She just smiled.

Getting five boys quieted down and in their respective beds was as easy as getting puppies to stay in a basket. One was always popping up to get a drink of water or visit the bathroom. Just when all seemed still, Wyatt came downstairs to double-check the contents of his backpack. Ted all but exploded. "Couldn't that have waited until morning?" He and Roxanne had pulled apart at the sound of footsteps on the stairs. There was just enough time for Ted to zip his pants and Roxanne to move to the end of the couch and pick up the newspaper.

"I didn't want to forget," Wyatt said. "*Jeez.*" He shuffled through some papers and then zipped up the pack and headed up the stairs, footsteps pounding for added emphasis. Normally, of course, they would have been glad to see their son acting conscientiously toward his schoolwork. Tonight it wasn't appreciated.

Having sex on the couch didn't seem like an option anymore. Roxanne was too nervous. She led Ted up the back staircase to their bedroom so they wouldn't have to pass the twins' room. Hopefully the sound wouldn't carry, but if it did it couldn't be helped.

Once they were behind the locked door, their efforts were frantic. They stood kissing, Ted grinding his pelvis against her, Roxanne effortlessly unbuttoning his shirt. She pulled the fabric out of his waistband, undid the last two buttons, and then pulled away from him and helped him slide his shirt off and undo his belt buckle. "Well, look at that," she said, sliding a knowing hand into his trousers.

Ted pulled her to him and clumsily attempted to unbutton her shirt, but it took way too long. She pushed his hand away and pulled the shirt over her head instead. The rest of her clothes came off without her even realizing it, as if she had willed them gone.

He whispered compliments about her body. It was as if he hadn't noticed the weight she'd gained since they were married.

When it came time for them to come together, he hesitated, and she knew he was thinking of the box of condoms in the top dresser drawer. "Do you think we need protection?" he asked.

"No," she said and reached down and guided him to her. Relief flooded over his face. She knew his question involved timing. What he really wanted to know was if she might be ovulating. But that wasn't the question he asked, so it wasn't the one she answered.

When they were finished, they lay intertwined together. "So what gave you this idea?" Ted asked. He lay on his back with one hand under his head, the other arm cradling Roxanne.

"I wanted to see the look of pleasure on your face," she said, tracing a figure eight on his chest with a rounded fingernail. In truth, she wasn't sure what prompted her increased sex drive. Hormones? The fact that they were long overdue? The sight of the muscular guy on the infomercial for the ab machine? Impossible to say, really.

"I saw some of that on your face too," he said. He sighed with great satisfaction. "Ahh, Roxanne, won't it be great when the kids are older and we have more time to spend together? No more diapers, no more bottles, no more plastic toys in the bathtub. We won't have to read to them—hell, they probably won't even be home. They'll be at basketball practice and part-time jobs and at their girlfriends'..."

"Ted Bear, are you trying to make me cry?"

"What?"

"They won't even be home? That's the saddest thing I've ever heard." Roxanne thought about an empty house: no footsteps on the stairs, no music coming from the twins' room, no babies giggling or toddlers singing "Old McDonald."

Ted pulled her closer. "You know what I mean. It's not that they aren't great kids. It's just so much right now. There's so many, and it's so constant. Imagine going out and not having to get a babysitter. Or traveling, just the two of us. Remember how we always talked about that?"

"A trip would be nice." Roxanne felt a wave of drowsiness wash over her. "San Francisco?"

"Sure," Ted said. "And Italy and the Baseball Hall of Fame and all those other places we want to see. We'll hit 'em all."

They lay companionably for the next few minutes, listening to the rush of the wind outside and the soft hiss of warm air coming from the radiator. The glow from the streetlight washed against the blinds.

Roxanne was fading into sleep. Without opening her eyes, she slid away from Ted and moved onto her own pillow. "We could go on trips and take the kids," she said. "The boys would like the Baseball Hall of Fame." Saying this took all the energy she had left, but it seemed an important thought to suggest to Ted.

"We could," he said. "But not for a few years yet. It'll be easier when they're all a little older. We have lots of time."

CHAPTER TWENTY

Roxanne was in the middle of changing Ferd's diaper when the doorbell rang. There was no point in hurrying. Friends or relatives would know to try the door and walk right in. Anyone else was probably selling something and could just go away as far as she was concerned.

This visitor was persistent though. Now the ringing of the doorbell alternated with a sharp rapping on the door, making whatever it was sound urgent. Roxanne headed down the stairs, Ferd straddled over her hip. It was midmorning, and though the twins had successfully exited the house on time, fully clothed and with lunches and homework even, she and the three younger boys had gotten a late start and weren't dressed yet. She knew her hair was bed-head wild and that her powder blue chenille robe, worn at the elbows and tied with a frayed knot at the waist, was not her most attractive look, but whoever stood on the other side of the door was clearly not going away until she answered it.

"Mama, it's a lady," Monty yelled from the living room. He stood on the top back ridge of the couch for a better view of the porch. How many hundreds of times had she told him not to climb on the furniture? It wasn't so bad that Monty was doing it—he was five after all—but recently Gregory had started following suit, and his balance wasn't nearly as good. Before she knew it, Ferd would be scaling the furniture as well, if he were anything like his brothers. Ted's sister Clara thought it was funny. She claimed Ted and Roxanne were raising a troupe of circus acrobats. Of course, Clara could laugh—she wasn't the one who had to apply ice to bumped heads or make umpteen runs to the emergency room for stitches.

Roxanne opened the door and instinctively swung the hip holding the baby away from the cold. On the porch stood a woman holding a clipboard and wearing business attire: dress coat, nylons, and sensible navy blue pumps.

"Yes?" Roxanne waited for what was sure to be a Jehovah's Witness spiel. She was prepared to accept a copy of the *Watchtower* to placate this woman, but that would be the end of it. There was no way she'd allow her to come past the threshold. The thought of debating theology today or any other day didn't have much appeal.

"Are you Roxanne Bear?" The woman glanced at her clipboard as she spoke.

Roxanne nodded and changed her assessment of this woman from Jehovah's Witness to census taker. Definitely an improvement. She much preferred being counted than converted.

"I'm Virginia Wynn from Pellswick County Social Services," the woman said. She held up a card like it was a badge. "We've had a report of child neglect in your home. I'm here to do a follow-up interview. I have a few questions for you."

Roxanne stood silent. Her mind reeled—*What?* This was unbelievable. In a moment this woman would laugh and admit that a friend of Ted's had devised the whole thing as a joke. Not a very funny joke. "Child neglect?"

"Yes." The woman's voice was almost apologetic. "Anytime there's a report of a child at risk, we're obligated by law to investigate the claim. May I come in and ask a few questions? It won't take long."

"Who complained about us?"

"I'm not able to divulge that information." Virginia Wynn put her identification card back in her pocket. She stood on the porch as if this was the only thing in her day planner.

"Do you have a search warrant?"

"You're not being charged with any crime, Mrs. Bear. This is just an informal interview." She lowered the clipboard and tucked it between her arm and her side. "You don't have to let me in, but if you don't, I'll just be back with a court order. It might be better to just take care of this right now."

Roxanne stood indecisively for a moment. The social worker had already seen her in her robe. The baby perched on her hip wore stained pajamas. That couldn't be undone. The creaking of the couch springs from the living room gave away the fact that Monty was jumping on the couch in front of the picture window. Presumably the sight of his little kindergarten head could be seen bobbing up and down even from the street. She debated her options. She could send this woman away, frantically clean up the house, and then what? The house never stayed clean for very long anyway. And the tension of not knowing when this woman might return with a court order might just kill her. No, better to let her in and take her lumps. Certainly they couldn't take her kids away because she hadn't taken a shower yet. That wouldn't even be reasonable.

She swung the door open and gestured for the social worker to come in. As Roxanne made room for the woman to pass, she glanced around the entryway and saw it through new eyes. Not a pretty sight. The walls, freshly painted when they first moved in, were now scuffed and dented. On the floor, besides the usual dog hair and toy clutter, one of the younger boys had strewn a bag of Cheetos, some of which were ground into the throw rug. Ah well, it couldn't be helped at this point. Luckily, it wasn't real dirt. That would have been embarrassing.

Roxanne suggested they sit in the kitchen. It was the only room in the house that was currently in good shape, seeing as she'd scoured the kitchen sink and taken care of the dinner dishes the night before. Even the counters were fairly clean, except for a stack of paperwork and Wyatt's ant farm. The floor was in pretty good shape as well—no sticky spots that she knew of.

But they didn't stay in the kitchen for long—that was the bad part. Mrs. Wynn wanted to see the house, so they went from room to room with Roxanne nervously making commentary and offering excuses for clutter and unmade beds. In the twins' room a window was open a crack, letting in a bitterly cold draft. Roxanne closed it without comment and nonchalantly pushed Lego pieces under the bed with the side of her slipper. The baby was still slung over her hip, his little body clinging to her side. The other two boys had followed them upstairs. Monty trailed at a respectable distance, while Gregory clung to the side of her bathrobe.

Mrs. Wynn lingered in each room, making notations on her clipboard and asking questions. Who slept where? Did she ever go out and leave the children alone? What hours did her husband work? How did they discipline their kids? In the bathrooms she flushed each toilet and checked the faucets. In the bathroom closest to their bedroom, Ted had left two condoms, still in their wrappers, on the shelf above the toilet, but Mrs. Wynn didn't comment on this show of responsibility. In every room she opened closet doors and glanced over the contents. It was, Roxanne decided, like having some weird realtor looking over the place. One who could decide from the surface of things whether or not you were a good parent.

In the hallway the social worker had a few more questions regarding a specific incident.

"Mrs. Bear, do you remember an occasion when one of the younger boys climbed on top of a vehicle in the driveway? Why wasn't an adult with him?" It hit Roxanne then. The afternoon when Gregory danced on top of the van—that's what this was all about. Who could have called and reported them? Fussy Mrs. Williams next door? That wouldn't have surprised her a bit. The old lady was always throwing the boys' toys back over the lot line. One time she even gave Emmett a white plastic garbage bag and suggested he pick up the yard to surprise his mother. One of the Bear boys voluntarily cleaning up—that would have been a surprise. Later she found the plastic bag tied to a broom handle out in the yard. The boys had used it as a surrender flag for one of their war games.

Roxanne stumbled over an explanation for Gregory's presence on top of the van. An adult was with him—Ted was, in fact, shoveling the driveway at the time, but he wasn't, unfortunately, keeping a close eye on the boy. "You know how men are," she said and realized how lame that sounded as soon as the words came out of her mouth. "We got him down right away," she said. "He wasn't hurt at all. And we gave Gregory a good talking to. He knows it's dangerous, and I can promise you it will never happen again."

Mrs. Wynn nodded and gave her a thin-lipped smile. She headed down the steps without saying a word. At the bottom of the stairs she opened the front hall closet. Roxanne took advantage of this lull to turn on Nickelodeon and get the two boys situated in front of the TV. She kept her fingers crossed that the show would keep them occupied.

"Can I ask," Roxanne said finally after she joined the social worker in the foyer, "what you are looking for, exactly?" The baby, who'd refused to leave her arms, was almost asleep, his little head resting against her shoulder. Despite the situation, Roxanne couldn't resist kissing his downy head.

"We're not looking for anything in particular." Mrs. Wynn scribbled something on her clipboard even as she spoke.

"But here you're judging me as a mother, and I'm thinking you could take my kids away. So you must be looking for something." The injustice of it all made Roxanne's cheeks flush—the curse of being fair-skinned.

"My job with the department of social services requires that I investigate any report that comes across my desk. I take the health and welfare of the children in this county very seriously." She spoke as if this was a prepared speech she'd given many times. "Our goal has never been to separate families. This is only done in extreme circumstances. More often we refer parents to community resources and services that can assist them in dealing with stress, child behavior issues, and also introduce them to discipline techniques they may not be familiar with."

"Yeah, yeah, yeah." Roxanne tried to keep the impatience in her voice to a minimum, but it was almost impossible. "I understand that. But we're not one of those families. No one's stressed here. The kids aren't stressed. Ted's not stressed. I'm *really* not stressed—if anything, just the opposite. Everyone says I'm very laid back."

"I can see that," Mrs. Wynn said dryly.

"And my kids are very well taken care of. They are my life. I wouldn't do anything to harm them. If anything, they could use a little more discipline." What was she saying? Would this woman think they let the kids run amok? "But we've never whaled on them or anything," Roxanne amended. "We don't do drugs. We don't own guns. We hardly drink at all, just now and then. Honestly, we're very good parents. I know so many people who would vouch for us."

"I'm sure you do." The social worker slipped the clipboard under her arm and pulled on her gloves, a signal, Roxanne was sure, that the conversation was over. "Thank you for your time, Mrs. Bear."

"Thank you," Roxanne said, and then she wondered why she felt compelled to thank someone who'd invaded her house and made her feel like a child abuser. "Is there anything else? When will we know the results?"

"This wasn't a test, Mrs. Bear," Mrs. Wynn said. "We're not Pricewaterhouse. Nothing needs to be tabulated. As far as I'm concerned, everything appears to be in order. If we have any other questions, we'll be in touch. Otherwise, you just have yourself a good weekend." She smiled at Roxanne and extended a hand. Shaking hands always struck Roxanne as being an awkward gesture between women, but it wouldn't do to screw this thing up now, so she clasped the social worker's fingertips with her left hand (Ferd's sleeping body occupied the right) and gave it a cursory shake.

Roxanne stood in the doorway and watched the older lady make her way down the front walk. She reminded herself again to ask one of the older boys to shovel the pathway to the house when they got home from school. So far her strategy for snow removal—waiting for it to melt—hadn't been successful.

Skyla and Nora walked down the sidewalk as Mrs. Wynn walked to her car. Skyla gave the woman a quizzical look and then glanced at Roxanne. *What gives?* her expression asked. Roxanne shrugged.

When Skyla reached the door, she jabbed a thumb toward the street. "Did we interrupt something important?"

"Come on in," Roxanne said, letting them pass. She pushed the door shut behind them and found herself fighting back tears. Nora peeled off her coat and boots. The sound of the television in the next room caught her attention, but she stayed by her mother's side.

"So who was that? New friend?" The amusement on Skyla's face disappeared when she saw that Roxanne was crying. "What's wrong?" As if the words had punctured a dam, tears spilled down Roxanne's face and she began to sob. "Is someone hurt? Did someone die?" Roxanne shook her head and sobbed. Her chest heaved convulsively, and she tried to speak but couldn't get enough air to get the words out. Ferd, still asleep with his head resting on her shoulder, trembled from the movement. His eyelids fluttered, and he shifted on her hip.

Nora pulled on her mother's jacket. "Mama, what's wrong?" Her sweet little face looked up in concern.

"I'll take care of this, Nora. Go watch Nickelodeon with the boys." Skyla turned Nora in the direction of the living room and gave her a nudge in that direction. Nora hesitated and looked at Roxanne again. "It's okay, Nora. Just go," her mother said.

Skyla stepped out of her winter boots and reached for Ferd. "Let me lay the baby down. You go wipe your eyes." Roxanne relinquished the sleeping baby, unwrapping Ferd's little fingers from her hair. She stood and watched while Skyla eased the baby over her own shoulder and headed up the stairs.

By the time Skyla returned, Roxanne had washed her face with a cold washcloth and blown her nose. The lack of a morning shower was hitting her full force. She felt as grungy as if she'd just returned from a week of camping in the woods. "I feel better now," she said, shuffling into the kitchen with Skyla following behind her. Roxanne pulled out a kitchen chair and indicated that Skyla should sit.

"You want to tell me what that was all about?" Skyla's voice showed her distress. "Or not?"

Roxanne took a tissue out of the sleeve of her robe and blew her nose, making a honking sound. "Real ladylike, huh?" she said and folded the tissue and put it in her bathrobe pocket. "I'm sorry about the breakdown. I'm not sure what came over me. I hardly ever cry. In fact, I'm more pissed off than anything." Then she told Skyla the whole story, starting from when she thought the woman was a Jehovah's Witness until the end of the story when Skyla and Nora came up the walk. She finished by telling Skyla her suspicion that Mrs. Williams had called social services and reported them.

"I'm just so damn mad," Roxanne said. "What a bitch. It's unbelievable someone would do that. When we moved in, she seemed so nice." She wiped her eyes with the back of one hand. "She brought over cookies and said, 'Welcome to the neighborhood'—blah, blah, blah. I totally bought it. Now I have half a mind to go over there and tell her off."

"Maybe it wasn't her."

"Who else could it be? No one across the street would have called. And you can't even see our driveway from the other side of the house. Your house and Mrs. Williams's house are the only ones that would have been able to see the van where it was parked. No, it had to be her. Bitch." Roxanne spat out the word. "Oh, Skyla, why can't people just mind their own business?"

"I don't know." Skyla often wondered the same thing. "If it means anything at all, I think you're an excellent mother."

"Thanks." Roxanne took the wrinkled tissue out of her pocket, put it up to her nose, and gave one resounding honk. "What gives her the right to judge me?" Roxanne was just winding up now. Skyla nodded sympathetically and let her vent.

While Roxanne was going on about neighbors and families and injustices in the world, Skyla's mind strayed back to the day that caused all the trouble in the first place. She knew it fell on a weekend day. It was snowing, and she and Roxanne were talking on the phone when Thomas alerted her to the fact that Gregory was on top of the van. She remembered stirring soup and seeing Thomas's head jut through the kitchen doorway. He'd just come in from outside. She could picture him, glasses steamed up, his goofy Waldo hat askew. She tried to remember the reason he was outside. It was all a little sketchy.

And then she knew.

He was outside because he had been over to Mrs. Williams's house to feed the cat while the old lady was out of town. Mrs. Williams wasn't even home the day Gregory was on top of the van roof.

"Roxanne," she interrupted. "It couldn't have been Mrs. Williams who called. She wasn't even home that day. We were taking care of her cat while she was in Chicago visiting her son."

Roxanne sighed. "You know what, Skyla? I don't even care who it is. It could be anyone, if you think about it. Now every time I go outside I'll think the neighbors are watching my every move. I'll have to turn into one of those perfect TV moms. No more yelling at Wyatt to get his ass in the car, no more letting the kids climb that big tree in back. That tree drives Mrs. Williams crazy, you know," she said, leaning forward across the table toward Skyla. "She's asked me about three times if I think it's safe for them to be up so high."

"It is pretty high up." Skyla herself had her own doubts about the wisdom of letting Wyatt and Emmett hang on ropes two stories above ground level. It wouldn't be so bad if they weren't always pretending they were going to let go and jump.

"I know, but what is life without risk? Should people not go on trips or get married or drive cars? For God's sake, I could keep them out of the tree and they could kill themselves tripping down the stairs."

"I guess."

"Besides." Roxanne drummed her fingertips on the tabletop. "How I raise my kids is my own damn business." She shook her head. "Just last week Ted was saying he could get a promotion if he was willing to transfer to the Columbus office, and I was all like, 'Columbus? No way!' Ted made a big argument for moving back to Ohio so we'd be closer to our families when he was the one who wanted to move away from them in the first place. 'Let's move to Wisconsin,' he said. 'It will be an adventure,' he said. 'Do you want to live your whole life in one spot?' He drives me crazy." She reached up and pushed the hair off her forehead. "We're all settled here finally. I love this house, and the kids just got adjusted to a new school. I don't want to start all over again, but after what happened today, I can tell you that Columbus is starting to sound mighty fine. I'd move tomorrow if I could."

Skyla tried to imagine Elm Street without the Bear family. There really would be no point in living there anymore. "Don't say that. I couldn't stand it if you left. Who would I talk to?"

Roxanne waved a hand dismissively. "We could still keep in touch. There's e-mail and phone calls and visits back. It's just an idea, anyway. I don't know if the job's even still open. I'll have to get Ted to find out."

There was a silence while Roxanne considered the idea of moving and Skyla sat quietly in dismay. "I spent a summer in Columbus once," Skyla finally said. "And I can't remember a thing about it, so it couldn't have been that great."

"Maybe not remembering is a good sign. Nothing bad happened to leave an impression. It's one of those boring but good places to raise kids like Des Moines or Indianapolis."

"Or Pellswick, Wisconsin."

"Like Pellswick, Wisconsin, was until some busybody ruined it for me." Roxanne pushed her chair back from the table and stood. "I hate to ask you, Skyla, but I desperately need a shower. Could you heat up pizza for the kids' lunch and watch everyone while I jump in the shower? It's in the freezer. You know where everything is."

She nodded and watched Roxanne walk toward the back stairs. "You know," Skyla called out to her, "it doesn't sound like social services is going to do anything. This whole thing will just fade away. We'll be laughing about this later on."

"I don't think so," Roxanne said and headed up the stairs. The sound of her slippers made a soft, steady shuffle on the hardwood stairs.

❋ ❋ ❋

Skyla parked the car directly in front of the high school's front door, even though the sign clearly designated it a no parking zone. The sign was intended to keep the lane clear for buses, which weren't due to pick up the kids for a few more hours.

Besides, what she had to say to Thomas would only take a minute. She'd be gone before a tow truck could even be called.

The high school was a red brick building with a flat front and rows of square windows on each of its three levels. The classrooms had been updated over the years, but the exterior looked the same as it had when it was built sixty years before. Skyla barely gave the building a glance as she climbed the concrete steps leading up to the double doors. She slid her hand up the railing required by code, but which Thomas said was straddled by the students more often than used for support. One of the older teachers thought the teens were regressing and playing horsey, but Thomas knew better—a person didn't have to watch MTV more than once or twice to realize they were simulating sex acts for comic effect. On either side of the steps were overgrown forsythia bushes that doubled as ashtrays for students who (Thomas joked) believed they were immortal.

Skyla bypassed the office, where visitors were required to sign in. The portly secretary, who was on the phone, spotted her through the doorway and gave a friendly wave, no doubt remembering her from the staff Christmas party. Skyla wasn't in the mood to wave back but managed a perfunctory nod.

The determined click of Skyla's heels echoed on the linoleum as she made her way down the hallway to Thomas's room. As she passed classrooms, students' heads bobbed in her direction.

Thomas's room was the last door on the left. Approaching the open door, she heard the hum of the large freestanding fan he ran all year round, claiming the ventilation in the old building was poor and that the white noise helped those students who were easily distracted. Skyla had questioned the ventilation issue once.

It seemed to her that a fan would just move the same air around and around, circulating disease-causing, airborne bacteria, but he had a lengthy scientific reason why his way was preferable.

She rapped and Thomas stopped talking mid-sentence. His marker, held in midair, pointed at the word "cosine" on the white dry-erase board. "Just a minute," he said to his class when he spotted her standing there.

"Whoo hoo, Mr. Plinka's got a girlfriend!" one of the boys in the front row called out. He was slouched back in his seat, legs sprawling into the aisle. "That's his wife, you idiot." This from a girl in the back.

"Don't look like any wife I ever seen."

Thomas shushed them and joined Skyla in the hallway. He rested a hand on her arm, which she shook off. "What's wrong?"

"What do you think is wrong?" Usually Skyla hated mind games. It was irrational, she knew, to make someone else responsible for your emotions. But she wasn't feeling rational—in fact, she was seething.

"I don't know." His mouth had that infuriating slack-jawed look he used to express bewilderment.

"The department of social services came to Roxanne's house today." She watched his face for some sign of knowledge, but all she saw was puzzlement.

"Why?"

"Don't act like you don't know anything about this." Skyla's voice rose in volume. She'd intended to confront him in a calm manner, but emotion was overtaking reason.

"I said I didn't know anything. Why would I?" He looked nervously into the classroom, where several students were throwing paper footballs back and forth to each other.

"Someone reported Roxanne and Ted for the time Gregory was up on the van. Child neglect or endangerment or something. They came to the house and asked a bunch of questions and checked out the house. I've never seen Roxanne so upset."

"I'm sorry to hear that," Thomas said, although he didn't look sorry at all. He looked amused. "But I'm not surprised that someone called. Not everyone appreciates Roxanne's freewheeling parenting style like you do. Some people might even think she's a little on the sloppy side."

"So that's why you called and reported her?"

"I didn't call and report her. Why would you think I had?" He used his best defensive voice, the one that usually made her back down, but it wasn't going to work this time.

"So you're telling me that you had nothing to do with this social services thing?" Skyla was irate. "After everything you've said about them—all the crap about Roxanne reading the *National Enquirer* and being low class, and how they let Buddy wander the neighborhood and pee on our lawn and, God forbid, turned it yellow so it's no longer *perfect*." She framed the word "perfect" with fingered quotation marks. "And then there was your reaction to the erection Christmas card, which I *told you* was an accident, and your constant comments that their yard is always a mess and how you don't like her watching Nora because you think she's irresponsible. And then there was the time Gregory was on top of the van. I swear to God we were the only ones standing outside who saw that whole thing happen. After all that, you're going to tell me it wasn't you who called?"

"It wasn't me who called."

"But you were the one who told me about it. You were checking on Mrs. Williams's cat that day." She said it as if trying to jog his memory.

"I remember it happening, Skyla. And that's all I know. I didn't call social services. I told you that already."

"I just find that very hard to believe."

The expression on his face shifted to a frown. "And I find it hard to believe that my wife would interrupt me at work to accuse me of something I didn't do. I'm not a liar, Skyla. If I'd called social services, I would have told you." Thomas pushed the bridge of his glasses up with his middle finger. He looked back into the classroom, where the buzz of student's voices was steadily increasing in volume. "Now if you'll excuse me, I have to get back to teaching a class. It's what I do, remember?" He turned his back on her and walked back into the classroom, pulling the door shut behind him. Through the door's window she saw him tap his fingertips together, a gesture he used when he needed to collect himself. "Okay, everyone," he said, "break's over. Time to reenter the wonderful world of mathematics." There was a collective groan before the students settled down. Skyla watched for a moment and then turned and went down the hall, the click, click, clicking of her heels breaking the silence.

CHAPTER TWENTY-ONE

Audrey didn't feel like spending her birthday with Gram, but it was the only offer she had and better than nothing. The alternative, going grocery shopping and doing laundry on her special day, was unimaginably dismal.

At least the day started out on a positive, birthday-like note. Walt rolled over in bed, gave her a kiss, and wished her a happy birthday. When she shuffled into the kitchen to set up the coffee, she discovered Jeffrey arranging peach-colored roses in a vase on the table and propping a card up alongside them. The roses were frozen from being left out in his car all night, something that, as he explained it, couldn't be avoided. "I had to leave them out there. It was a surprise." They didn't look any worse for being subjected to the freezing temperatures, but only time would tell if there would be long-term repercussions.

Walt had promised they'd go out for dinner for her birthday. "No cooking for the birthday girl," he'd said over coffee, but she had the feeling he was more interested in the prime rib at Bob's Steak House than in making her feel special.

Dennis called too, right after Jeffrey left for work. He'd wanted to confirm that she got the card and necklace, which of course she had since he'd allowed plenty of time for delivery. Such a thoughtful son. They chatted for a few moments, but Dennis couldn't talk for long because he had to get back to work. That was disappointing.

Thomas and Skyla didn't call at all. Apparently they thought they'd covered it when they had Walt and Audrey over for dinner a few days before on a Sunday. They'd presented her with presents, and Skyla had actually baked a cake, a domestic skill Audrey hadn't known her daughter-in-law possessed. They lit the candles on the chocolate cake and sang "Happy Birthday," but it didn't have that birthday feel, being four days early and all. Not to mention that Thomas and Skyla seemed to be in a snit about something, with Skyla snapping at Thomas in a way Audrey had never seen before.

It started after they'd sung and before they'd cut the cake. Thomas sent Nora off to wash her hands and then politely let Skyla know that she'd brought out the wrong knife to cut the cake. Skyla responded with a venomous look and silently disappeared into the kitchen. She'd returned with knives of every shape and size cradled in her arms—steak knives, carving knives, butter knives, and one that looked like it could subdivide a cow carcass. "Here," she'd said, dumping them on the table. They clattered against one another, startling Walt, who hadn't been paying attention. "One of these should be perfect for the job. God forbid we use the wrong one." Her sullen look reminded Audrey of a rebellious teenager.

Walt and Audrey exchanged worried glances then, but Thomas just picked up a medium-sized serrated knife and proceeded to slice through the cake. He whistled while he did it, and Skyla left the room. Audrey half expected her not to return, but when she returned with Nora she acted like nothing had happened. Walt was the one who finally carried the array of knives back into the kitchen, wrapping them expertly in two linen napkins so that it resembled something a person might take camping or hunting. After that Thomas was his same quiet but personable self, but there was an edge to Skyla. She was pleasant to her in-laws and Nora, but she wouldn't talk directly to Thomas. Clearly something was wrong between those two. The air was thick with tension.

Audrey speculated on the reasons for the strife. She imagined scenarios ranging from affairs for each of them to the stress of Skyla's working at that disreputable bookstore. She hoped they weren't getting a divorce. Such messy things and so hard on the children. So common, though. Just recently at the grocery store she'd overheard a woman say her son was getting divorced because his wife had discovered she was gay. How do you discover such a thing? They made it sound the same as stumbling across an old pair of shoes in the back of a closet. Audrey tried to imagine Skyla in the arms of another woman, but the thought made her shudder, and she quickly swept it out of her mind.

Wednesday, her actual birthday, started off with good tidings but quickly faded to nothing. After Jeffery's roses and Dennis's phone call, the day looked like it was going to proceed like any other. Walt drank coffee and settled down to work on the crossword puzzle. When she suggested they go out for a birthday breakfast at the local coffee shop, he looked puzzled. "I thought you wanted to go out tonight," he said. As if a person couldn't go out to eat more than once a day. He lacked enthusiasm for any pre-dinner celebrations and even held firm in his tradition of withholding her presents until that evening. Audrey had moped then, wondering why things never turned out the way she wanted.

When the phone rang at ten thirty, Audrey answered it to hear Gram's chirpy voice singsonging, "Happy birthday, Audrey!" It was a welcome sound. At least something was happening to keep the birthday momentum going. Gram was calling from the beauty parlor on her new cell phone, a gift from her boyfriend, Mike. She'd just finished getting coiffed, as she put it, and wanted to take Audrey out to lunch. "Anywhere you want!" she said. "It's your special day." Mercy, how could anyone be so unrelentingly cheerful? It just wasn't normal. Audrey pushed these negative thoughts aside and accepted Gram's offer with gratitude.

Gram said she would pick Audrey up after her usual appointment with the psychic, but Audrey had another idea. "I think I'll come along," she said, "and wait for you. I can browse in the store." Her need to get out of the house overrode her disapproval of Mystic Books.

When Gram and Audrey arrived at the bookstore, the owner greeted them as if they were old friends. They'd barely stamped the snow off their boots when Risa Towers scurried out from behind the counter to exclaim over their appearance and clasp Gram's hands. "It's so good to see you. And looking so well, too!" she said. "So well, so well." Risa complimented Gram on the brooch pinned to her heavyweight bouclé coat and then turned her attention to Audrey and pressed her hand. It was an oddly intimate gesture from an acquaintance, and Audrey wasn't comfortable with it. If it had been a handshake, at least there would have been a definite ending to it. The storeowner's hand was light and knobby, and Audrey wanted to push it away but didn't want to be rude. Instead she released it to gesture around the store and comment on how good things looked. They kibitzed about the appearance of the store for a few minutes until Risa asked their opinion of the new window display.

"As usual, Skyla's outdone herself," Gram said. Her voice was proud. A person would have thought Gram herself was responsible for Skyla's talent. Audrey felt a pang of guilt. She wouldn't have noticed the window except that Gram pointed out the Valentine's Day motif as they walked past. She begrudgingly conceded that the display was beautiful. The background was draped red velvet. In front of the fabric's folds, roses and satin pillows framed books of love stories—not the cheap dime-store romances, but poetry and Shakespeare in leather-bound volumes.

"Your daughter-in-law is very talented," Risa said. "Lady Luck was smiling down on me the day she walked through my door. It was truly my lucky day."

Audrey nodded even though she didn't believe in luck. People made their own luck, as far as she was concerned.

No one else was in the store, and Risa didn't seem inclined to let them walk past. She talked about the weather; she listed off the contents of the store's newest shipment of boxes and rambled on about the hardware store owner's wife's pregnancy. Her voice went on and on until Audrey no longer heard words but a continuous stream of sounds. Risa was an imposing barricade for such a small person. Audrey didn't remember her being so voluble during past encounters. Of course, that was when Risa's husband, Bert, was alive. He had talked enough for both of them.

Gram was the one who finally made the break, thank heavens. Audrey was afraid that without the occurrence of a major event like an earthquake or robbery they'd be stuck talking to the little white-haired woman all day, but Walt's mother knew the ropes. "I'll let you get back to work," she said. "I'm sure you have much to do." With a wave of her hand she dismissed Risa and wheeled around before another word could be spoken. Gram grasped Audrey's elbow and steered her toward the back. "Such a lovely lady,"

Gram whispered. "But a little chatty. If I were you I'd wait back here, otherwise you might get cornered again."

Audrey didn't want that to happen. It was bad enough the first time around. She watched Gram disappear behind the partition where the psychic resided. The black lacquer panels that divided the bookstore from the fortune telling area seemed symbolic of something evil—black being the color used by rebellious teenagers and devil worshippers. Maybe it wasn't as serious as all that, but why hide in the back of a store if your activities are on the up-and-up?

Audrey knew from her previous visit that the two rows of bookcases in front of the psychic's area were the perfect hideout: tall enough to shield her from the storeowner and close enough to hear the conversation between Gram and that woman. She got into position and listened. "Madame!" Gram said in that excited, imagine-meeting-you-here voice she always used. It irked Audrey to no end. Of course Madame was back in the corner—where else would she be? And not only that, Gram had an appointment, so duh, as Jeffrey would say.

She shook her head. To Gram all of life was one big, happy surprise. Mercy, what a way to live.

Audrey picked up a book on plant life and leafed through the illustrations while listening to Gram and the psychic exchange pleasantries. The horticulture guide in her hand was written specifically for Wisconsin gardens. She paged through it looking for perennial flowers to add along the front walkway this spring. Walt grumped that flowers so close to the house attracted bees, but there'd never been any stinging incidents, so Audrey ignored his concerns. Yes, the bees buzzed around when they sat out on the front stoop in the evenings, but it was more likely they were attracted to his beer than her black-eyed Susans.

Behind the partition Audrey heard the shuffling and laying out of cards. The smell of incense wafted from the direction of the partition. It was unpleasant—a smoky, woodsy scent like the smoke from an old Christmas tree burning in a bonfire. Madame shuffled the cards and told Gram that her aura was blue and green. "Very good—very good," she said. Those colors meant that Gram was sensitive and caring, a truly kind and generous person. Audrey harrumphed to herself. Who wouldn't want to hear they had that kind of aura following them around? There was no fool like an old fool. Audrey shut the book and slid it back into place on the shelf.

Madame told Gram that good things were ahead for her in her immediate future: travel, family gatherings, good health! Audrey rolled her eyes while Gram clucked approvingly. But, Madame cautioned, Gram might want to take a multivitamin and extra vitamin C in the coming months, or she might get hit with one of those nasty colds that so often come with the changing seasons.

"We women take care of everyone else and so often forget to take care of ourselves," she said.

"Isn't that the truth," Gram said.

For the summer months Madame predicted Gram would be spending time on a lake, a fun outing with soft waves and sunny skies. This was a safe bet, Audrey thought. If you lived in Wisconsin and could stand upright, chances were good you'd be near a lake when the weather got hot. That prophecy would apply to most of the people in the state. She rolled her eyes after she heard Gram murmur something about how wonderful that would be. How could anyone eat what this woman was cooking?

Also, Madame continued, she saw a gathering for Gram that summer. An important gathering. Either a reunion or wedding or something of that manner. The psychic's voice became animated with excitement. Gram would get a chance to visit with someone she hadn't seen in a long time. Many of her questions would be answered. It would be a wonderful, joyful day.

Something to look forward to, Audrey thought sardonically. Another no-brainer. Who didn't go to some large gathering during the summer months? And didn't running into old friends or acquaintances come with the territory? From behind the screen Gram mused as to what that occasion would be. She didn't have any reunions or weddings coming up that she knew of. "Just remember I said it," Madame said. "Keep it in mind so you can validate it later." Audrey couldn't believe how gullible her mother-in-law was. Wait until she told Walt. She could almost see the smirk on his face.

Madame and Gram chatted a bit more about health issues and the weather. Gram's appointment seemed more a social visit than a revealing view into the future. Frankly, it didn't seem worth thirty-five dollars. Audrey would have given her a dollar fifty for the vitamin advice and called it a day.

Her ears perked up when she heard her mother-in-law speak her name. Gram was telling the psychic that it was her daughter-in-law's birthday and that they were going out to lunch to celebrate. "Ahh," Madame commented, "your daughter-in-law is an Aquarius. A very interesting sign. Aquarians have strong personalities—they're honest and loyal, original and independent."

"That's Audrey to a T," Gram said. She sounded pleased.

All of those traits could fit any number of people Audrey knew, Aquarian or not. Although she was willing to concede that independent and loyal were her trademarks.

She stiffened when she heard what Gram suggested next. "It would be great if you could give Audrey a reading." Oh no. She held her breath waiting for the response.

Madame thought it was an excellent idea. In fact, the time slot right after Gram's appointment just happened to be open, a lucky break since normally she was booked all the way through. Gram exclaimed at this amazing coincidence and added that she would pay for it. "It can be one of her birthday presents." Clearly, the two women decided, it was meant to be.

From her hiding spot behind the bookcase, Audrey cringed at the direction the conversation was taking. Mercy, how did this happen? Couldn't a person just wait quietly without getting dragged into something awkward? Why didn't Gram just keep her big mouth shut? This was worse than having some idiot waiters singing "Happy Birthday" to you at a restaurant.

"I'll go get her," Gram said, and Audrey heard the scrape of a chair being pushed backwards, which could only mean that she was on her way.

Audrey surveyed the store for an escape route only to spot Risa coming down the aisle toward her. She was trapped from both sides. If she were a rabbit, she'd be emitting a high-pitched scream right now.

"Oh here you are, Audrey." She heard Gram's voice at the same time she felt a hand on her arm. "I have a wonderful surprise for you." Audrey turned and saw Gram's smiling face. At the same time Risa was coming at her from the other side. The storeowner's mouth widened as if to speak, and Audrey knew that once that started they'd be hard-pressed to stop it.

A quick decision was needed, so Audrey pretended not to see Risa and turned to Gram. The lesser of two evils, in this case.

"I'm glad you ladies are still here," Risa said with delight. "I wanted to show you some gift items we just got in stock."

"We'd love to see them, but we don't have the time," Gram said. She snapped her fingers as if to say *oh darn*. "Madame is going to give my daughter-in-law a special birthday reading, and then we're off to lunch!" She patted Risa's shoulder. "Maybe another time." Risa beamed broadly, and Audrey couldn't help but think that some people were so easily pleased.

Risa nodded. She turned and walked back toward the front of the store.

"Are you ready to go? I'm starving," Audrey said and began to button her coat. Maybe Gram would forget the whole psychic reading idea and they could be on their way.

"Oh, no," Gram cried. "I wasn't just saying you had a reading. I meant it." Her eyes shone. "We're in luck. Madame has an open appointment, and when I told her about your birthday, she said she could squeeze you in. My treat."

Audrey reluctantly found herself seated next to Gram at the psychic's table. She rested her hands on the gold lamé tablecloth while Madame Picard greeted them and shuffled the cards with the efficiency of a Las Vegas blackjack dealer. "So today is your birthday. Happy birthday." She cut the deck and shuffled again. "A birthday can tell so much about a person." Madame wore long earrings—fake stones clustered together like grapes. The lavender-colored gems swung with every movement of her head. Audrey noted how perfectly her lips were outlined in ruby lipstick—dark slashes against alabaster skin.

The psychic deftly laid cards on the table and then stopped to study what she had done. "Hmmm," she said, her forehead furrowing.

Gram leaned forward to get a better look at the cards. "Oh, my," she said, her expression concerned. At least twenty cards were spread out on the table, each illustrated with a medieval-looking sketch: a skeleton, a dagger, young lovers, and other scenes. "This doesn't look good."

Audrey squirmed in her seat. Mercy, what was this about? Where was the lake news and the watch your health warnings? It was her birthday, for heaven's sake. How hard could it be to predict something? Seeing presents, cake, and growing older would be a good start.

"Hmmm," the psychic said. "You have some interesting changes coming up in the next year or so." She tapped on a card showing a young couple embracing. "The strong and stable love of your life will be your rock through this treacherous storm."

"That would be Walt," Gram said in a knowing way, her eyes widening.

"What storm?" Audrey questioned. Heavens, a minute ago everything was going fine in her life. This woman was setting up problems she didn't have or need.

Madame continued. "Boundaries in your life are not as clear as they were in the past. You've been feeling thirsty, hollow, unfulfilled. Your creative pursuits of the past were not appreciated, and you're not sure how to replace them." She pointed to a card that had some kind of star-shaped symbol.

It was true that Walt and Jeffrey didn't appreciate her efforts at home, but Audrey was used to that by now. Great meals that took hours to prepare were consumed with nary a comment. The house was organized and cleaned in an efficient manner, and no one said a word. She prided herself on not making an issue of things, but without a doubt, it would be nice to get some positive feedback from time to time.

"Your health looks good, except for those headaches you get from time to time." At this Madame looked up and held her hands on either side of her head. "Pressure headaches. Feels like a vise grip." Audrey felt her face flush. She didn't think she'd ever mentioned her headaches to Gram—or anyone else besides Walt, for that matter. Suffering in silence was her style. How did this woman know how her head felt? Could it be a lucky guess?

Madame lowered her hands to her side and leaned toward Audrey. She spoke as if talking to a friend. "You know what helps those? Take a hot bath and at the same time put a cold compress on the back of your neck. It has something to do with the vascular system and your nerve endings." She shrugged. "I don't know why it works—it just does. Anyway," she said, suddenly all business, "as far as health is concerned, you're trying to schedule in some fitness time for yourself on a regular basis—a walk, some swimming, a visit to the gym. You're feeling some resistance on this front at home, but you need to follow through." She reached over to Audrey and placed a hand on her wrist. "Maybe you take up golfing, join a bowling league, I don't know. Whatever you do, it's going to make you feel better."

Audrey nodded. She'd been considering joining the Y. In fact, she had broached the subject of getting a family membership to Walt just the other night. "I don't think we'd ever use it," he said, and that had been the end of it.

"The upcoming vernal equinox will magnify your nonconformity. With your personality, if someone pushes you, you're more likely to push back than walk away." Madame held a palm up and pushed against an unseen force.

"So true," Gram said.

"You have a strong personality, which is good, but watch it. Sometimes it works against your best interests. You know what I mean," she said and looked directly at Audrey. "Sometimes in life we need to just let things go, let other people have their way, even if we're sure we're right."

Audrey tried to think of what she could mean. If anything, other people took advantage of her good nature, not the other way around. "I'm not sure I understand. I get along fine with everybody."

"It's not always a matter of getting along," Madame said, shaking her head and making her jewel-clustered earrings shimmer. "Sometimes it's internal. Aquarians get to be like dogs hanging on to a bone. They get an idea, and it's hard for them to rethink their ways. They can do it though." She pointed one long, skinny finger at Gram, who nodded. "Aquarians are tough cookies. If they try, they can realign their way of thinking for their own good."

Madame shifted her attention back to the cards and rearranged them. She spoke of the benefits of broadening one's world and trying new things. Audrey listened politely. The psychic was talking so quickly it was hard to grasp everything she said. She touched on finances and future travel plans and something about a new friendship. She talked and talked until Audrey had trouble keeping it straight in her mind. If only she'd thought to write it down from the beginning! That way she could have shown it to Walt later. It would have been interesting to hear his opinion about the whole thing. Meanwhile, Gram was agreeing with everything like a visiting evangelist was in town and she was the Hallelujah Chorus.

"Progressive Aquarians are always looking ahead," Madame said. "It's good to plan, but don't let the planning take the place of doing. You know what I mean."

Gram nodded vigorously. Audrey managed a tight-lipped smile.

"The doing is everything." Madame gathered up the cards and shuffled them again. She cut the deck and arranged cards in a pinwheel design. "The most important thing you should take away from this table is the key to becoming whole. You, Audrey, have a void in your life. You need to fill that void." Madame held her hand above her head as if indicating the height of someone taller than herself. She raised her eyebrows. "It's like this—when your void is filled, you're up here." She lowered her hand to chin height. "Right now you're down here. Not good."

Audrey watched this visual presentation wordlessly. Madame rested her hands on the table and then, seeming to lose interest, stared at the space above their heads. Audrey was suddenly aware of the murmur of voices in the front of the store and the classical music playing through the ceiling speakers.

Gram finally broke the silence. "And how does she fill her void?" She was leaning against the table, purse on her lap, head propped in one hand like a tired student slumping on a desk.

"There's really only one way. Correcting the error of her ways. She needs to find the person she wronged recently and do everything in her power to make up for what she did. Once that's done, everything will fall into place and her life will improve." Madame tapped her long nails against the tablecloth like she was plinking on the keys of a piano. "It's a matter of karma. You did something to cause someone else pain, and you won't be released from your own pain until you make it up to them."

Audrey stiffened. "I don't know what you mean." She inwardly cursed her tendency to blush when she lied.

"I think you do."

Audrey held on to the edge of the table and tried to keep her breathing even. This woman seemed to know so much about her: the headaches, her desire for fitness, the void in her life, and now this? Who could have told her? Skyla or Gram would be the logical link, but neither of them knew anything. Mercy, where was all this coming from?

"You need to right your wrong," Madame repeated. "Once that's done, good things will happen for you. Otherwise—" She made a guttural slicing noise as she gestured a slashing motion across her neck. "Not so good. The bad karma follows you around." She glanced at her watch. "Alrighty then. Time's up. It was so nice to meet you, Audrey." Madame extended her hand. "Have a very happy birthday."

Gram nudged Audrey, who shook Madame's hand without much enthusiasm. Her mind was on voids and righting wrongs and wondering why Gram and this psychic couldn't just mind their own business and fix their own karma. For heaven's sake, everything in her life was fine half an hour ago. In the space of thirty minutes, it had all gone to hell.

CHAPTER TWENTY-TWO

Skyla waited on the other side of the screen while Madame finished talking on her cell phone. The conversation was heated—she was telling the person on the other end that he had to clean up the dog vomit because there was no one else to do it and he couldn't just leave it. Madame sounded aggravated. "Dammit, Andrew, all I can say is it better be cleaned up by the time I get home. Good-bye."

Skyla stuck her head around the corner. "Trouble at home?" Madame was seated at the table, the cell phone next to her folded hands.

"Yes," the psychic sighed. "My lazy grandson is visiting for God knows how long, the dog is dying, and no one can do anything without me." She smiled, revealing a row of perfectly aligned teeth, a shiny white contrast to her crimson lipstick. "Same old, same old." She stuck her cell phone into the shoulder bag hanging over the back of her chair. "So, little Skyla, what is new with you?" She clicked her long fingernails together—today they were painted with splashes of colors, each nail a tiny Jackson Pollock canvas.

"Risa told me you gave my mother-in-law a reading this morning," Skyla said. "And I'm dying to hear what happened." She unbuttoned her sheepskin coat as she spoke, slipped it off, and slung it over her arm. "Tell me, Madame." Skyla did her best Madame Transylvanian accent. "What did you see in Audrey's future? Will she win the lottery? Travel to exotic lands? Continue snooping around my house?"

Madame twisted the wrapped silver bracelet around her wrist. The bracelet was the image of a coiled snake with outstretched tongue. "Well, you've got Thomas's mother figured out, all right. She's a definite sourpuss."

"You think?" Skyla reveled in having her opinion confirmed by someone outside the family. The closest Thomas came to saying anything negative about his mother was that she had "issues." He also admitted she clearly favored Dennis, but that wasn't news. Everyone from the neighbors to the owner of the local grocery store knew Dennis was her pride and joy. Audrey still referred to him as her baby boy. Skyla wondered if he'd ever be old enough to escape that term of endearment.

"Not a happy woman. And a bit of a skeptic, would be my guess." Madame smirked. "But I did a number on her. She doubted me coming in. But going out she wasn't so sure." She gestured toward the front of the store. "I did an outstanding job, if I do say so myself. I had a few flashes of insight, and judging from her expression, I hit the nail on the head."

"Like what?"

"I gave her a little food for thought. Something for that grim face to ponder besides herself." Madame patted the sides of her bouffant hairstyle. "So different from your Gram, who's such an upbeat person. That's a woman who paves her own path with happiness, I can tell you that much."

Skyla nodded. Gram was a joy to be around—there was no disputing that. "Details. I want details. What did you tell Audrey? What did she say?"

"Oh, little Skyla." Madame's fake accent mysteriously reappeared. "You know I can't divulge what was said. All is private behind this screen." She drew up her lips in a Mona Lisa smile and placed a forefinger up to her lips. "Shh."

"Right," Skyla said, shifting her coat to her other arm. "So you won't even throw me a bone? It would give me such a thrill."

Madame shrugged. "Just a variation of my usual midlife crisis spiel. One size fits all, or your money back. It's been getting good results for me. I figure if it ain't broke, why fix it?"

"That's all you'll tell me?" Skyla was disappointed even though she had a pretty good idea what the psychic's midlife crisis spiel was: an outpouring of gobbledygook with an emphasis on exercise, vitamins, and extending yourself to others. A person didn't have to hang around the back of the store stocking shelves for too long before they overheard most of the routines. "That's all you're getting out of me." Madame stood up. "I think I have time for a quickie smoke before my next appointment. If Mrs. Erickson gets here early, would you come get me?"

"I will." Skyla extended her arm and offered her coat. "If you hang up my coat on your way."

Madame sighed. "Nothing for free in this world. Everything for a price."

CHAPTER TWENTY-THREE

Roxanne got up in the middle of the night to pee and on impulse stepped onto the old bathroom scale. She studied the quivering needle until her eyes registered the weight, and then she did the subtraction. *Yes!* Three pounds less than the week before. Unbelievable. She stepped out of her slippers, bent at the waist to move the scale closer to the toilet, and hopped back on to see if the house's uneven floors were playing tricks on her. *Ching, ching, ching*—it settled at the same number. She wondered if she should run to Wal-Mart in the morning and get one of those digital scales. They were easier to read, but were they more accurate? She really didn't know, but there was something official looking about numbers lit up in red. Oh, screw it. Good news was good news. Why mess with it?

Roxanne was so happy she could have hugged herself. Even without the benefit of a pregnancy test, she'd bet money she was going to have another baby. With each of her previous pregnancies, she'd lost weight the first trimester—a good thing, Ted said, considering all the weight she gained after that. Well, would he want her to starve herself and produce an unhealthy baby, she'd asked him. It wasn't a threat exactly, just putting it all in perspective.

Besides the recent weight loss, she'd felt nauseous and fatigued, and her period was only two days late. For such a teeny thing, this baby sure was causing a lot of trouble. Maybe it would be twins again. What a wonderful thought! Roxanne almost hated to think it—she might jinx herself. It was true that with Wyatt and Emmett she had the worst morning sickness of any of her subsequent pregnancies. Twice the hormones or something— she couldn't remember exactly why. But she'd gladly do it all over again if she could have twins. Or triplets! Even better. Wouldn't that be a hoot? People always rose to the occasion when you had triplets, doing shifts at your house for feedings, bringing meals for months on end, donating baby clothes and disposable diapers. Triplets got way more respect than twins.

Besides, she didn't know how many more babies she could sneak past Ted. Triplets would bring the score up to an acceptable eight. Still four babies short of her hoped-for twelve, but she could live with eight. Yes, eight seemed like a decent size family: a tribe, a herd, a houseful. She could live with eight. And if even one were a girl, she would thank the Lord and call it a day.

Roxanne pictured little dresses hanging in the closet, all ruffles and smocking, and those little hats—what were they called? Oh, yes, bonnets! That was it—matching bonnets for every outfit. She'd finally get to make that Barbie birthday cake she'd been dreaming about for eons. The magazine page was crumpled from repeated handling, but the print was still legible and the picture just as adorable as the first day she'd spotted the article at the dentist's office. She'd folded the magazine and slipped it into her diaper bag to take home and read later. Roxanne had never decorated a cake, but these were guaranteed to be easy. The Barbie doll in the photo had blonde hair, which would be perfect if her new daughter had hair the color of her brothers.

Wait until she told Skyla she was pregnant! Roxanne tried to imagine the expression on her face when she told her the news. Skyla would think she was insane. Oh, this was going to be so much fun. And the great thing about being pregnant now was that she hadn't packed all of Ferd's things away yet.

Ted would have a fit initially, she knew that from past experience, but he would come around. He always did.

She shuffled back to the bedroom and kicked her slippers off so exuberantly they skidded across the floor into the corner. By the glow of the streetlight through the curtains, Ted's covered body looked like an Indian burial mound.

"You okay, baby?" Ted was groggy. He lifted his head halfway off the pillow. He spoke as if it was difficult to open his mouth.

Usually Roxanne broke pregnancy announcements gradually. She'd buy new receiving blankets and leave home pregnancy kits out on the kitchen counter. Give him time to get used to the idea, that was her method. Tonight though, she was too excited to keep the news to herself.

"My period is two days late," she whispered. She climbed in next to him and curved her body against his.

"Hmm." Ted rolled onto his side and punched his pillow into a cylindrical shape and settled back down.

"I think I might be pregnant."

In the distance she heard a siren's wail. Ambulance or fire truck? It was hard to say, but she said a quick prayer for the victims, a childhood habit. "Did you hear me, Ted? I think I'm pregnant."

"I heard you," he said. "But I doubt you're pregnant. You've been late before. And we've been so careful." He yawned and rubbed his eyes.

"Well, except for that one time." A silence hung between them.

Just when she thought he wasn't going to respond, he said, "But you said it was okay that time." He didn't sound happy.

"Well," she hedged. "Nothing's one hundred percent."

He rose up on his elbows. "You mean to tell me we weren't covered that time?"

"We might not have been."

"You've got to be kidding, Roxy." He smacked his forehead with the palm of his hand. He was always so dramatic. "Why is this happening?"

"Ted, don't overreact. We don't know for sure yet, and even if I am pregnant, it's not such a horrible thing. I could use the clothes Ferd just outgrew, and the boys love babies—"

"Roxanne, you are certifiable." His voice was getting louder. "We're over our limit for kids as it is. I can't take it anymore." She shushed him. The way he was carrying on he was bound to wake up one of the boys.

"Where are you going?" she asked as he slid out of bed and padded over to the closet. He pulled his plaid bathrobe off the hook and put it on. If he were in a better mood, she might have joked about the way he fumbled around looking for the openings in the sleeves.

"I can't sleep now," he said. "I'm going downstairs to read. The middle of the night is the only time a person can get any peace around here." Roxanne heard his footsteps recede down the hallway and debated following him, but then she decided against it. With any luck she, at least, could get some sleep. There was no point in both of them being awake.

CHAPTER TWENTY-FOUR

Audrey didn't believe in karma, bad or otherwise, but how else to explain her bad luck since her birthday outing with Gram? Mercy, it was like that psychic put a curse on her. In the last few days she'd burned a roast, forgotten to take the library books back, and was late for a dental appointment. So unlike her. Unbelievable.

The ruined roast was the worst of it. Why, she hadn't overcooked anything since she was a newlywed, and she'd never seen a kitchen fill up with smoke that way. The smoke detector went off despite the fact that she opened the window and turned on the stovetop fan. Then when she stood on a chair to remove the battery, she lost her footing. In a panic, she grabbed at a framed picture hanging on an adjacent wall and knocked it to the floor, causing the glass to shatter. Luckily, she regained her balance and was able to free the batteries from the unit and get off the chair without breaking her neck. It was a close call, though.

"Having a senior moment, Mom?" Jeffrey asked when he entered the room a minute later. He was not known for his empathy, but surely even he could see how flustered and upset she was.

"I forgot to set the timer," she said. Her hands shook. In the haze of smoke the room looked foreign, like an alternate kitchen in a parallel, off-kilter universe.

"I thought I smelled something burning a while ago," he said and left the room.

Walt came in moments later. "Holy moly." He stepped over the shards of glass on the floor, lifted a magazine off the counter, and waved the air toward the open window.

She stood and clutched the batteries in her hand with such fierceness that her fingernails dug into her palm. "I don't know what happened," she said. Even to her ears it sounded like someone else's voice. "Something's wrong with me. And yesterday..." She paused to take a gulp of air. The room seemed to be closing in on her. "I had to pay library fines, and the day before I arrived at the dentist half an hour late. I was sure my appointment was at one o'clock. That's what I wrote on the calendar..." Her voice trailed off.

Walt lowered the magazine and turned to look at her. "You look whipped, Aud." His voice was uncharacteristically tender. "Why don't you go sit down in the living room, and I'll take care of things in here." He spoke as if he had doubts about her mental health.

"But what about dinner?" Her eyes were suddenly heavy. Was it just from the smoke?

"I'll have Jeffrey pick up some carryout. Just go sit down," he said. He opened the door to the pantry closet and came out with a broom and dustpan. "I mean it. Go. Put your feet up. I'll let you know when the food gets here. Is Italian from Pepino's okay?"

She nodded and headed for the living room.

Sinking into the couch felt good. Audrey couldn't help but feel that this was just the beginning of a bad turn in the road of

her life. One day a burned roast, the next day what else? A diz-
zying succession of disturbing possibilities whirled in her mind,
and she trembled. She didn't believe in karma, not really—in fact,
she wasn't even really sure what it was. But maybe, just maybe,
there was something to this "what goes around comes around"
thing. It might be best just to nip this whole thing in the bud—
right her wrongs, as the psychic said. Right her wrongs. Not such
a big deal. She could do that without much trouble at all. Tomorrow she would pay a visit and make amends. Just to be on the safe
side.

CHAPTER TWENTY-FIVE

Roxanne was sitting on the toilet in the first-floor powder room when the doorbell rang that morning. She ignored it. Two weeks had passed since the visit from social services, and while nothing had come of it ("Let them try and take my kids," Ted had thundered when he'd heard about it), she was still wary. She'd spent the last two weeks assessing her parenting abilities and life in Pellswick. She lost sleep wondering which neighbor could have turned them in. And why? Couldn't they have come to her if they were concerned about the kids? Some days she was pissed off, and other days she was pissed off and depressed. Ted promised to look into transferring back to Ohio and even asked the management at work about it. The higher-ups said they'd let him know.

It would be hell to move again, especially if she was pregnant, but she'd do it in a minute. Life was better before strangers started invading her world. Who'd have thought answering a door could put a person's whole world into such a tailspin?

The doorbell rang again, and she shifted impatiently. According to the previous owners, this bathroom was originally a room for storing vegetables, which explained its Lilliputian size and lack of windows. Sometimes, leaning over the sink to wash the babies' hands and faces, she got a whiff of something resembling damp earth and tulip bulbs, and she imagined this space occupied by wooden storage bins filled with turnips, carrots, and onions. Today the thought of root vegetables made her stomach churn, and the persistent doorbell ringing made it even worse.

Could she have gotten the stomach flu from Skyla? Both Nora and Skyla were sick—down for the count. Roxanne's theory was that Nora had brought the virus home from school with her, a little something extra nasty to carry along with her backpack and mittens. But it was just as likely that Skyla picked it up at the bookstore. Just the day before Roxanne had called to see how they were doing, and Skyla had sounded miserable. "I haven't been this sick in years," she said before excusing herself to throw up. Roxanne was sympathetic. She would have been more sympathetic if she had known it felt this bad. What she originally thought was morning sickness was turning out to be stomach pain in a big way. She hoped having the flu wouldn't hurt the baby.

Whatever she'd eaten the night before was majorly disagreeing with her. Her innards had threatened to spew out either end for several hours now, but nothing happened yet. Her body was torturing her. She wondered if making herself throw up would help.

The doorbell rang again. She sent rude thoughts in the direction of the front door. *Go away. Leave me alone. Just go away.* A mental hex.

"Mama." Monty's voice came from the other side of the door. "There's a lady at the door."

"It's okay, Monty." She tried to sound reassuring. "Just go and play. She'll leave."

"She says she wants to talk to you."

Roxanne had a sudden thought. "You didn't open the door, did you?"

A pause. "Just a little bit."

Dammit, how many times had she told the kids not to open the door? Didn't anyone listen to her? "Okay, hang on." Roxanne scrambled to get herself together and presentable. She left the top snap of her jeans open and didn't bother tucking her shirt in. She headed toward the front door knowing she'd be back in the bathroom as soon as possible.

"Yes?" Roxanne opened the screen door a few inches. An older woman holding a plate covered in aluminum foil stood on the porch. She didn't care what the deal was, this lady had thirty seconds tops to explain her business.

"I'm Audrey Plinka." As soon as she said the words, Roxanne recognized her as Skyla's mother-in-law, she of the older-lady curled hairstyle and the grim mouth.

Roxanne was relieved. "Skyla and Nora aren't here," she said. "I don't know where they are. Bye-bye." She started to close the door.

"Heavens, no. Wait, wait." Mrs. Plinka held up her hand like the school crossing guard. "I'm not looking for Skyla and Nora. I came with a peace offering and to apologize." She lifted the plate so it was level with Roxanne's chin. "I made banana bread."

The words "banana bread" made Roxanne's stomach turn inside out. "I'm sorry," she said and clutched her midsection. "But could you come back another time? I'm really sick." She turned on her heel and made it to the bathroom just in time. The front door was still open, but that couldn't be helped. Maybe Skyla's mother-in-law would close it or Monty or Gregory would think to shut it. If not, she had to feel better at some point, and she'd do it then.

Roxanne hunched over on the toilet seat and vaguely wondered about the banana bread peace offering. She remembered the day Mrs. Plinka came charging up the front walk insisting that Nora come home with her. Skyla was right, her mother-in-law did have a condescending, controlling way about her, but it was nothing that couldn't be handled. In fact, Roxanne felt bad shooing Nora in the house and sending Mrs. Plinka away. The older lady had looked crestfallen, and there was something pathetic about the way she trudged through the snowdrifts back to her car. And now here she was bringing baked goods to apologize for the curt way she'd spoken to Roxanne. How sweet was that?

Skyla had been adamant about not having Thomas's mom babysit for her, something about how she always tried to take over. To Roxanne, having someone take over sounded ideal. "What does she do?" she'd asked.

"Anything she wants," Skyla said with a frown. "One time when Nora was a baby, Thomas and I went to a movie, and when I came back she'd folded the laundry, washed the dishes, and reorganized my pantry closet." Skyla clearly didn't see this as an advantage. "After that, Thomas and I decided no more. It wasn't worth the free babysitting to have her worm her way into our lives."

※ ※ ※

Audrey stood on the Bears' front porch holding the plate of banana bread and wondered what to do next. This was not how the atonement was supposed to go. She shifted from side to side and peered through the door. A toddler walked into view carrying

203

what looked like a ball-peen hammer. He had the soft curls of a cherub, but he grinned like a hellion as he swung the hammer back and forth. He walked and swung, narrowly missing walls and his brother, an older boy of about four or five who stood just inside the door and stared out at her. Audrey opened the door wide enough to insert the plate. "Could you put this on the kitchen counter for me, please?" She directed this to the older boy. He listened with wide eyes and then turned and disappeared.

This was getting to be ridiculous. All she'd wanted to do was drop off some bread and say she was sorry. Why did everything have to be so involved?

Audrey let herself in and called out as she entered. "Hello. I'm just going to put the bread in the kitchen, okay?" She didn't hear a response, but she didn't care at this point. She slipped off her shoes and navigated her way toward the back of the house to the kitchen. "Mercy," she said. In all her years she'd never seen such a messy kitchen. Dirty dishes filled the sink and spilled onto the countertops. The floor was strewn with dry cereal and smeared with something that looked like marshmallow cream with dog hair embedded in it. The kitchen table was covered with paperwork and a two-foot-high Popsicle stick art project that looked like a half-finished birdcage. Catalogs and newspapers were stacked in the corner by an overflowing garbage can.

Audrey shook her head. Where would a person even begin?

The little boy who'd watched her through the front door now peered at her from the doorway that led into the living room.

"Hello," Audrey said. "What's your name?"

The little boy was silent.

She tried again. "I'm Nora's grandma."

"My mama is sick," he said and stepped closer.

Audrey nodded. No doubt the woman was hung over—that wouldn't have surprised her a bit. Pathetic how some people lived. Especially when they had children. Still, it was sad to see these little ones adrift without anyone to guide them.

"I'm hungry." Now the smaller boy, hammer still clutched in his hand, appeared next to the older one. The bigger boy pointed to his brother. "Gregory's hungry too. We need breakfast."

"You didn't eat breakfast yet?" Audrey glanced at her watch. It was almost eleven o'clock. The little boys looked expectantly at her. Oh, for heaven's sake, why did everything have to fall on her shoulders? She sighed. There was no way she could walk out of this house until these boys were fed. Well, they were lucky she was here and so capable. "I'll see if I can find something for you around here," she said. "You." She pointed at the older boy. "Find your mother and tell her I'm getting you breakfast. And you—" She leaned over and took the hammer out of the younger one's grasp. "Give me that. It's not a toy. You could get hurt." Her tone was sharper than she intended. The boy's face crumpled. "That's a good boy," she added. "Now go and play, and I'll call you when breakfast is ready." The two boys left the room.

Audrey turned away and opened the refrigerator door. Surprisingly, the inside was clean, though sparse. Grocery shopping in this house must not rate any higher in importance than cleaning. Still, there was cheese, eggs, jelly, and orange juice in the fridge and bread and waffles in the freezer. A meal could be put together with almost no trouble at all. Good thing Walt wasn't expecting her home in time for lunch. She had a feeling she was going to be here for quite a while.

CHAPTER TWENTY-SIX

Three days later Skyla waited for Thomas to come home from work. She stood next to him while he took off his coat and unwound a woolen scarf. A muffler was what he called it—she didn't know why. It was so like the Plinkas to use the uncommon version of words. At their house a couch was a sofa and margarine was oleo. It had confused Skyla at first, but she grew used to it. Now the problem was remembering not to use the Plinka words when talking to regular people.

Thomas greeted her and started talking about his day. He hung his coat and scarf in the closet and yammered on about the traffic and the next day's weather forecast. She stood with folded arms and waited for him to finish. Everything was always about him. He could be so clueless.

It wasn't until he asked Nora's whereabouts that Skyla spoke. "She's at Roxanne's," she said. "Playing with the boys."

"At Roxanne's?" He raised his eyebrows questioningly. "I thought…" The look on her face stopped him mid-sentence, but she knew what he was about to say. *I thought we agreed Roxanne wasn't going to watch Nora anymore.* Which wasn't quite true. He alone had decided Nora couldn't go to the Bears' without Skyla, something about it being a safety risk, which was absolutely ridiculous, of course. Roxanne was a good person, a loving mother. Skyla felt comfortable leaving her daughter in her care. Yes, there had been an incident at the Bear house involving the paramedics recently, but Nora wasn't even there when Emmett threw the steak knife at Wyatt, so why Thomas felt compelled to keep bringing that up was beyond her.

Skyla held her hands up like a maestro dictating a rest. "Don't worry. Nora's just fine. Your mother is watching her." She watched the look on his face—the expression of fake bewilderment that wouldn't fool anyone—and said, "So I hope you're happy. You've officially managed to screw up everything good in my life." She wanted to turn on her heel and leave the room in the dramatic way that worked so well in movies, but then she would have missed his reaction.

He looked at her for what seemed to be a long time, weighing a response. She knew he was incapable of blurting out whatever came to mind.

Finally he spoke. "Skyla, you are a puzzle to me lately." Thomas took off his glasses and wiped them on the bottom of his shirt. Without them he didn't look quite himself. "First you say Nora's at Roxanne's, then you say she's with my mom, and then you accuse me of screwing up your life." He put the glasses back on. "For God's sake, you're starting to sound like my students. I have no idea what you are talking about."

"I stopped over at Roxanne's after school to visit, and your mother was there babysitting for the boys." Skyla spoke slowly.

"She said she was helping Roxanne out. I was stunned, to say the least. I tried to get Nora to come home with me, but she wanted to stay and play."

"My mother is babysitting for Roxanne?" He looked incredulous. Under other circumstances she might have believed this news was a shock to him.

"I called Roxanne on her cell, and it seems that your mother's been there the last three days helping out. Just showed up at her door one morning when Roxanne was sick and took over, like she does. Roxanne thinks she's a gift from the angels. Her new best friend."

"How did this happen?"

"If I had to guess, I'd say someone who knew both of them arranged it." Skyla didn't even try to disguise the bitterness in her voice. "If I had to guess, I'd say someone wasn't happy with his wife having a life of her own. If I really had to guess, I'd say that you never want anything to change, so you took my friend away from me by trying to get social services to take away her kids, which made her want to move. And then to add insult to injury, you put your mom on the case so that there was no room for me anymore."

"That's the most ridiculous thing I've ever heard. I didn't know anything about any of this until just now, and I still don't understand it."

"But wait—there's more." Even to Skyla her words sounded like something from an infomercial, but she was on a roll now. "Since I can't have Roxanne watch Nora, I can't work longer hours, which means I have to be home taking care of the house just like you wanted in the first place."

"Back up a minute," Thomas said. "I'm still digesting my mother babysitting for Roxanne. I can't even imagine them in the same room together."

"You don't have to imagine it." Skyla could feel her cheeks getting flushed. "You can just walk over there and see it for yourself. I don't talk to Roxanne for a few days because Nora and I are sick, and while I'm out of the picture, your mother completely takes over. What a coincidence. In three days she completely cleans Roxanne's house, cooks meals, and gets Roxanne caught up on the laundry."

"But how do they even know each other?"

Skyla ignored him. "I suppose when the new baby comes she'll be the live-in nanny. They'll probably name it Audrey if it's a girl." She rolled her eyes.

"Roxanne's having another baby?" This time she could believe he was genuinely surprised.

Skyla nodded, teeth clenched. "She's at the doctor right now getting the test, but she's already sure. She didn't even do a home test because she didn't want to waste the money. I suppose Audrey will hear all about it before I do."

"Well, well, well. Another baby," he said. "Just what they need." He shifted his stance to do what she knew would be a John Wayne impression. "Round up the horses, pilgrim—it's raining babies at the Bears' house." He grinned, and Skyla regarded him with a cold look. *Round up the horses, pilgrim—it's raining babies at the Bears' house?* That didn't make sense at all, not to mention he didn't even sound like John Wayne. Still doing the imitation, this time with thumbs hooked through his belt loops, he said, "Will wonders never cease?" How typical of him to make a mockery of her concerns.

"So that's all you have to say?" This conversation was going nowhere. Her world was crumbling around her, and she was looking for an explanation. All she'd gotten so far were platitudes and denials. In John Wayne's voice, no less.

"You know more than I do." He pushed his glasses up with the tip of his pointer finger like he was shooting himself in the head. "I guess the full story will come out eventually."

"So you're not behind this?" Her frustration was rising. "You can't tell me why your mother mysteriously showed up at Roxanne's house offering to help her?"

"No, Skyla." He sighed theatrically. "I didn't ask my mother to clean your friend's house. I didn't call social services. I didn't hire a moving company and force the Bears to move back to Ohio. I didn't get Roxanne pregnant. And frankly, I'm tired of you accusing me and acting like a shrew."

She felt her blood pressure rising. A shrew? *A shrew?!* How typical that Thomas wouldn't even lower himself to use the word "bitch." "I am going to find out what this is all about," she said through clenched teeth. "I will not have my life manipulated by you and your family. I've had it."

He looked so self-righteous she wanted to slap his face.

"Duly noted," he said.

CHAPTER TWENTY-SEVEN

The only doctor Roxanne trusted completely was her obstetrician, Dr. Davy. All the rest of them annoyed her with their poking and prodding and personal questions. Why go looking for trouble? In her opinion, it was best to leave well enough alone.

The day she went for her annual exam and pregnancy test, Dr. Davy was nowhere in sight—off birthing a baby, no doubt, giving some couple a gift of unimaginable happiness.

Roxanne knew the pee-in-the-cup routine. She'd done it before and knew the doctor wasn't involved, but it was a rip-off that she wouldn't even get to see Dr. Davy afterwards. The receptionist, who looked like she could be a high school senior, said the associate would do the exam. These annual checkups were no-brainers. If Roxanne could give herself a Pap, she could practically phone the whole thing in. Still, it didn't seem right to be in this office and not see Dr. Davy, with his neatly combed-back hair and name embroidered above the pocket of his white lab coat. His absence made her feel anonymous. You'd think her status as the mother of the most beautiful babies Dr. Davy ever birthed (he'd said so himself) would give her preferential treatment. For one fleeting moment Roxanne considered leaving and rescheduling for a time when Dr. Davy would be there, but then she dismissed the thought. It was rare that she had someone to cover for her during the day.

Instead of preferential treatment, a nurse's aide gave her a labeled paper bag and an empty plastic cup before directing her to a bathroom. The size of the room made her nervous—as if to over satisfy the legal code, it was large enough to accommodate a fleet of wheelchairs. The sink, raised-seat toilet, and a shelving unit were against one wall. Underneath her feet an expanse of black and white honeycomb-shaped tiles stretched three yards from the base of the toilet to the door. Adjacent to the toilet a pull cord dangled near a sign that read, "Pull in case of emergency." Roxanne often wondered what would happen if she did pull it, but she managed to suppress the urge every time.

She urinated into the cup as instructed and then wiped the sides with toilet paper. Did everyone have this aiming problem, or was it just her? It wasn't really the kind of question you'd ask most people, although Skyla would tell her straight if Roxanne remembered to bring it up the next time they had coffee. She set the cup in the paper bag, placed it on the shelf intended for samples, and washed her hands. The young receptionist called her name as she walked out to the waiting room.

Right on schedule—now that was something that didn't happen very often at a doctor's office. Once she was alone in the exam room, Roxanne slipped into the gown so the opening faced the back. She contemplated teasing Dr. Davy when she started coming in for her next set of prenatal visits. Isn't it odd, she'd say to him, that the one time you're not in the office, they manage to keep right on schedule? Today was a good day for everything to go well, what with Skyla's mother-in-law babysitting and all. Audrey had assured her that she'd raised three boys of her own and it wouldn't be a problem, but the Bear boys had provoked more than one babysitter to the brink of a breakdown. Audrey seemed up to the task, but Roxanne didn't want to push it. She'd already done so much, covering for Roxanne when she had the flu and getting the house in order. Any objections Roxanne might have had dissolved as she held her aching midsection in the bathroom. With her family so far away, she'd almost forgotten how nice it was to be taken care of.

It was a miracle, really, everything Audrey had accomplished in three days. Like a housewife wizard, she turned a gigantic pile of dirty laundry into folded piles of pressed clean clothes. Thanks to her whirling-dervish mop, the kitchen floor didn't have a sticky spot on it. The countertops gleamed. In each room there were now traces of Audrey—from the newly vacuumed carpeting to the packaged meals labeled and tucked in the freezer. Heaven sent, the woman was, standing on the porch with her foil-covered plate just when she was needed most. Ted thought this outpouring of help was odd. "She's doing this to piss off Skyla and Thomas because they've shut her out," was his take on it. "You'd better watch it, or you're going to lose your friend." Roxanne heard the warning but didn't believe it. Yes, it was odd that Audrey was doing so much for her when they barely knew each other, but there was a reason she showed up at their house to begin with, and the rest of it unfolded because Roxanne was sick. Anyone might have jumped in and helped, given the circumstances. Besides, Audrey was so sincere, and Skyla didn't seem to care.

"Better you than me," Skyla said when Roxanne told her everything that had happened since their last talk. Besides, now that she was feeling a little better, this would be the end of it. Audrey wasn't going to keep coming forever, although it would be nice if the house could stay this clean all the time.

The med tech came in to get her weight and blood pressure and the date of her last period. Roxanne tried to initiate a conversation about her unconfirmed pregnant state while the woman was taking her pulse, but her words were waved away and she let it go. The young associate doctor bustled into the room as the med tech left. He said a perfunctory, "Good afternoon, Mrs. Bear," glanced at her chart, and got right down to business. Assembly-line medicine is what Ted called it. Working as a pharmaceutical sales rep, Ted had his own opinions about the medical profession. This doctor went through the motions of the exam without the banter she enjoyed with Dr. Davy. The silence was a relief. The idea of small talk with another ob-gyn while she lay on her back, feet in the stirrups, felt like cheating.

Finally it was over, and Roxanne was allowed to sit up. Her legs dangled over the edge of the examination table, and she was suddenly self-conscious of the patch of leg hair her razor had missed and her chipped toenail polish. She put her legs together and leaned forward, hands on her knees.

"Do you know?" she asked. "If they have the results of my pregnancy test yet?"

He had the clipboard in hand and was near the door. It was clear he had been about to say, "See you next year" and move on to the next patient. Her question seemed to take him by surprise.

"You're not pregnant," he said. "Why would you think that?"

"Oh, but I am." Roxanne struggled for an explanation. "I've had five babies, and believe you me, I know how it feels. I just took the test because they wouldn't schedule a prenatal appointment without it."

There was a moment of silence, and then he said, "You can check at the front desk on your way out if you'd like, but I can tell you right now that you're not."

She held her breath. Oh, where was Dr. Davy when she needed him? Clearly this man (was he even a doctor, for God's sake?) couldn't tell his ass from a hole in the ground. Of course she was pregnant.

"Your cervix wasn't blue," he said. He unclipped her folder and opened it to her paperwork, running a finger over the surface. "And you had a period just last month."

"It's a week late."

He cocked his head to one side as if thinking of what to say next. Finally he spoke. "Menstrual cycles," he said, "can and do vary." She listened politely while he continued with a lengthy explanation of the intricacies of menses and decided not to argue. Better to go home, buy a home pregnancy kit, and then schedule an appointment with her real doctor. She and Dr. Davy would laugh about this later.

"Stress can affect your cycle." He was rambling now. Typical of a man—when you least want them to talk, you can't shut them up. "There are many factors that can influence cyclical timing. Some women even believe planetary forces like the phase of the moon or the tides can cause a delay." He smiled condescendingly. "Of course, modern science has yet to confirm that."

"Interesting," Roxanne said. She was aware of the moistness of her bare bottom against the paper shield on the table and wanted to wipe herself and get dressed. She spotted a box of Kleenex on the counter next to the sink, left there, no doubt, for that express purpose. "Well, thank you, Doctor. It's been a treat." She held out her hand, which he stepped forward to grasp.

He shook her hand and started to speak, but then the expression on his face changed. "Tell me," he said, "how long have your eyes looked like this?" He put the clipboard down on the counter and then turned back to cup her chin in his hand. He lifted her face so that she saw only the ceiling. With his pointer finger he pulled the skin below each of her eyes.

"I know I look like hell. I just got over the flu and haven't slept for shit, excuse my French." She gave a little half laugh. "Although generally I don't look much better."

This new young doctor didn't respond to her joking the way Dr. Davy did. His face showed concern. "The whites of your eyes are yellow, which is a sign of jaundice. I think we should take a blood sample."

What was this all about? "My youngest had jaundice when he was born," she said. "You aren't going to make me lie naked under a light are you?" She said it in jest, but the doctor didn't smile.

"It's not usually serious in newborns," he said. "But in adults it could indicate any number of things. We'll take a blood sample and send it to the lab, and you'll need to make an appointment to see your internist as soon as possible. They'll run some tests."

"Like what would it be?"

"It could be any number of things." He hesitated. "It could be anything from gallstones to something more serious. Without tests, I really wouldn't want to speculate."

Well, la-de-freakin'-da. Dr. Maybe-It's-The-Moon-Making-Your-Period-Late wouldn't care to speculate why her eyes were yellow. This appointment was not going well, not well at all. She knew she should have rescheduled and waited for Dr. Davy.

"Just wait here, and I'll have Brenda come back in to draw some blood. Just sit tight."

He exited and there she sat, conscious of her dangling legs and the looseness of her breasts behind the thin cotton gown. Roxanne was cold and wondered if there was any reason she couldn't get dressed. Certainly they wouldn't be drawing blood from her vagina. Ha!

She scooted her butt forward on the table and eased her way down to the vinyl floor. Reaching behind her, she held the gown shut and crossed the room to the molded chair where she'd left her clothing neatly folded, underwear on the bottom, purse hanging off the back. On the wall right above the chair hung a small mirror. Roxanne leaned over the chair and widened her eyes for inspection. Man oh man, he wasn't kidding—they did look yellow. How long had they been like that? She pulled the lids up and then down. Her eyes felt kind of itchy too, now that she thought about it. Gallstones, did he say? Hard to believe that some little stones in the center of her body could give her the eyes from hell. She tried to remember what she knew about gallstones. They were really painful to pass, she knew. Or was that kidney stones? She would have to look it up when she got home.

Roxanne grabbed her purse off the back of the chair and backed up until she felt her rear rest against the edge of the examining table. She fumbled in the main compartment, bypassing the fruit snack wrappers, the box of Band-Aids, and the TV remote control she carried with her at all times because otherwise it just got lost. At the bottom she found her cell phone. It was encrusted with graham cracker crumbs, but otherwise it was in good shape—battery charged and everything.

She pushed the buttons to dial home and put the phone up to her ear. "Audrey? This is Roxanne. I'm really sorry, but they're so screwed up here it looks like I'm gonna be stuck here awhile longer."

CHAPTER TWENTY-EIGHT

The next afternoon found Skyla feeling out of sorts. She walked the length of Mystic Books, feather duster in hand, and took swipes at light fixtures and shelves without noticeable results. There were no signs of cobwebs or misplaced books either. Even the back of the store was immaculate. Nothing truly needed doing. If a customer didn't come in soon, she would fall asleep on her feet.

"Why are you sighing, little Skyla?" Madame Picard asked from where she stood next to the folded partition. "Life is so hard?" Madame was wearing a multicolored head wrap today. It was a new look she'd discovered on a mannequin at the museum store. People half expected a turban anyway, she said, and this way she could blow off doing her hair if she was in a hurry. In true Madame fashion, her nails, earrings, and outfit coordinated with the head wrap.

Skyla hadn't realized she was sighing, but it wasn't surprising the way things were going. "Life's not that hard. I just need a different one."

"A different life?" Madame dropped the fake accent and sounded amused. "Do you want mine? My arthritis is acting up, and my washer just broke down."

"No, you can have it. I'm just feeling…" She searched for the right word. "Restless. Nothing seems permanent."

"Nothing is permanent," Madame said and laughed. "You're just figuring this out now?"

Skyla didn't answer. She'd thought some things were permanent. How could life have deceived her? She had clung to Thomas like a life raft when they first met. She admired his levelheadedness, his sense of order. The initial physical attraction between them was intense; just his gesture of taking off his glasses and the promise of what was to come had been tantalizing to her. She liked his quiet confidence. Thomas didn't have anything to prove. He was a man of great integrity, returning money the cashier had overpaid and holding doors for young mothers pushing strollers. She admired that. But mostly she was struck by his sense of tradition, his belief that things should be a certain way. He was so settled, so sure. They dated only a short time before she decided Thomas was just what she needed. They set a wedding date right after that.

As a married couple, they agreed about most things and especially how to handle his mother. Audrey was meddlesome but well-intentioned, Thomas had said right before he'd taken her home to meet his family—just let her have her say and then do whatever you want. They laughed about Audrey's attempts to take over their lives. She and Thomas were a team. Or so she thought. Now Thomas and Audrey had linked up against her, and Roxanne had gotten drawn into their trap. And she'd thought Roxanne was smarter than that. For crying out loud, Roxanne had not only found out that she wasn't pregnant, but she'd also learned that she had some other health problem—gallstones or something like that. And who had heard about it first and helped Roxanne through this crisis? Audrey, of course. It was all so unfair. Skyla had been left out.

This was all new to her. Growing up she never had time to get mired in relationships. She'd barely cast her line in the water, it seemed, when it was time to pack up and move on. How had she gotten so firmly entrenched in this life? She'd put down roots before she realized the permanence of it all, and with Nora and the passing of each year she became more anchored. She thought of her single years with longing. Didn't she have some plan to go to New York or Paris and take the art world by storm? Or was that just the way she remembered it now, after the fact?

"It seems to me," Skyla said finally, "that you just can't count on the people you love."

"Oh, Skyla, hearing you say that makes me so sad," Madame said. "It's always been my experience that the people you love are the only ones you can count on."

CHAPTER TWENTY-NINE

Roxanne had thought a negative reading on a pregnancy test was the worst news she could get in a doctor's office. That was before she found out she had cancer.

She and Ted sat on one side of a massive glass-topped desk in the oncologist's office (who knew they had such luxurious offices?) while the doctor sat opposite, his face grim. Under different circumstances she would have commented on the room: the richness of a tall mahogany cabinet on one side, the gold-framed diplomas that hung opposite, and a picture window behind the doctor's desk that faced a courtyard with a fountain. Through the window she saw two women dressed in salmon-colored scrubs sitting across from the fountain smoking cigarettes. They leaned toward each other as they talked and laughed as they exhaled, puffs of smoke drifting lazily around them. The mood inside the office didn't match the images outdoors.

Roxanne heard the doctor say the word "cancer" and gripped the armrest of her chair. She knew any news requiring Ted's presence wasn't going to be good, but she wasn't prepared for this.

She was aware of breathing in and out and her heart picking up speed, but she made pains to keep a straight face. Fear, like a live thing, clutched at her throat with a spiny claw. She swallowed and pushed the fear away, blinking back tears. Roxanne listened politely to the doctor, but she wasn't completely there. Part of her had floated up to the ceiling and was looking down at the nice young couple getting the unspeakable news. Such a horrible, sad thing. Roxanne viewed herself as a stranger might and noticed the blonde hair spilling over her shoulders, the white knuckles gripping the chair, and the way her head moved up and down in acknowledgement of what was being said. She kept her fear contained. Over and over she thought, *It can't be true, it can't be true, it can't be true.* A mental mantra to ward off this evil. Her other self, the one hovering up around the ceiling, took it all in. *She's trying to keep from losing it,* she thought about herself, and then she wondered if this disassociation meant she was going insane.

"But it's curable, right?" Ted asked. "We can beat it?" He reached over and covered Roxanne's hand, a shield of warmth over her chilled fingers. She wanted to see the expression on his face but knew if she turned her head to look at him she would lose her composure.

"We're talking about pancreatic cancer," the doctor said, almost apologetically. "It's very aggressive. But there are treatment options." Roxanne seemed to have lost her voice, even as Ted's became stronger. The two men volleyed words like chemotherapy, anti-nausea drugs, and surgery back and forth between them while Roxanne, suddenly tired and overwhelmed, sat glued to the chair. *Why is this happening?* she thought. And then she wondered, *Who will take care of my babies?*

Outside the window, in the courtyard, the two women snuffed out their cigarettes and rose up off the bench to get back to work.

In as much time as it takes to smoke a cigarette, a person's life was changed forever.

⁕ ⁕ ⁕

Time went at a different pace after Roxanne was diagnosed. Outdoors life went on. The snow, by now a gray slush, melted and was not missed by anyone. The sound of rushing water through the sewer grate let everyone know Lake Michigan would soon inherit the last dregs of winter. Spring arrived and brought with it cool rains and sunny-colored daffodils. The maple trees that lined Elm Street came to life and sprouted tiny fist-like buds that unfolded into leaves.

Inside the Bear house, each day had new significance. Roxanne had always been so healthy—it was hard for anyone to believe she was now seriously ill. Sure, she'd had backaches the last few months and a touch of diarrhea here and there, and yes, she'd lost some weight, but if anything she'd never looked better. Even when she came home from the ob-gyn's office that first day, Audrey had dismissed the yellowness of her eyes. "Barely noticeable," she'd said. "Probably just something you ate."

But it wasn't something she ate. Instead, it was something devouring her.

Surgery was ruled out right at the start. "It's spread to the lymph nodes, lungs, and liver," Ted told Skyla when she appeared at the door holding a pan of lasagna. "Stage IV, they call it. It's wrapped around some blood vessels and is unresectable." He said the words matter-of-factly, but he looked like he was going to cry.

"Can't they do anything?" she asked and immediately regretted the question.

"They're going to start chemo next week. Gemzar." He said the word as if she'd know what it was. She nodded, and he reached through the open door, took the pan of lasagna, and retreated into the house. Skyla stood on the porch for a few minutes for good measure. When he didn't return, she went home.

"It doesn't sound good," she told Thomas when she got home. She had set aside her anger at him, not knowing if it was gone for good, but sure that she didn't have any room for it at the moment. "Ted looks like a zombie, and Roxanne didn't want any company."

Thomas was sitting at the kitchen table cutting up chicken nuggets and green apples for Nora, who watched him with wide eyes and drank from a glass of chocolate milk. He sliced in slow, even strokes while Skyla repeated what Ted had told her.

"Poor guy," Thomas said. "I'd be devastated if I lost you."

"He's not going to lose her," Skyla said. She was indignant. "Don't even say that. Roxanne's going to beat this thing." She twisted a lock of hair around her finger. "Why would you even say such a thing?"

"It's just—" Thomas hesitated. "Pancreatic cancer is really vicious, and you did say it was stage IV." He set down the knife and poured ketchup onto the plate. "All set, honey," he said to Nora and then stood up and walked over to where Skyla stood. "I hope she's cured, I really do." He put his arms around Skyla, and for the first time in weeks she didn't feel like pushing him away. "I just think you should be prepared if she isn't."

"It's just too horrible to even think about." She pressed her face against his shirt, and the tears came despite her best efforts. "Too horrible." Her lower lip trembled, and her chest heaved uncontrollably. Skyla sobbed so hard her eyes grew bleary. She unsuccessfully tried to sniff back a runny nose. Everything flooded out at once.

With her face pressed against Thomas's chest and his arms wrapped around her, she was shut away from everything but the sound of his heartbeat and her own whimpered cries. She heard Thomas's muffled voice reassuring Nora that everything was fine. Then he guided Skyla up the stairs to the bedroom and helped her lie down on the bed. He disappeared for a minute and came back with a box of Kleenex and a crocheted afghan. She gratefully took a tissue, sat up, and blew loudly. Then she settled back down on the pillow. As if they had rehearsed it, Thomas put the Kleenex on the nightstand, covered her with the afghan, sat next to her, and stroked her hair.

"Why did this happen?" she asked.

"I don't know." The feel of his hand raking gently through her hair was almost hypnotic.

"It's so unfair."

"Yes."

"Why Roxanne? Of all people, why her?" Skyla swallowed hard. It felt like she had a golf ball in her throat. "I mean, Roxanne *is* life."

"She's been a good friend to you." Thomas moved his fingers over her scalp. It was calming. Her body relaxed into the bed. His words sounded so sincere that she didn't point out that this statement contradicted his previous opinion of Roxanne. Maybe he had changed his mind.

The bed seemed to absorb every ounce of energy she'd ever had. "Maybe I'll just take a little nap," Skyla said.

And Thomas, who generally frowned on sleeping during daylight hours, said, "I think that's a good idea." He patted her head one last time and got up and lowered the blinds. It was a comforting gesture. "Just sleep," he said and pulled the door shut.

※ ※ ※

Ted's parents, his sister Clara, and her daughter Analisa came from Ohio to help Roxanne through chemotherapy. Because Clara was a nurse, she became Roxanne's caregiver, while the in-laws handled the kids and household chores. Ted cut his hours and only worked half time. It took three and a half adults to replace one Roxanne, Thomas pointed out with what seemed to be a new respect.

The Bear boys doubled up on bedrooms to accommodate the relatives. Roxanne's parents and brothers came sporadically as well, but they never stayed more than a day or so, which Ted told Skyla was just as well. "They're a pain in the ass. Her brothers complain that we don't have beer in the house, her mother carries on about her arthritis, and her father falls asleep in my recliner." He threw up his hands in disgust. "They hardly pay any attention to Roxy and the kids. I don't even know why they come."

The Bear house was fuller than ever and yet seemed emptier. The boys appeared to have forgotten their penchant for wildness. The house was quiet.

Too quiet, Skyla thought. Her hours at the bookstore had decreased, and she had time to visit every day. She brought soups and homemade bread that Roxanne rarely ate and flowers that seemed inadequate. She never knew what to expect. Some days Roxanne was up to visitors and was a gaunt version of her old exuberant self. "Look, Skyla," she said one day, sticking a leg out from under the covers. "Clara gave me a pedicure." Her toenails were painted ruby red and covered with small white hearts. "The hearts were Monty's idea."

"We've been busy," Clara said. Something about the open-faced way she smiled reminded Skyla of Ted.

"I see that. Very nice." Skyla was suddenly shy. Not that long ago she and Roxanne had talked nonstop. Now it was hard to know what to say. Besides telling Roxanne she was so, so sorry this was happening, they'd never discussed her disease—never even mentioned the word "cancer." Skyla was afraid saying the word out loud would give it power.

Sometimes when she came to visit, Roxanne was asleep or spending time with her sons, and Skyla felt like an intruder. Even Buddy the dog, once Roxanne's greatest aggravation, found his place on the floor next to her bed and became a comforting presence. Skyla watched from the edge of the room as the younger boys sat on the edge of the bed and colored or Wyatt and Emmett showed Roxanne their spelling tests and graded projects. Once, Skyla walked in on an improvised puppet show. Monty and Gregory crouched at the end of the bed and waved their sock puppets back and forth. The puppets mostly wrestled and hit each other. Roxanne smiled and clapped. "Don't I have talented children, Skyla?" she asked, and Skyla, her heart breaking into a thousand pearl-sized pieces, could only nod. Roxanne applauded again and laughed—a throaty chuckle that Skyla hadn't heard in a while. "I definitely see professional wrestling in their future. I heard that Stone Cold started with puppet shows when his mother was sick." Monty, the older of the two, popped up from the end of the bed. "Really? Cool!" Skyla stood in the corner by the window and made small talk for a suitable length of time before she left. Seeing Roxanne was hard, but not seeing her would be harder still.

On some days Roxanne had more energy and was up and dressed and walking around the block with her sister-in-law at her side, shades of her old life. Skyla watched them from her living room window and wished she were the one walking beside Roxanne, holding her elbow for support. It was a selfish thought.

"I think she might be getting better," Skyla told Thomas. "It's like the chemo is killing the cancer."

Thomas didn't say anything—trying not to get her hopes up, she knew. He was of the opinion that Roxanne was just buying time, though he had enough sense not to say as much to Skyla. It came out in other ways though. Just the week before they had gone to visit Thomas's parents, and Audrey had said, "Thomas tells me your friend Roxanne is gravely ill." Gravely ill. The words rubbed like steel wool.

"Yes," Skyla said. "She has pancreatic cancer."

"What a shame." Audrey took bread out of the oven while Skyla sliced tomatoes on a cutting board on the counter. "A shame," she repeated. "Such an energetic young person. And all those boys." Skyla continued looking down at the tomato, sliding the blade through the firm red orb in even strokes. "Tell her I'll keep her in my prayers, would you?"

"Sure." Skyla scooped up the slices, set them on top of a bowl of greens, and then reached for a cucumber. "I'll tell her." But she wouldn't.

❅ ❅ ❅

As the weeks went by, Roxanne's bad days outnumbered the good until one Saturday Skyla knocked on the door and was greeted by a somber-looking Clara. "It's not the best time for a visit," she said. She looked tired, and for the first time Skyla realized how hard this was for Clara. Somehow, she'd thought nurses were more comfortable with illness, used to it even.

"Is she sleeping?"

"No." From behind Clara the sound of crying could be heard, an adult man wailing in a way that pierced her heart. Ted. "We've had bad news. The last CAT scan showed that she's no longer responding to the chemo." Clara's eyes were moist. "In fact, it's spreading."

"I see," Skyla said, and because something was blocking her throat she couldn't say another word. It was as if the shattered pieces of her heart had traveled up to where she swallowed.

"They recommended hospice care, and we're going to do it here. Ted thinks it's important for the kids to spend the time with her." Skyla was aware of the sound of a lawnmower off in the distance and a car making its way down the street. It didn't seem right that the planet was still turning and people were going about their mundane tasks, oblivious to the fact that Roxanne was slipping away. "We're ordering a hospital bed and are going to set it up in the dining room."

"That's a good idea."

"Ted's going to call Roxanne's parents. They'll want to be here."

Skyla choked back a sob. Crying was such an ugly thing, she thought. If only she could stop. She seemed to have no control of herself anymore.

"I'm so sorry, Skyla." Now Clara was crying. She wiped her eyes with the back of her hand. "I'm really sorry." She seemed to be saying it as much for herself as for Skyla.

"How much…" The words caught in Skyla's mouth. Clara leaned against the doorframe as if she was not in a hurry to go back inside where Ted sobbed and Ferd now wailed. Skyla could hear other noises too, the sound of Ted's mother comforting someone (the baby? Ted?) with a "there, there" and the television playing the theme from *Gilligan's Island*. Skyla tried again. "How much longer does she have?" Saying it out loud meant she could no longer deny it was true. The words burned in her throat and felt like betrayal.

"It's hard to say for sure," Clara said and shook her head sadly. "Not enough."

"I'll come back tomorrow," Skyla said. She thought, *Oh please God, let her be here tomorrow. Please—I will never ask for anything else ever, ever again if I can just see Roxanne one more time.* She had a feeling God didn't strike bargains, but it didn't hurt to try.

Clara nodded. "That would be better. I'll tell her you stopped by."

Skyla nodded, and Clara went back into the house, pulling the door shut behind her.

CHAPTER THIRTY

Skyla visited Roxanne every day. She trudged down the sidewalk between their houses and up the path to the Bears' front door. She sat by Roxanne's side and watched her friend gradually slip from this world to the next, helpless to do anything about it.

The hospital bed was set up in the middle of the dining room, directly beneath the cut-glass light fixture that looked like a punch bowl. Roxanne slept under white sheets just feet from the foyer where visitors came and went. Those making appearances included neighbors, relatives, and the burly priest from St. Charles Church on Chimney Street (the Bears weren't Catholic, but they didn't turn him away). No one stayed long. Roxanne's worn look and the tortured appearance of her husband were more than most people could bear.

Roxanne was now thinner than a person should be, and her hands were cool to the touch. When she spoke, it was with much effort. She didn't waste a word. Skyla wanted to reach out and pull her firmly back into this world, somehow transfer her energy to her friend. If it were possible, she would gladly have given some of her life to Roxanne, donated years the way work friends contribute sick days to stricken colleagues. If it were possible, she would have done it. Instead, Skyla chattered about what was going on in the world. As if it mattered.

Clara was the only one who updated Skyla regarding Roxanne's physical condition. She confided in her in a way that made Skyla feel like part of the circle. Roxanne was in rapid terminal decline, Clara said, and her body was in the process of shutting down. "We're keeping on top of the pain," Clara said. "That's important."

While Clara tended to Roxanne, Ted and his parents walked around the house in an emotional haze. They vacillated, Skyla knew, between unrealistic hopes for a miracle and complete despair. They lived on prayers and not much else. When she asked Ted how he was doing, he replied with terse statements: "Not so good," he'd say, or "Could be better." Once she found him sitting at the kitchen table, coffee mug in hand, face unshaven and eyes vacant. "Why is this happening?" he asked. Skyla noticed then that he'd lost weight as well—his face was gaunt, and his eyes looked sunken. "Just a few months ago she was fine. Why would God do this?"

Skyla wasn't sure he was talking to her, although she was the only one in the room. "I don't know," she said softly. It didn't make sense.

The Bear boys, influenced by the mood of the house, were oddly quiet. Wyatt and Emmett were uncharacteristically kind to their little brothers and Clara's daughter, Analisa. As if they instinctively knew their role in their mother's illness, they kept the younger children occupied: gave them piggyback rides, built Lego forts with them, and walked them to the park. The house had an air of waiting.

"She's having a good day today, so now is the time," Clara said to Skyla one Saturday, "that we really need to pay attention." She'd met Skyla at the door and was wiping her hands on a dishcloth. The smell of cinnamon rolls wafting from the kitchen meant Ted's mother was baking again. Clara spoke in a hushed voice. "Whatever Roxanne says has significance." She shook her head. "We can learn so much from her."

Skyla wasn't sure what that meant. Roxanne was dying. What good could come of that? What knowledge was worth her life? Clara gave Skyla's arm a pat and retreated into the kitchen. Skyla unbuttoned her jacket, draped it over the stairway railing, and walked toward the dining room, where Wyatt sat reading to his mother from the morning paper. Skyla stood in the doorway to let her eyes adjust to the dimly lit room. Since her last visit, things had been rearranged: a nightstand and lamp were now next to the bed, and a dozen yellow roses stood in a green vase on the ledge of the built-in china cabinet. Two Mylar balloons, both of them with "Thinking of You" messages, grazed the ceiling in the corner. The shades were partially drawn, but the small lamp on the table next to the bed (Skyla recognized it as the Noah's Ark lamp from Ferd's room) cast a yellow glow. The sight of Roxanne curled up in her white cotton gown illuminated by the baby lamp made Skyla clutch her hands to her chest.

Wyatt held the newspaper in front of him and read, "And then Dogbert says, 'How about a wide-eyed and innocent child who loves you unconditionally?' and Dilbert says, 'Tiny weasels.'" He lowered the paper and grinned at his mother.

Roxanne managed a small laugh. "That's a good one."

Skyla stood motionless and wished herself gone from this room. Why did joy always have to be overshadowed by pain? She wondered if it would be possible to retreat in silence. How many steps would it take to reach her jacket? How much farther was the distance to her own house, where no one was dying and she could pretend that life went on as usual? She took a step back, and the floorboards sighed from her shifting weight.

"Skyla?" Roxanne raised her head from the pillow. Her voice was small. "Hey." She patted the side of the bed. And then it was too late to leave gracefully, too late to whisper to Clara that she didn't want to intrude or that Roxanne seemed too tired to talk. There was nothing left to do but take the seat that Wyatt offered and settle in for a visit.

Wyatt eased past Skyla, the newspaper still clutched in his hand. "Is there anything else you want, Mom?" Wyatt asked, stopping under the arch that led into the foyer. Somehow he had grown up while Skyla wasn't looking and was now all arms and legs and husky voice. When had that happened?

"I'm fine, baby." Roxanne managed a half smile, and Wyatt left the room with the newspaper trailing from his fingertips, the bottom edge grazing the floor. She turned her attention to Skyla and lifted her hand from the bed just high enough to wave her fingertips toward Wyatt's back. "So tall."

"Looks like he's grown a foot," Skyla agreed. Amazing the way she and Roxanne both noticed the same things. Like looking through the same microscope. "Overnight practically. Emmett too."

Roxanne said, "Such big boys." She eased herself farther back on the propped pillows so that her head was slightly elevated.

"And they're only in middle school. They'll be giants by the time they reach high school. At the rate they're going, they'll bigger than Ted. You wait and see."

Roxanne's face turned solemn, and she nodded.

The silence in the room smothered Skyla like a blanket, and she bit her lip. How insensitive could she be? Roxanne wouldn't be around when the twins were in high school—she might not even be here next month or next week. The seasons would change, and the boys would keep growing older and taller. Already it was spring. Winter boots and coats were packed away. Outside it smelled like sunshine on damp earth, and tulips and daffodils were poking their heads above the soil. Next year it would all happen again. But it would happen without Roxanne. No mother to ruffle the hair of the older boys or cuddle the babies. No Roxanne to help them with their homework or read them bedtime stories. Ted would sleep alone, and Skyla would pick up the phone only to realize that her friend no longer existed on this earth. Skyla looked at the wall and blinked back tears. She would have slammed her hand in a door if it would take back the words.

"Waiting and seeing isn't an option," Roxanne finally said. She looked calmly at Skyla. "I don't have that much time." She spoke with much exertion.

"Don't say that," Skyla said. By some miracle she managed to keep her voice steady, but the tears were spilling out faster than they could be wiped away. "Medical technology is always coming up with new things. No one knows for sure."

"I'm sure." Now Roxanne's voice was just above a whisper. "Did Ted tell you I wrote letters for the boys? For after?"

Skyla shook her head and wiped her eyes with the edge of her sweater. "No."

"Clara and I planned everything." She closed her eyes, and Skyla noticed the delicate veins on Roxanne's eyelids and the gentle way her chest rose and fell as she breathed. No one spoke for a few minutes, and Skyla's own breathing followed the pattern of her friend's until she felt they were almost one and the same.

"What am I going to do without you?" Skyla said at last. She couldn't mask the anguish in her voice. "You're my only friend."

She was aware of how selfish this sounded. Certainly she had less of a right to grieve than Ted and his boys, but it seemed that the world was a better place when it was reflected in Roxanne's eyes. Nothing would be the same without her.

"I worry about you, Skyla." Roxanne's eyes were still closed.

"You do?" The irony of Roxanne worrying about her was not lost on Skyla.

Roxanne nodded with her eyes still closed. "You still think you're a little orphan girl all alone in the world. It's not true." She folded her hands on top of the sheets. "You have everything you need. Lots of people care about you." She swallowed.

"None like you."

"Well, of course. There's nobody like me," Roxanne said and snorted in a way that startled Skyla into a laugh. Roxanne opened her eyes as though the snort surprised even her and grinned. "But even without me, you're covered."

Skyla stared at Roxanne through bleary eyes and spoke with admiration. "Roxanne Bear, you are an original."

"Don't forget me."

"I could never forget anything about you." Skyla swallowed hard.

"Good. I'd like to think it all counted for something," Roxanne said. And before Skyla could assure her that of course it all counted for something, that Roxanne's life made an enormous difference, Roxanne closed her eyes and yawned. "I'm so tired. Can we talk later?" Her words were drowsy, barely decipherable.

Skyla pulled the blanket up around Roxanne's shoulders like tucking Nora in for the night. She stood over Roxanne for a few moments, stroked her pale cheek, and watched the shallow way her chest rose and fell with each breath. "Good-bye," she whispered.

CHAPTER THIRTY-ONE

Skyla thought she'd be notified when Roxanne was about to die. The phone would ring, and it would be Ted urging her to come quickly—Roxanne was slipping away and wanted to speak to her one last time. She would hang up, and without even stopping to put on a jacket, she'd run to the Bear house to be with her best friend during her last moments of life. What she saw and heard would remain with her forever and would soften the blow of losing her friend. Her made-up scenario resembled a movie death more than real life, and having survived the passing of both her parents, she knew death wasn't particularly cooperative as far as timing went. Still, it only seemed fair that she would see Roxanne one last time.

She wasn't with Roxanne when she died that Sunday night. The phone never rang. As it turned out, no one at the Bear house even thought about Skyla. She had to find out on Monday morning when she unknowingly went to visit Roxanne, one hand carrying a cling-wrapped plate of pumpkin muffins, Nora at her side holding the other hand. She rang the doorbell with her elbow and told Nora to wipe her feet on the mat. Clara opened the door with a grim look on her face.

"What is it?" Skyla asked.

"Come in and we'll talk," Clara said, and it was then Skyla knew.

Clara related the details as they stood in the foyer at the base of the stairs, her head tilted in a sympathetic way. Roxanne had died peacefully in the hospital bed in the dining room the night before, Clara told her. The adults, knowing the end was near, had gathered the children into the room, and all of them, Ted and his sons, Clara and her daughter, Roxanne's parents and in-laws, surrounded Roxanne's bed. The three youngest boys climbed up onto the bed to hug her, and Wyatt and Emmett leaned over to rub her hands and kiss her cheek and whisper words of love. Roxanne had been given a shot of morphine less than an hour before. Shortly after they said their good-byes, she was gone.

Roxanne had passed away quietly, with love all around her, Clara said. It was good that her boys played a part in her passing—it gave them closure. Skyla listened to the words but had trouble processing them. Nora had already drifted away from her mother to follow the sound of Cartoon Network, and Clara had taken the muffins when they first walked in. Skyla's hands had never felt so empty.

"Time of death was eight oh-two," Clara said. Skyla tried to remember what she'd been doing at 8:02. The dishes? Giving Nora a bath? Reading the paper? How had something so immense happened without her realizing it?

"Eight oh-two," she repeated. The words came out of her mouth without any thought on her part. Now Skyla knew what people meant when they said they were numb.

"She died peacefully, Skyla," Clara said. "She wasn't in any pain."

Skyla turned to look into the dining room even though she knew her friend was no longer there. The white sheets on the hospital bed were rumpled, but there was no trace of Roxanne left behind. Skyla wondered when they'd taken her body away, but then she realized it really didn't matter. "I don't know what to say."

"It's a hard thing," Clara said.

Skyla swallowed again. "How's Ted holding up?"

"He's out making arrangements for the service right now. Roxanne already wrote the obituary and made some other decisions, so that should make things easier. My mom and dad took the older boys shopping for dress clothes." Unspoken were the words *for the funeral.*

Skyla stood and twisted her hands as if waiting for someone to tell her it wasn't true. She was reminded anew of the feelings she had when her father died—the devastating sense of being cast adrift, the heart-sinking feeling that nothing would ever be the same again.

Clara broke the silence. "There's so much to do today and tomorrow. I'll let you know the details about the service when I know for sure." She squeezed Skyla's arm, a gesture meant to be consoling, Skyla knew, but it didn't help much. Hugging Clara would be the socially correct thing to do under these circumstances, but she didn't much feel like it. Even small talk was too much effort.

"I'd better be going," Skyla said.

"Thank you for coming," Clara said. The words sounded practiced to Skyla's ear.

Later on, Skyla couldn't remember prying Nora away from the Bears' TV set and walking home from Roxanne's house.

Grief-stricken, she somehow managed to make Nora lunch. She spread peanut butter and jelly on bread and sliced the stacked layers in a perfect diagonal as if her DNA had been programmed for sandwich making. As always, she checked Nora's backpack and dropped her off at school. She wasn't scheduled to work at the bookstore that day and suddenly couldn't remember what she ever did with her free time. There was a Roxanne-shaped void in her life, and Skyla wasn't sure how to fill it.

Or if she could.

CHAPTER THIRTY-TWO

Thomas and Skyla arrived at the memorial service a little late—dropping off Nora at her little friend Lindsey's house took more time than Skyla had anticipated. Lindsey's mother was the type who liked to talk but didn't have much to say. Her topic that evening was the tragedy of Roxanne's death, and from there the conversation morphed into a commentary on the uncertainty of life and the fact that rumor had it the Bear boys were wild things. Clearly, Lindsey's mother was providing a guarantee for her own mortality—the inference being that she would not die young because her children were well behaved. The criticism of Roxanne's parenting skills irked Skyla. "Roxanne was a wonderful mother," she finally said in voice that indicated it wasn't up for debate. "And a good friend."

"I'm sure she was." Lindsey's mother was backpedaling now. "I didn't mean to say she wasn't."

Skyla left it at that. Thomas was sitting in the car, engine running, and she didn't want him waiting any longer.

Mortenson's Funeral Home was crowded. Ted stood at attention, just past the open oak casket where his wife's body lay, her head resting on a white satin pillow. He solemnly greeted the line of visitors as they came through, shaking the men's hands and hugging the women.

"Are you okay?" Thomas whispered to Skyla as the line edged closer to the casket. He held her elbow with a reassuring firmness. Without him at her side, she wasn't sure she could have kept going.

She nodded and looked away. The Bear boys were almost unrecognizable in their dark suits and slicked-back hair. Wyatt and Emmett were mingling among the guests. Roxanne would have been proud of them. Monty and Gregory were involved in a game that required popping out from behind a heavy blue velvet curtain that ran along one wall. They were the only bright spot in a room filled with people moving slowly and speaking quietly.

Skyla stood silently in front of the casket, relieved that Thomas wasn't spouting any funeral platitudes about the loved one being at peace or in a better place.

Roxanne wore a floral print dress, which wasn't her usual style. With her eyes closed and her face slack, there was no evidence of the woman who smiled relentlessly at her babies and roared with laughter at the antics of her older boys. A semicircle of floral arrangements filled the space behind the casket. Skyla wondered what they did with the flowers after the service— it would be wasteful to throw them away. Even as the question passed through her mind, she was ashamed of thinking such a thing during Roxanne's funeral.

"Are you ready?" Thomas's words interrupted her thoughts. He nodded toward Ted, who stood alone, having just finished talking to the people ahead of them.

Ted's face brightened at the sight of them. He reached for Skyla's hands and encased them in his, like he'd captured a butterfly. Skyla couldn't utter a sound—she was so afraid she'd start to cry.

Thomas spoke. "We're sorry for your loss. Such a tragedy." It was so like him to choose a traditional condolence, as if he'd memorized phrases from an etiquette book. For once, though, Skyla found it comforting.

"It's been a nightmare," Ted said. He shook his head from side to side. "The boys and I, we'll never get over it."

Skyla found her voice. "I'm sorry." Ted's hands were warm around hers, and his grip was firm. There was no sign he'd be letting go.

"Everyone's been wonderful." He looked around at the crowded room. "I can't believe who all's shown up. The kids' teachers, the soccer coach, all the neighbors. Even the mail carrier." Ted let go of Skyla's hands. "And you guys have been so great through this whole thing. It's meant a lot. And your mom," he said to Thomas. "What a great lady. I really mean that. I don't know what we would have done without her." Ted cleared his throat and continued. "Yeah, Audrey was incredible. All the laundry she did, and the meals she dropped off. Just snuck in and out of the house leaving things. And you probably know she's at our place right now watching the house and the dog. It was her idea. I guess sometimes houses get broken into during funerals. She thought someone should house-sit, just to be on the safe side." He shrugged. "Anyway," he said, running his fingers through his hair, "I just wanted you to know I appreciated everything you did for us."

"She dropped off meals?" Skyla couldn't help sounding astonished.

"I guess you didn't know," Ted said. "She said it was her way of making up to us for the whole social services thing. Audrey felt real bad about calling and turning us in. What a crazy misunderstanding. Roxy was pissed off at first, but they both joked about it after a while."

Skyla's thoughts reeled. Audrey was the one who reported Roxanne to social services? Audrey? She glanced over at Thomas. His expression was neutral.

"Oh look," Ted said. "The Jensens made it." A couple behind them pressed forward. Ted gave Thomas a final clap on the shoulder. "Glad you came. Thanks."

Thomas murmured something under his breath and led Skyla off to the side. "Here?" He pointed to an overstuffed couch along one wall. Skyla sat.

"How long have you known," she said finally, "that your mother was the one who called social services?" The question hung in the air. She turned her head to see him sigh.

"For a while." He looked down at his hands and flexed his fingers. "I talked to her after that day you met me in the front hall with steam coming out of your ears."

"The day she babysat for Roxanne," Skyla said. "When Roxanne was at the doctor's office."

"Yes, that day." Thomas turned to face her. "I was upset you were mad at me, so I asked her outright what was going on."

"You didn't seem upset I was mad. You did a John Wayne impression, if I recall correctly." The memory still chafed at her.

"I know," he said. "I'm sorry. You just looked so enraged, and I honestly didn't know what was going on." He reached over and rested a hand on her forearm. Her impulse was to pull away, but she sensed he had more to say and waited. "I never saw you so mad. You looked like you wanted to claw my eyes out. I guess joking around wasn't the right way to handle it."

"So you asked your mom what she was doing at Roxanne's?" Skyla said.

"Yes, I thought it odd she was at their house babysitting. So I called her and asked what the story was." He sighed. "She got all defensive right away and started muttering something about karma and atonement. I still don't know what that was all about. But when I pinned her down, she told me she was the one who called social services. She'd been driving by our house that day and saw Gregory on top of the van. After reporting the Bears, she had regrets, so she stopped over at their house to drop off banana bread and apologize. Roxanne was sick that day, and she stayed to help. That's how it all started."

"Banana bread? She thought banana bread would make up for it?" Skyla was incredulous. "She's unbelievable."

"Well, that's what happened, believe it or not."

Skyla had a thought. "Why didn't you tell me it was your mother who called?"

"Mom wanted to tell you herself," he said. "I guess it's taking her a while to get up the nerve."

"And here I was blaming you all along, and you had nothing to do with it." Skyla felt a pang of guilt. "And I was so sure."

They sat side by side in silence for what felt like the longest time. Finally the time came to pick up Nora, and they had to go.

※ ※ ※

Later that night, Skyla awakened to the sound of Thomas returning to bed. The illuminated numbers on the nightstand clock said 3:46. "Where did you go?" she whispered.

"Just getting a drink of water and checking on Nora," he said.

"Hmm."

He nestled under the covers and drew her close against him. Between the streetlight's glow and the nightlight in the adjacent bathroom, she could just make out his features—the firm chin and narrow nose, the eyes that looked naked without his glasses.

"I was thinking," he said.

"Yes."

"About what my mother did for Roxanne and Ted. That was really nice."

She didn't answer at first. Then she said, "Well, it was the least she could do after calling social services and trying to get them in trouble."

"I know," he said. "That part was terrible." Skyla knew that the pause meant he was formulating his thoughts. If he were wearing his glasses, he'd be adjusting them at this moment. "But I think," he finally said, "that we've all done something like that. It's human nature. You use poor judgment or act impulsively and then regret it later. At least Mom tried to make up for what she did. You have to give her credit for that."

"Hmm."

"And now that it's in the past, I don't see any point in dwelling on it."

"Just let it go."

"Exactly."

"Like it never happened."

"Not like it never happened." He cleared his throat. "We all know it happened. But talking about it won't serve any purpose. Better just to let it go and give her credit for doing the right thing.

For her, that was big. I don't know if you noticed this, but my mother's not known for her people skills."

"You don't say."

"Could you cut me a break, Skyla?" He sighed. "I know I haven't been there for you in the way you needed me to be. I'm sorry Roxanne died. I'm trying as best I can to make things right between us. I just hate it that you're always mad at me."

She shifted her legs under the weight of the comforter. "I'm not mad at you, really. If I'm mad at anyone, it's your mom. Why couldn't she have just minded her own business? Roxanne was my friend, not hers." It felt good to let it all out.

"I understand why you're upset," he said.

"Sometimes I just don't know how to feel anymore." She swallowed hard. "Everything is falling apart, and nothing is the way I thought it would be."

"How can I help?" His tone was kind.

She stared up at the ceiling and blinked away tears. "I don't think anyone can help. I lost my friend. My best friend. My only friend." And then, without warning, she began weeping. Thomas wrapped one arm around her and reached for the tissue box he kept on the nightstand. He handed her a tissue. Skyla blotted her eyes and then blew her nose with a gentle honk. She buried her head in his chest and thought of everything she'd ever lost. "Oh damn," she said in between sobs.

He leaned over and kissed her hair and then whispered in her ear. "Let me be your friend."

CHAPTER THIRTY-THREE

A week after the funeral, the boys and Buddy returned to Ohio with their grandparents. Nora and Skyla walked over to the driveway to say good-bye as the twins and Ted loaded suitcases into the back of two rented minivans. Skyla had pictured an emotional scene: the younger ones wailing at the thought of leaving home, Wyatt and Emmett giving her teary-eyed hugs because she reminded them of the mother they'd lost. The reality was they said good-bye as dispassionately as if she'd been the mail lady. Without Roxanne, she had no role in their life. Or perhaps they were all cried out. She knew better than most that once a child lost his mother, every other sadness paled in comparison. When the two minivans backed down the driveway, Skyla caught a glimpse of Gregory's little hand waving good-bye. The sight of it made her eyes misty. It was all so final.

With his family gone, Ted was left behind to attend to the details of emptying the house and getting it ready to sell. He'd arranged a transfer to the Columbus office so he and the boys could be closer to family. Skyla went to see him one evening after dinner to offer to help with the house.

"Hey, Skyla," he said when he opened the door. He gave her a half smile and then ushered her inside. She was taken aback by the bareness of the front entryway. The scent of lemon oil was faint but unmistakable. The floor was so clean it gleamed, and the walls had been stripped of family photos and children's artwork. It didn't feel like Roxanne anymore.

Skyla stood in that space and twisted her hands nervously and said the words she'd practiced on the walk over. Was there anything she could do to help? Did Ted want her to pack boxes or mow the yard after he left and before it was sold? She was relieved, of course, when he said no, that it was all arranged. The offer was made, but she didn't have to follow through.

"It's hard to believe she's gone, isn't it?" Ted said after what seemed like a long lapse in the conversation.

Skyla nodded.

"I keep thinking she just ran to the store or something. I wake up at night and reach over, and she's not there."

"It's just not right."

"No, it's just not right."

The words hung in the air, and Skyla was suddenly aware of the sound of ticking coming from the mantel clock in the living room. She had never noticed it before. She glanced at Ted, who looked down at his feet and sighed. "I guess I should be going," Skyla said and took a step toward the door.

"Wait, Skyla," Ted said and struck his forehead with his palm. "I almost forgot. I have something for you. Wait here." He turned and loped up the steps, two at a time. She held on to the newel post, jiggled her foot against the tile floor, and waited.

He seemed to be gone for a long time. Just when she was about to call out, she heard his footsteps heading back toward the stairs. "I keep forgetting," he said, coming down the steps. "I've had so much to think about. This is for you." He held out a sealed business-sized white envelope. She looked at him questioningly. "Go ahead. Take it," he said. "It's from Roxanne."

"Oh," said Skyla, suddenly without words. She turned the envelope over to see her name written in dark blue ink and underlined twice. Roxanne's handwriting.

"I kept meaning to give it to you," Ted said, as if she'd asked him for an explanation. "There was just so much going on." He ran his fingers through his hair.

"Thank you," said Skyla, overtaken with shyness. "Thank you very much."

"You're welcome."

There was an awkward lull where she wondered if she should give Ted a hug, but the moment passed without either of them moving. Skyla finally said, "You take care now," and gave a quick wave before heading out the door with Roxanne's envelope clutched in her fingertips.

"Good-bye, Skyla," he called from behind the screen door.

She was halfway down the porch steps when she was struck with a question. "Ted?" she called out, retracing her steps in his direction. She held up the envelope. "Did my mother-in-law get one of these?"

"A letter? Well, no." Ted spoke apologetically. "It was just for the family, you understand. And you. Not that she didn't like Audrey," he said quickly. "And we really appreciated everything she did, too. But the letters were just for the ones she left behind."

She held the envelope up in the air. "Thank you again," Skyla said and headed home to read it.

✳ ✳ ✳

On the day the movers came to the Bears' house, Skyla was home standing upstairs in the cupola with Roxanne's letter in hand. She'd looked at it dozens of times since Ted gave it to her, reading and rereading the sentences that filled one side of the single sheet of stationery, finding Roxanne in the words, but wishing there were more. In between readings she refolded it carefully at the creases and stored it in her jewelry box for safekeeping. Parts of it she had memorized—*People are the only things that matter,* Roxanne had written. *There's a lot of love out there, Skyla, if you'll just let people into your life. Open your heart.*

She leaned against the window with the envelope clutched in her hand and watched as a crew of brawny men in T-shirts and jeans loaded Roxanne's possessions into a truck. The kitchen table with the crayon marks, the baby dresser with the stenciled lamb on it, the disassembled bunk beds—all of them came through the front door. She watched the men wrap the pieces of furniture in cream-colored tarps and fit them in the truck with the precision of watchmakers. She stood in one place for what seemed like hours and didn't leave the window until everything was loaded up and the van pulled away. Then she headed to the phone to dial Audrey's number.

CHAPTER THIRTY-FOUR

Audrey wanted to know Skyla's opinion of the paint job at the Bears' old house. Gold siding with olive green shutters. The new owners had turned it into a tribute to the Green Bay Packers.

"It's pretty dreadful," Skyla said, dipping a dishcloth into sudsy water. She wrung it out and wiped the kitchen counters. They'd just finished tidying up the kitchen after Sunday dinner, a new tradition that was working out well. This week it was Skyla's turn to host and cook, and next time it would be Audrey's. It seemed to Skyla they were both making more of an effort. Sometimes she even found herself picking up the phone to ask Audrey's advice on household matters. Their relationship, if you wanted to call it that, was coming along. Skyla continued, "Yellow and green aren't too bad on a sweatshirt, but for a whole house?" She made a face. "No thanks."

Audrey leaned back against the counter. The sun passed through the window at an angle, bathing her sandaled feet in yellow light. "It doesn't even look like Roxanne's house anymore."

"You've got that right." She returned to the sink, set the dish-cloth over the faucet, and rinsed off her hands.

Audrey continued, irate. "Mercy, what were they thinking? I mean, what kind of people would paint their house like that? If you're lucky, you won't be seeing too much of them."

"Actually, I've met them already. They're a really nice couple." Skyla turned to face her. "I took some cookies over when they first moved in. The husband has a landscaping business, and she's a nurse. They're adopting a baby girl from China. I really liked them."

"Oh," Audrey said, momentarily taken aback. "Did you tell them about Roxanne?"

"No, I didn't," Skyla said, looking down and tracing the outline of a floor tile with the toe of one shoe. "They were so excited about the house. I didn't want to burst their bubble. I'm sure someone else will tell them, if they don't already know."

From the living room came shouts of joy from the men, who were watching some sports event. Walt was yelling, "Yes, yes, yes," and Thomas was exclaiming, "All right!" Skyla could picture them jumping to their feet, fists punching the air.

After the uproar in the other room died down, Audrey spoke. "A baby girl from China, you said?"

"Yes." Skyla tilted her head and said, "Doesn't it seem fitting that there'll be a little girl in Roxanne's house? She'd have liked that."

They both were silent for a moment, thinking of Roxanne. Audrey said, "Did I ever tell you how badly I wanted a girl? I was so disappointed when I wound up with three boys."

"Really, that's funny. I can't imagine Thomas having a sister. Three sons just seems right for your family."

"I don't know if it's right, but it's what I got, anyway. Things work out the way they do, it seems. A person doesn't have a choice. But sometimes it works out for the best, anyhow. Like how I never would have picked you for Thomas, and here you turned out to be just right."

"You wouldn't have picked me for Thomas?" Skyla asked, amused.

"Well, no," she said. "You weren't Thomas's type at all. He's so steady and predictable. And you—well, I had a lot of trouble figuring you out. You'd lived all over the place and done everything. And now," she said, "it's like you've always been part of the family."

"Part of the family," Skyla repeated.

"Mercy, it's hard to imagine a time when you weren't around." Audrey absentmindedly picked up the dishcloth and wiped the counter Skyla had just cleaned. "And just when I'd given up on having a daughter." She sighed. "Funny how things turn out."

A daughter? Audrey thought of her as a daughter? Really. She watched as Audrey scrubbed at a nonexistent spot, and Roxanne's words came to mind.

There's a lot of love out there, Skyla, if you'll just let people into your life.

People are the only things that matter.

Open your heart.

Audrey paused in her work to glance in Skyla's direction. "Seems like sometimes life gives you what you need instead of what you want, if you know what I mean."

"I know exactly what you mean." Skyla leaned against the counter and thought of the mother she had lost and all the women who had mothered her since: the neighbor women from her childhood, her teachers, and now Audrey, imperfect and meddling, but dependable and caring. She watched as her mother-in-law wiped the faucet and then polished it with a dry dishtowel. So typical, always bustling around, imposing her way on things. The odd thing was that Skyla no longer found it insulting. She smiled and rested a hand on Audrey's shoulder. "Why don't you leave that, Mom, and go sit down? I'll get to it later."

ABOUT THE AUTHOR

Karen McQuestion's essays have appeared in *Newsweek, Chicago Tribune, Denver Post, Christian Science Monitor,* and several anthologies. Originally self-published as a Kindle e-book, *A Scattered Life* became the first self-published Kindle book to ever be optioned for film. McQuestion lives with her family in Hartland, Wisconsin. You can visit her website at www.karenmcquestion.com.

Reading Group Guide
A Scattered Life by Karen McQuestion

1. Thomas and Skyla are very different people. What was the initial attraction? Do you think their marriage works? Why or why not?

2. Skyla grew up without a mother. Audrey always wanted a daughter. In theory, they should have gotten along well. Why didn't they, and who was at fault?

3. Roxanne describes her parenting style as "very laid back." In your opinion, is she too laid back? What are her strengths and weaknesses as a mother?

4. If you were Skyla, would you have let Audrey babysit for Nora? Would doing so have helped their relationship, or would it have hurt it?

5. Madame Picard said, "Most people have everything they need to be happy." Do you agree or disagree? And why?

6. Do you think Audrey called social services out of genuine concern for the Bear children, or did she do it out of spite?

7. Gram is happy-go-lucky; Audrey has a negative outlook. Do you believe these traits are inborn? And if so, do people have the ability to alter their disposition?

8. Madame Picard admits she's not a psychic—she tells clients she's an "intuitist." Despite this assertion, she seems to be playing the role of a fortune teller. Is she a scam artist, in your opinion?

9. Did Audrey overstep her bounds by pitching in and helping out at the Bear household when Roxanne was sick?

10. How did the death of Skyla's parents affect her? Do you think her attitude is understandable, given the circumstances?

11. The reader never sees Roxanne's letter, although Skyla does recall a few sentences. What do you think Roxanne hoped to impart to her friend? Do you think the author should have shown the whole letter?

12. Do you feel that Audrey redeemed herself by the end of the novel?

13. What do you see in the future for Skyla and Audrey?